BROKEN INSTRUMENT

WRECKED ROOMMATES SERIES

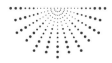

KELSIE RAE

D1519545

Broken Instrument
Cover Art by Cover My Wagon Dragon Art
Editing by Wickedcoolflight Editing Services
Proofreading by Stephanie Taylor
Published by Twisty Pines Publishing, LLC
April 2022 Edition
Published in the United States of America

1

FENDER

My palms are sweaty, and my heart rate spikes as I drag my hands along the back of the brunette's head. She opens her throat and dives in deeper, practically swallowing my cock while I squeeze my eyes shut, trying to lose myself in the feel of her lips wrapped around me.

This should feel good.

And it does.

But the closer I get to coming, the more I crave it. Not the woman in front of me, but the high. The oblivion. The moment when all the heavy shit doesn't make me feel like I'm suffocating anymore.

I *can't* crave it, though. Not anymore. Not after rehab. Not after everything I had to give up because I couldn't keep my addiction in check.

It's funny.

On paper, it sounds easy. Don't do drugs, or it'll ruin your life.

But what happens when your life is in shambles *before* you start using a handful of white pills and a bottle of dark brown liquor to cope with the day-to-day shit? It doesn't feel like you're giving up quite as much.

Because what's there to give up in the first place? If anything, it feels like you're finally able to breathe. To let go. To not *feel* quite so deeply for a few minutes.

And I was so tired of feeling.

That's what I was addicted to. That's what I wanted to ease for a little while. That's why I popped those little white pills. Why I drank straight from the bottle. It's why I shot heroin into my veins, and why I woke up in a hospital bed not so long ago.

It's also why the band I created, Broken Vows, is now touring across the country with my older brother as the lead singer instead of me. It's why I recently spent time in rehab, and it's why I can't even enjoy the feel of this random brunette's mouth as she swallows my cock. Because even though it feels good, I know how much *better* it could feel if I was high.

My stomach tightens at the thought.

I want it.

I want it so damn badly.

I rest the back of my head against the bathroom stall's door, tangle my fingers in the stranger's hair, and pull her off me. With a soft pop, my hard dick slips out of her mouth, and she looks up at me.

"Something wrong?" she questions, her dark lashes fluttering, and the corner of her hazel eyes smudged with dark liner.

I shake my head, tuck myself back into my pants, and offer to help her up.

She takes my hand and smiles wickedly, proving my poker face really is worth all the years of practice I spent controlling it.

"Should we take this back to my place?" she asks as her

blood-red fingernail wipes the edge of her mouth. The sight should turn me on. But all I feel is empty inside. Empty and wanting. But not for her. I don't want her. She's sexy. Don't get me wrong. But she's somehow…faceless. Not a person, but an object. And I hate it. It's not me. Not who I am. Not who I want to be. It's like she's a means to an end who can't even get me there without the help of my addiction.

Fuck.

"Can't," I grunt. "Thanks, though."

Her perfectly drawn brows furrow. "But you didn't--"

"Yeah." I scrub my hand over my face. "I know. Have a good night."

"You sure?" Her fingers drag down my chest and toy with the waistband of my recently buttoned dark jeans. "I could--"

I grab her wrist. "Leave. Now."

Her breath hitches as she tugs her hand away from me and races toward the exit like a bat out of hell. The bathroom door slams against the rough brick wall, her heels clicking against the tile floor before silence settles over the bar's bathroom.

If only my unsettled soul could quiet so easily.

With my chin to my chest, I fist my hands at my sides and count to ten, reminding myself of every single fucking reason I can think of as to why I shouldn't call Marty--my half-brother turned dealer. Why I shouldn't track him down and buy a few pills. Only a few. Just enough to get me through the next few weeks when I know it'll only cause me to spiral more. Shoving my hands into my hair, I tug at the roots--hard--and push the stall door open with all my strength. It slams against the wall with a reverberating crash as I make my way to the sink and wash my hands with scalding hot water, though it does shit to wash away my past mistakes.

Shoving my hand into my pocket, I pull out a fun-sized bag of M&M's and rip the package between my teeth. The pieces fall in a cacophony of a rainbow as I pour the entire bag into my mouth and chew mechanically. Not sure how they became my new vice or why I started eating them by the handful when I was in rehab, but they're the only thing that curbs my dry mouth when I'm craving something stronger. Or at least, they usually do. Right now, they taste like sawdust. My annoyance flares as I avoid my gaze in the mirror, crinkle the wrapper into my fist, and toss it into the trash.

In a daze and not ready to go home, I head to the bar and collapse onto the nearest stool, ordering a shot of Jameson. I'm not addicted to alcohol. Or at least not any more than anyone else in this bar. But I'm not stupid either. I know it's the first step to spiraling. To giving in. To becoming the weak, broken lead singer of my band.

Old band, I remind myself. Right now, I'm not sure where we stand.

I chose Broken Vows as its name for a reason. I'm not exactly great at keeping promises. Especially not ones that are so damn hard to keep.

The sound of glass clinking against the bar top startles me, bringing me back to the present as the bartender sets my order in front of me. I blink slowly and stare at the amber liquid.

It's taunting me. Daring me to drink it. Promising to numb me the way I'm desperate to be numbed. I swirl my finger around the small rim, the familiar itch begging me to grab hold of the tiny glass and swallow its contents whole.

And it would be so easy to do.

Sure, there are rumors about why I left Broken Vows a few months ago. Why they're touring across the country while I took an extended leave of absence as their lead singer and guitarist before showing up on the porch of my old place.

River, Milo, Jake, and my brother, Gibson, and I used to all room together. I moved in with my friend, Buddy, when the proximity to Gibson, aka Sonny, became too much.

It feels like a lifetime ago. When things were simple, yet oh so complicated at the same time.

Before River and Milo's little sister, Reese, was cast in a Hollywood movie. Before Broken Vows took off, my brother fell in love for the first time with an innocent little coworker named Dove, who wound up touring with us as the co-singer in the band. Before my addiction consumed me and tore apart everything we'd been working for. Before I had to let go of my dreams because I was pissing on everyone else's.

Yeah.

It really does feel like a lifetime ago.

So much has changed since then. Hell, I've only been gone for a little while, but half my roommates have moved out, Milo's now a dad, and his girlfriend and new daughter are living across the hall from me.

Yup. A lot has changed. And I have no idea how to handle any of it.

I shouldn't have come back.

But I didn't know where else to go.

I *had* nowhere else to go.

Which led me here. To SeaBird. Desperate to get away and breathe for a little while. But realizing being around alcohol, a live band who doesn't hold a candle to Broken Vows playing on the stage where we used to play, and the temptation of a one-night-stand--which is apparently a trigger for me--is enough to drive a guy insane.

And I *am* going insane.

The fact I'm actually considering drinking the beverage in front of me is enough evidence to put me in a crazy house.

It should be easy.

To give it up.

Especially after everything it's cost me.

So why am I considering throwing away all the progress I've made?

Because you're weak, a little voice inside my head reminds me. And I hate the voice almost as much as I hate the alcohol in front of me.

The barstool next to mine squeaks softly as a pair of suit-covered arms taint my periphery.

"They're shit, aren't they?" he says.

Confused, I look at the stranger. When I recognize him, I barely bite back my groan.

It's Hawthorne.

The guy who almost turned Broken Vows down but extended an invitation to tour with Organized Chaos after I begged my father, the infamous Donny Hayes, to intervene. Without him, Hawthorne would've never caved and given Broken Vows another chance after I screwed everything up by almost missing our audition 'cause I was too busy getting shitfaced at home. I guess it's one benefit to having a rockstar as your dad.

The irony isn't lost on me since it's what screwed me over in the end, anyway.

Regardless, my dad stepped in and convinced Hawthorne to give us another chance. Without him, my brother wouldn't be living out my dream with his girlfriend by his side. And even though I'm happy for him, it doesn't stop the bitterness from flooding my mouth.

It should've been me.

Sucking my cheeks between my teeth, I look over my shoulder at the shitty band playing a cover of Aerosmith and go back to staring at my untouched drink.

"I keep telling Chuck to stop hiring the wanna-be's, but I guess not everyone's Broken Vows, huh?"

I scoff and drop my chin to my chest but stay quiet. Chuck's the owner of SeaBird and is one of the most supportive bastards I know. If it wasn't for him, Broken Vows wouldn't have had anywhere to perform and would've never wound up on Hawthorne's radar. Not sure it matters anymore, but––

"How've you been?" Hawthorne prods.

Without bothering to look at him, I mutter, "Fan-freak-ing-tastic. You?"

He pauses, though I can feel him looking me up and down. "Better than you."

I glare at him and turn back to my untouched drink.

"You gonna drink that?" he asks.

Tearing my gaze from the alcohol, again, I twist on my seat and demand, "What are you doing here? Are you checking on me or something? My dad send you?"

"No––"

"Coming to hear the local bands?" I wave my hand toward the stage but don't look. I can't. Not again. It's too much. The reminder of all I'm missing. All that was taken from me. No. All I let go because I was too weak to control myself. Still, Hawthorne's presence brings too many memories and emotions to the surface. I can only handle so many. Then I'm left more itchy and raw than after my encounter with the girl in the bathroom. And my self-control is only so strong.

I clear my throat and get to my feet. "Are you trying to find the next big thing? Don't let me interrupt––"

"I'm here because Sammie needed to do some inventory before we could grab takeout."

His response makes me pause.

"Sammie?" I push, mentioning Chuck's daughter and the

7

favorite bartender at SeaBird, who I was surprised to *not* see pouring drinks when I'd first walked in.

"Yeah. We started dating when I came to check out Broken Vows the first time."

"Oh."

I hadn't noticed.

"Yeah. Speaking of which, I asked Gibson about you the other day. He said he hadn't heard from you."

Aaaand, there he is again. My brother. The golden boy.

I shrug one shoulder and reach for the glass, my thumbnail turning white from gripping the thing too hard. I let it go and wipe my sweaty palms on my jeans. My gaze remains zeroed in on the shot glass still within reach.

"You're not going to hook up with them for the end of the tour?" he presses, leaning onto his elbows to get a better view of my blank expression.

Again, I stay quiet, but my jaw's tight.

"Does Gibson even know you're out of…?" He clears his throat and drops his voice low. "Last I heard, you were still… on hiatus. Does Gibson know you're home?"

"Doesn't matter. He should be focusing on the tour."

"Fender, they miss you––"

"Stop," I snap. "Just stop. I'm not going to call Sonny and beg to meet up with Broken Vows and finish the tour."

"Who said you'd have to beg? From what I've gathered, the plan all along was for you to rejoin the tour as soon as you were released from…" Again, his voice trails off as his gaze darts from one end of the bar to the other. And while I know I should be grateful for his secrecy, it only pisses me off more.

God forbid anyone finds out I'm a fuck-up.

I scrape my hand over my face and sit back down, resting my elbows against the countertop, mirroring Hawthorne's stance as I steeple my fingers against my chin. "Yeah, well. There was a change of plans."

"Does Gibson know?"

"It doesn't matter what Sonny does or doesn't know. He should finish the tour without me. He and Dove have great chemistry. The fans are loving them. The music is dope. Let's leave it at that."

"And you?" Hawthorne asks.

"What about me?"

"Now that you're out, what are your plans?"

Tongue in cheek, I don't say a word. Honestly, I don't know what to say or what he expects to hear.

"You still playing?" he prods.

"Why do you care?"

"Because you have talent––"

I scoff and lift my hand to silence him. "If I had so much talent, I wouldn't have needed to call in a favor and have my dad convince you to give Broken Vows a shot––"

"It wasn't a lack of talent that made me hesitant, Fender, and you know it." His gaze narrows, daring me to argue with him.

But he's right.

I hang my head as the reminder washes over me. I *do* know. The reason he was going to pass on Broken Vows was because of me. Because I was a loose cannon. Because I couldn't be trusted. Because I wasn't reliable. Because he knew my addiction would inevitably get in the way of my music. And he was right. It did. But the worst part is where it left me.

Fucking broken.

And alone.

So damn alone.

"I understand why you haven't reached out to Gibson," he

adds carefully. "But I want you to understand something. Your future as a musician isn't over."

Another scoff slips out of me. He reaches over and grabs the shot glass in front of me. "As long as you stay clean," he finishes, his gaze pointed. "Think you can do that for me?"

No.

I hold his stare and watch him bring the hard liquor to his lips, swallowing my temptation before setting the empty glass back down on the bartop. He digs into his suit pocket, pulls out a shiny black business card, and places it beside the empty shot glass. "Call me."

"I'm retired," I hedge.

"From Broken Vows? Maybe. But from the music industry in general?" He tsks. "It's in your blood, Fen. People don't retire from what's in their DNA. Bury it? Sure. Run from it? More often than you'd think. But they don't retire from who they are. Call me. Give yourself something to live for again. Because this?" His astute gaze slides over me. "Is hardly what I'd call living."

He gets to his feet and leaves me alone while making me second guess my reason for living all over again.

2
FENDER

With my shoulders hiked up to my ears and my head down, I rock back on my heels, blown away that I'm actually here.

I shouldn't be here.

This is a bad idea.

But I'm lonely. And even though I'm not gonna be having sex with anyone in the near future, it would still be nice to talk to someone. To *not* be alone.

A muffled dog's bark echoes from down the hall as I lift my hand and tap my knuckles against the familiar apartment door.

It's late. I shouldn't be here. But I didn't know where else to go. Yeah, Milo's at home. But he has his girlfriend. His baby girl. He doesn't need my shit.

To be fair, neither does Trish, but I can't help myself.

Shoving my hands into my pockets, the dog's barking from down the hall grabs my attention again for a split second before the door in front of me creaks open.

With wide eyes, a gorgeous Trish peeks through the crack in the door, her jaw dropping when she recognizes me. The door closes, followed by the rustle of the metal chain lock unlatching, and my only casual yet consistent hook-up stands in front of me.

Trisha folds her arms to keep her pert nipples from playing peekaboo through her dark silk nightgown, looking uncomfortable to find me here. Especially when the last time we spoke, I ended things without even bothering to give her an excuse.

"Fen?" Her voice is quiet. Nothing but a breath as my name leaves her lips.

My smile is tight as I rub my hand over my head. "Hey, Trish. Long time, no see."

She glances behind her shoulder like it's a nervous tick and steps further into the hallway and closing her apartment door until only a crack is left. "What are you doing here?"

Excellent question.

What the hell am I doing here?

I clear my throat and rock back on my heels. Again. "Uh, yeah. Just wanted to stop by."

She smiles, but it doesn't reach her eyes. "It's good to see you."

"You too. How've you been?"

"Good. I've been…good. Listen––" Barking cuts her off as she glances down the hall and looks up at me again. "You weren't answering any of my calls. I tried to reach you."

"I know."

"And the one time you finally decided to return my call, you ended things," she reminds me.

"I know," I repeat.

"So…no offense, but what are you doing here?"

"I…" I scrub my hand over my tired face. "Can I come in?"

With a hesitant nod, she drops her voice low and says, "Only if you stay quiet. I, uh, I have company."

I hide my surprise with a look of indifference and dip my chin. "Okay."

She pushes the door open, and I follow her into her apartment. I don't miss the way she keeps the door from closing or the way her eyes keep darting toward her bedroom as we huddle in the small entryway.

"So?" she prods. "Where've you been? Last I heard, you were on tour, and then you disappeared––"

"I know. I, uh…" I drop my gaze to the ground. "I was in rehab."

Silence dominates before a whispered, "Oh," echoes through her tiny apartment.

"Yeah." I look up at her. "I missed you, though."

A sad smile tugs at her lips. "I missed you too, but…" She peeks over her shoulder again toward the closed bedroom door.

"But what, Trish?"

"But I've been seeing someone," she admits, her voice hushed.

I should feel disappointed. Hell, I should feel jealous. But if anything, the same numbness only settles into my bones a little more.

"Is he in there?" I ask, my head tilting toward her bedroom down the hall.

She nods. "I'm sorry––"

"Don't be. Does he treat you right?"

Her smile softens, finally giving a glimpse of the one I fell for all those months ago when we first started hooking up. "Yeah. He's a good guy. An architect, actually."

I laugh. "An architect, huh?"

She nods.

"Good for you, Trish."

"You mean that?"

I nod.

"Thanks," she replies.

"You happy?"

Another nod.

"Then, I'm happy for you too."

"Thanks," she repeats. The dog's barking reverberates through the shared wall to her right again. She rolls her dark almond-shaped eyes. "I swear, Hadley's going to be kicked out of her apartment if she doesn't get rid of––"

Hinges squeaking from the hall cut her off. The shadow of a man appears from the apartment across the hall from Trisha's. A three-hundred-pound, sixty-year-old with a massive beer belly and a gray combover wobbles out his front door and into the shared hallway. Like he's off to battle, he marches toward the source of the barking, and Trisha pales.

"Shit. She's in for it now," she mutters under her breath, peeking through her still-open door. I follow her gaze as the asshole waddles down the hall, his footsteps heavy and jarring, toward the apartment beside Trisha's.

His sausage fingers pull into a heavy fist. He pounds on the door and bellows, "Hadley Rutherford! Open the hell up!"

The barking ceases as I look back at Trish with an arched brow.

"The landlord," she clarifies under her breath, watching the scene unfold like an inevitable train wreck before remembering her manners. She shoves at my chest until the shitshow is hidden from sight, though I can still hear it perfectly clear through the open door. Ah, so we're out of sight but can still experience front-row seats at the shit show.

Sneaky, Trish.

Apparently, this isn't her first nosey-neighbor rodeo.

"Hadley Rutherford," the old man yells again. "If you don't open the door right this minute––"

Squeak.

I assume Hadley must've opened the door because a feminine voice replies, "Oh. Hey, Mortin--"

"Don't *hey, Mortin* me, Ms. Rutherford," the landlord interrupts. "I heard it in there. The dog--"

"It was my tv--"

"Don't give me any bullshit, Hadley. We both know you're harboring a dog in there." My hackles rise at the condescension in his voice, but I keep my feet planted where they are. "And we both know this building has a strict no animals policy. You've left me no choice but to evict you unless you can hand over the dog right this instant. I'll drive him to the shelter myself--"

"You don't understand," the soft voice argues. "If you would simply let me explain--"

"I don't want to hear any more about it. Now, give me the damn dog." The sound of his hand slamming against solid wood makes Trisha flinch. Another much louder and more protective dog bark echoes from inside the neighbor's apartment.

Trisha's eyes widen, and she covers her mouth as she peeks out the door into the hall, giving me permission to do the same.

"*Now*, Ms. Rutherford," Mortin orders, though it looks like he's backed up a few feet and is practically hugging the opposite wall. If I had to guess, the dog is seconds from attacking the bastard, and I'm not sure I'd bother to intervene and help him out if the dog did. He's a dick who's power tripping from his title as landlord. I only had to witness thirty seconds of this interaction, and it's easy to see.

"You don't understand," the neighbor argues. I can't see her, though. She's still hiding behind her front door and is speaking through the crack, probably to keep her massive dog from ripping off the landlord's head. Hell, it's what I want to do, and I'm not even involved in the shitshow.

Mortin spits, "I don't want to hear it--"

"But she isn't mine! She's my brother's--"

"I don't care who she belongs to. She is not welcome on the premises. Now, give me the dog or pack your bags." The threat is clear in his voice, and I lean forward and peck Trish on the cheek in a final goodbye.

"See ya around, Trish," I mutter, squeezing past her and into the hallway. My feet move on their own, bringing me closer to the chaos as if I have no control over my body until it's too late and my mouth opens. "Excuse me."

The landlord's jowls wobble as he glares at me with beaded eyes while a pretty brunette cowers behind her door with a pair of glasses propped on her button nose.

"Mind your own business," Mortin growls as what sounds like a bigass dog growls behind the cracked door.

"This *is* my business," I argue.

"Oh?" he challenges. "How so?"

"It's my dog." The lie tumbles out of me before I can stop it.

He jerks back, unconvinced. "Excuse me?"

"Hey, sis," I greet the stranger. Her hair is piled on top of her head in a messy bun, and a giant, holey T-shirt swallows her curvy body whole as I step forward and kiss her cheek. "Sorry I'm late, but thanks for watching Fido."

Stunned, her lips part as her dark lashes bat up at me. She glances at the landlord analyzing our exchange. With a forced smile, she clears her throat and replies, "Took you long enough."

"You're the dog owner?" Mortin demands.

I nod. "Yeah. I was out of town for the weekend, and my original sitter fell through. Thankfully, my sister's the best and agreed to watch Fido. Isn't that right, Hads?" I turn back to the gorgeous stranger and find her jaw still hanging open. She recovers a second later.

"Yup. So, if you'll excuse us, Mortin," she smiles sweetly, "I'll go grab Fido's leash, and my brother will be on his way."

Mortin folds his arms, resting his hands on his massive beer belly as his gaze shifts from Hadley to me and back again. "Dogs are not allowed on the premises. Even if it's only for the weekend." He points his sausage finger at me. "If it happens again, your sister will be the one looking for a place to stay. We clear?"

"Yeah, we're clear."

"And if I hear any barking again, I'll call the police––"

"But––" Hadley starts, and I shake my head to cut her off.

"It's fine, Hads." I turn to the dick landlord. "It won't be a problem again."

His chin dips before he turns on his heel and waddles down the hall, leaving my pretend sister and me blanketed in silence.

"Fine?" she demands, still pissed. "What happens when she barks five minutes from now?"

I squeeze the back of my neck and force my gaze to stay on her face instead of traveling down her curvy frame. "I guess I didn't think that part through."

"Ya think?"

The superintendent's door opens again. The asshat pulls out a lawn chair and a book, making himself comfortable in the hall. When he catches us staring, he announces, "Take your time, Ms. Rutherford. I'll wait here until I see the dog escorted out of the building with my own eyes."

"You've got to be kidding me," Hadley seethes between her teeth.

"Chop, chop," he calls back at her. "It's late, and I'd like to get some sleep."

Her cute button nose scrunches as she bites her tongue.

Her fingers dig into my forearm, and she drags me into her apartment, slamming the door behind her.

Something massive bumps into the back of her legs, followed by a low growl that could make a grown man piss himself. I cover my crotch to keep the demon from neutering me and look down, hoping the animal will see I'm a good guy and not an intruder or something.

Using her curvy frame as a shield between the beast and me, Hadley lifts her hands and scolds, "Calm the hell down, Pix. He's a friend. He's not the asshole––"

My brows furrow as I take in the massive dog trying to squeeze between Hadley's legs. "Pixie?"

Hadley freezes and looks back at me, her frustration dissipating into thin air, replaced with a prickling awareness which, under any other circumstance, I'd guess would send Pixie into a full-blown frenzy. Probably one that would wind up with my nuts being eaten. But thankfully, the dog knows me.

Still.

It doesn't stop the tremor in Hadley's voice as she takes a slow step back and accuses, "How do you know my brother's dog?"

3

HADLEY

"**B**ud's your brother?" the handsome stranger asks. If I didn't know any better, I'd say he's surprised. But it's not like I can call his presence a coincidence. Not when Bud's been missing for who knows how long, and the guy in front of me decided to be my own personal savior seconds ago.

The hair on the back of my neck stands on end, and I cross my arms over my chest protectively. "How do you know my brother?"

He hesitates and squeezes the back of his neck, then squats down to pet Pixie, who took full advantage of my suspicion and finally squeezed past me to attack the stranger with kisses.

Kisses.

Apparently, a guard dog, she is not.

"Hey, Pix," the stranger greets her. "How you doing, baby girl?"

Pixie licks his offered hand, nuzzling against him as if they're best friends when she's usually less than friendly with strangers.

So the question is...why isn't she treating him like a stranger?

"How do you know my brother?" I demand once more, this time more forcefully.

Scratching behind Pixie's floppy dark ears, he says, "We met through a mutual...friend. He even let me crash on his couch for a couple of months. Didn't he, Pixie?" He moves his attention from her ears to under her drooly chin but keeps up with the baby talk. It shouldn't be adorable but kind of...*is.* "Yes, he did. Yes, he did. Aren't you the best girl?"

Pixie crowds him on the ground, her giant butt wiggling back and forth in a full-body tail wag of excitement. It eases a bit of my wariness. I mean...if she trusts him, he can't be too bad, can he? You know, with her dog instincts and all.

I chew on the inside of my cheek but unfold my arms as I watch them interact for another few seconds.

"What's your name?" I ask.

He looks up at me and pushes himself to his feet, offering his hand. "Fender. And you're Hadley?"

"How do you know my name?"

Hooking his thumb over his shoulder toward Mortin's apartment, he explains, "Your landlord wasn't exactly discreet when he came to yell at you, *Ms. Rutherford,*" he says, mimicking Dickhead Mortin's baritone voice. "You're welcome, by the way."

My lips pull into a thin line. "I haven't thanked you yet. It's not like I can actually let you walk out of here with my brother's dog, but I'm not exactly sure I have a choice anymore since you confirmed I have a dog here."

"Mortin didn't need me to intervene to confirm you had a dog in here," he reminds me. "Pix isn't exactly discreet."

I bite the inside of my cheek but don't bother to argue. The bastard has a point.

"So, where is he?" Fender asks. "Buddy?"

My upper lip curls. "Good question. You're his friend. You tell me."

"I wouldn't know. I haven't seen him lately."

"Oh?" I fold my arms, my frustration boiling just beneath the surface all over again as I take in the stranger who's turned my night upside down. First, he saved me, but now I'm not so sure it was a coincidence. Not when my brother disappeared, leaving his messes for me to clean up––again–– and I'm about to be evicted because of it.

Squeezing the back of his neck with one hand while petting Pixie with the other, the strange, albeit sexy stranger rocks back on his heels and shrugs one shoulder. "We don't exactly hang out in the same crowds anymore."

"You mean the drug-dealing felons kind of crowds?" I spit.

Surprise flickers across his face, but he covers it with indifference. "Something like that. Bud never mentioned you."

"Not surprised. We aren't exactly close."

He cocks his head to one side. "Then, what are you doing with his dog? Pix is his baby."

I bite back my annoyance. Little does this guy know, Bud has an actual child he neglected for years before he slowly started to come around. Until recently, when he fell off the face of the earth. Again.

"It was either me or the pound," I mutter, motioning to the giant, drooly beast.

Fender chuckles, low and throaty. "Bud would never send Pixie to the pound."

"Yeah. Well, when you go on a binge and disappear, leaving your dog locked in your apartment for a week until the superintendent calls your emergency contact, who happens to be your sister whom you haven't spoken to in months, I guess we'll have to agree to disagree."

Fender jerks back, confused. "What?"

"I'm sorry, did I not make myself clear? Bud went on a bender, disappeared, and left me to pick up the pieces. Again. Oh. And did I mention the fact that apparently, he hadn't been paying rent either? Which is why I couldn't stay at his place with the dog until he showed back up? Nope. The guy's in debt up to his eyeballs––"

"Bud disappeared?" he interrupts, still reeling, though I'm not sure why. If they were friends like Fender said, I would've thought he knew Bud's MO.

I shake off the thought and answer, "Yup. He disappeared, which I thought he'd grown out of since his ex mentioned he'd been turning his life around, but he fell off the wagon again. Ain't that a bitch? So, you know the mutual friend you mentioned? Maybe you could call him and see if he's seen Bud lately. Maybe ask him to remind Bud there are other people in the world, and he has responsibilities he needs to take care of." I motion to Pixie. "Exhibit A."

Fender clears his throat, avoiding my gaze as he scratches at the scruff on his strong jaw. "Sorry. I can't."

"Why not?"

"Because I'm not in that life anymore."

I roll my eyes. "Neither was my brother. Or at least he said so the last time I spoke to him."

"Bud was trying to get clean?"

"Bud was being Bud. Making promises he had no intention of keeping. Now, if you'll excuse me. I have to figure out what I'm going to do with his freaking dog now. Mortin's officially staking out the hallway––"

"I can take her."

My brows pinch. "Excuse me?"

"I can take her. You know, until your brother shows up again. That way, you won't get evicted, and Pixie won't wind up at the pound."

It would be easier if I said yes. If I lied to myself and said I haven't gotten attached to the giant butthead and our nightly snuggles. If I said I won't miss her gentle snoring or the way her entire body wiggles with excitement when I get home from the grocery store.

But the truth is, even if I *did* admit it out loud, she isn't my dog. If she were mine, I would consider moving into a new place. But our relationship is temporary. Like everything else in Bud's life. And I have no doubt he's going to do what he always does. He's going to show back up in a few weeks, acting like everything is hunky-dory. Like it's my job to carry the weight of his mistakes and decisions. Just. Like. Always.

It's a moot point, anyway. Pixie isn't only Bud's dog. Technically, she belongs to his daughter. He'd gotten her for Christmas one year as a gift for missing the previous one. And even though they go months without seeing each other, it's not like my niece is going to willingly hand over her sole reason for visiting her father to a stranger all because he dropped the ball. Again.

I bite my lip to keep from taking him up on his offer and shake my head. "You can't."

"But your land--"

"No. You don't understand," I interrupt. "Buddy's daughter--"

"Bud has a daughter?"

"Yeah. She loves Pixie. And yeah, she might have daddy issues, but I can't get rid of her dog because her dad decided to be an irresponsible asshole."

His trimmed fingernails scratch against his five o'clock shadow before he digs into his pocket for his cell. "What's your number?"

"Excuse me?"

"I'll text you my contact info so you can reach out whenever your niece wants to see Pix."

"That won't be necessary," I argue.

"Look. The way I see it, you can either let your landlord take Pixie to the pound, which'll piss off your niece and your brother whenever he decides to show back up, or you can let me watch her while keeping full visitation rights until your brother decides to get his head out of his ass, *or* you can keep her yourself and go apartment hunting. The choice is yours."

I click my tongue against the roof of my mouth, his options swirling around in my brain as indecision gnaws my lower gut.

"I can't just give her to you," I mutter.

"You aren't. You're passing along babysitting duties until Bud shows up again."

"Why, though? Why would you be willing to help?"

"Honestly?" He shrugs his broad shoulders, the dark blue henley making my mouth water as it stretches across his broad chest. "I have no idea. I guess I could use the distraction."

"From what, exactly?"

He looks down at the ground, shifting his weight from one foot to the other while reminding me of a little boy who failed a test or something.

"Life, I guess," he answers. There's something about the way he says it, though. The vulnerability. The resolution. The indecision. Like some twisted cacophony of mixed emotions urging me to dig a little deeper.

"You need a distraction from life?" I ask.

"Do you want my help or not?"

There's a sharpness in his voice this time. Like he doesn't want his acid tongue to hit its mark, but he's blindly wielding it to keep anyone from getting too close. And it only piques my curiosity more. After all, I'm a writer. I'm a sucker for a good story with juicy details. And tragedies? They're my specialty. But I don't question him further. I don't push him. Honestly, I think it's because it looks like he's already been bulldozed past his limits, and he doesn't need anyone else pushing him further. Not right now.

And he's right. I might not want his help, but I do *need* it.

It's like he said, if I don't take him up on his offer, I'll be homeless. It's not like I can keep hiding her in my apartment when Mortin knows she's here and is currently camping outside my door. And I'm not about to turn my life upside down for a dog who isn't even mine. Sure, she's cute, but I'm not going to let myself get attached any more than I already have. I can't.

She. Isn't. Mine.

"And you promise to give her back to Bud when he shows up? 'Cause this isn't the first time he's disappeared without saying where he's going or when he'll be back––"

"I know Bud," he tells me. "And I know Pixie. Don't I, girl?" Bending down, he scratches her ear again.

"Fine," I mutter. "My number's 555.332.0821."

He types the digits into his phone, and my cell dings on the kitchen counter with an incoming text message a few seconds later.

"There," he announces. "Now you know how to contact me."

"You sure you're okay taking her?" I ask, my attention drifting to the giant furball at my waist. She's part Mastiff, part Great Dane, with a side of...Husky, was it? Honestly, she's a mutt and kind of reminds me of Hagrid's dog from Harry Potter but with more drool. So. Much. Drool. And I hate how I'm second-guessing him taking her.

She's mine. At least, when Bud's gone, she is.

Sensing my hesitation, he says, "Only until Bud gets back or if you think of another solution. But right now, thanks to your landlord out front, I'm thinking this is the only one."

I swallow thickly, nearly choking on my guilt. I force a smile and give Fender a nod. "Okay. You can take her for the time being, but I'm going to keep brainstorming."

"All right. Does she have a leash or anything?"

I nod again. "Let me grab her food and stuff."

Rummaging around the apartment, I grab her things, put them in a paper grocery sack, and hand everything to him. "Here."

"Thanks."

"Don't mention it. We'll be in touch," I remind him.

His smirk is sarcastic but playful as he takes the leash from the bag and attaches it to Pixie's collar. "Can't wait."

4

FENDER

Cursing myself under my breath, and with a grocery sack full of dog food hanging from one arm, I climb out of my car and grab the door handle to the backseat. It's late. I'm exhausted. And all I want is to go home and collapse onto my bed when the hair on the back of my neck prickles with awareness. I pause and look over my shoulder at the dark street behind me.

Shadows blur my vision, playing peekaboo with my sanity as the distinct feeling I'm being watched overwhelms me.

It's probably from my conversation with Hadley about her brother. My own demons coming to haunt me for my past mistakes. I've always been a scared little boy afraid of his own shadow. I guess it's what happens when your mom disappears for days, leaving you alone in your trailer to fend for yourself.

But Bud's missing. And it doesn't feel right. Hadley might think it's his MO, but he was getting better. Or at least, it was the impression I got when he let me stay on his couch a few months ago.

Then again, who knows if he was able to keep his resolve? I'm sure as hell struggling on that account. Maybe Bud did too.

I'm not curious enough to ask Marty if he's seen him, though.

No. That door's closed. And I'm not stupid enough to open it back up.

Sonny and I might've fought about me cultivating a relationship with our dad and half-brother, Marty, but he was right about one of them.

Marty didn't care about me.

And recognizing that truth has been a hard pill to swallow. Even now, when I think about it, I'm afraid I might choke on it. The damn pill. The one saying I cared about him more than he ever cared about me.

I still remember the first time we met. When he reached out to Sonny and me a little while after we'd connected ourselves. You see, Marty knew about our dad, Donny. He'd always known he was the infamous rockstar's son. But me? I had no idea. Neither did Gibson, but at least he had a mom who looked out for him. Who wanted what was best for him. Mine? Well, she might have a good heart, but I got my blonde hair and vices from her. Well, technically from both my gene donors. Donny Hayes wasn't exactly any better in the beginning. But mom? She was a real class act. She had a thing for white pills and brown liquor, so when another brother showed up who wanted to connect, I couldn't wait to cultivate our relationship. To feel like I wasn't alone. To have a family. A real one.

I think it's why I clung to Sonny too. He was kinder than Marty, though. More guarded, sure, but more genuine. Once he realized I only wanted a brother, he opened up to me. We became friends, connecting through our passion for music and 90's movies.

Marty was the cocky one. The older brother who'd pretend to take you under his wing, only to push you toward trouble. Gibson wouldn't put up with his shit and wrote him off long ago. But me? I was too desperate for a family to care, and Marty wasn't afraid to play me like a fiddle.

And because I'm the broken brother, the one who was so desperate for his family, I ignored the red flags. The lies. The manipulation. All because I wanted to have the one thing I never did while growing up.

Loyalty.

Friendship.

And love.

I suck my cheeks between my teeth and shake off the thought––and the feeling I'm being watched––before opening up the backseat to my shitty beater because I liked spending money on my vices instead of saving it for something useful. Like replacing my 1980s car, which is obviously on its last leg.

A bright flash casts my shadow against the garage but disappears in the blink of an eye.

I twist around again, scanning the shrubbery lining the sidewalk in front of the house in search of the perpetrator but find it empty. Nothing but grass, trees, a dark road, and some shrubbery.

I could've sworn...

I shake my head and release a slow sigh when Pixie jumps out of the backseat and onto the driveway with a low growl in her throat as she places her massive body a foot or so in front of me, her dark brown eyes staring at the same shadowed street.

Another flash blinds me, and I rub at my eyes.

What. The. Hell?

After a few more seconds of silence, Pixie lifts her nose

into the air, sniffs, plops down on her haunches, and looks up at me, deeming the situation safe.

At least there's one benefit to having the big beast around.

"You think someone's out here?" I ask her, well aware of how crazy I sound. But I can't help it. It's too quiet. And I'm afraid the silence will only confirm I'm losing my damn mind.

Pixie looks up at me when no more flashes blind us, sneezes, and pees on the front lawn. Like she isn't worried anymore. Like I'm losing my shit for no reason.

"You're right. Everything's fine. Come on. Let's go inside."

I'm drained. Both emotionally and physically. And after everything that happened today? I could use some sleep.

With Pix by my side, we traipse up the steps and open the front door. The lights are off inside the two-story house, but low voices echo from the second floor, and Milo peers down from the balcony.

"Hey, man," Milo greets me. His brows furrow. "Wait. Is that a dog?"

"Yeah," is all I reply as I head up the stairs, too exhausted to give him an explanation. I can give him the details tomorrow.

When I reach the second floor, Maddie's voice echoes through Jake's open bedroom door. "So…yeah. That's how he's doing. Promising, right?"

"Do you know if he's spoken to Sonny?" someone else asks her, and considering the voice is coming from Jake's room, it doesn't take a genius to figure out who it belongs to.

But Jake's question pisses me off. It's like I'm some damaged little problem needing to be handled with kid gloves, and they don't even have the decency to confront me head-on. Instead, they're busy talking behind my back in hushed voices. I know they care, and they don't know how to show it. But if my friends think this is the solution, to talk behind my back, they have another thing coming to them.

"No, I haven't called Sonny," I announce from the doorway, not even bothering to hide my annoyance as I take in Jake and Maddie sitting on his bed. Jake's been gone for a couple of days. He had a business retreat or something, but he looks like shit. Like someone kicked his puppy. Which is saying something because the guy's been through the wringer over the past year or so.

Cutting him some slack, I sigh and add, "But if you have any other questions, you can ask *me*. We clear?"

Jake nods, staring at Pixie behind me with wide eyes and a slack jaw. I'd laugh if I weren't still a little annoyed they were talking about me behind my back.

Poor, broken Fender.

I hate it's how they perceive me. But what I hate even more? They're not wrong.

"Good," I return, looking down at the four-legged beast. "This is Pixie."

"Pixie?" Maddie asks.

"My friend's dog. I'm watching her for a while."

Milo and Maddie look at each other, and he grunts, "What's a while, Fen?"

Jaw tight, I repeat, "A while." I walk the rest of the way into Jake's room, the dog padding behind me, and peek through his window, still fighting the urge to grab a flashlight and search the premises for the lurker outside. There's no way I imagined those flashes.

Is there?

"Something wrong?" Jake asks, his voice quiet and strained. Probably afraid I'll finally snap and lose my shit on everyone. Even though he's only been gone for the weekend, a better friend would've noticed his absence more. But me?

I've been too lost in my own head to care. About anything, really.

The same quiet street taunts me from the window. I close the blinds and mutter, "No."

"You sure?" he prods.

"Thought someone was following me," I mutter under my breath. "But I guess I really am going crazy." Turning on my heel, Pixie and I head out of the room without another word and close my door quietly behind us.

When it closes with a soft click, I look down at Pixie, all rolls and drooly jowls as she scans the foreign room.

"So. Do you sleep on the floor, or...?" My voice trails off, waiting for her to take the lead.

With her light pink tongue lolling from one side of her mouth, she stops assessing the room and looks up at me. Like she's waiting for me to take the lead. Since, you know, I'm the human and all.

Right.

Gripping the neck of my henley, I rip it over my head and toss it into the dark woven laundry basket next to the door. Pushing my jeans down my legs, I climb into bed.

Pixie stays near the door, her tail wagging from side to side as she stares at me.

"Go to bed," I tell her, but she doesn't move. She just keeps staring at me with those giant brown eyes.

Waiting.

"What do you want? Go to bed."

Nothing.

With a sigh, I pat the gray comforter to my left. "All right, Pix. Come on."

Her heat is almost comforting as she jumps up, turns around in a small circle, and plops down next to me. She presses her side against my own and somehow manages to quiet the constant voices inside my head, telling me what a screw-up I am.

And for the first time in months, I sleep soundly without any assistance from drugs.

It's a freaking miracle.

5
HADLEY

"Don't hate me," Isabella begs as soon as I answer the phone.

Pressing my cell to my other ear, I stare blankly at the computer in front of me before swiveling in my rolling chair to give it my back. I can't deal with it right now, anyway.

With a sigh, I close my eyes and ask, "And why would I hate you?"

"I have to work this weekend, and since Bud's still missing and Mia's a handful on a good day, let alone when I have to leave for a few days, I was wondering––"

"Mia hates me," I tell her.

"She doesn't hate you."

She will after I tell her I had to give her dog to an absolute stranger, I think to myself, but bite my tongue, waiting for Bella, Bud's ex, to get to her point.

"She just…doesn't know you," Isabella adds a few seconds later.

"Mm-hmm."

Mia is Bud's daughter. She's also only a few years younger

than me and doesn't take kindly to the fact I'm her aunt or that I actually have rules when she comes to visit, unlike any time she stays with her dad.

I swear those two are practically twins. Both have no filter, no self-control, and no desire to consider their future or how their choices in the present can affect said future. Exhibit A: Bud was only fourteen when he got Isabella pregnant. Fourteen. She was also only fourteen, which means Mia was practically raised by kids.

But the worst part? She puts her dad on a pedestal. And even though Isabella has done a pretty good job raising her, I'm still terrified Mia will wind up like her dad. Selfish and an addict.

And me? I'm the aunt who likes to hold Mia's father to a higher standard and may or may not have had a bone to pick with the guy over the last few years. It's made my situation with Mia a little less than desirable. Especially when the girl is so freaking smart. She's also gorgeous, and funny, and... she has so much potential. But I'm terrified she isn't going to utilize any of it because she's too busy following in her dad's footsteps.

"You know I have no one else, Hadley," Isabella reminds me. She's an only child, and her parents kicked her and Mia out of their house as soon as she turned eighteen. They haven't spoken much since. Which means when Bud's MIA, I'm the only person Bella can rely on.

"I know," I mutter.

"Normally, I'd call Bud, but..."

"I know," I repeat. "For how long?"

"Only a couple of days, but it's a pretty big project I'm heading up in LA, which is great. But ya know, it'll be a little more traveling than usual, and considering the circumstances––"

"I get it." Slipping off my glasses, I pinch the bridge of my nose and let out a long sigh. "I'll help out however I can."

"You will?"

"Yeah."

"I'll talk to Mia again. I'll remind her who's the boss, make sure she's respectful and all that jazz, okay?"

Like it'll help.

I lean back in my chair and kick my feet out. "Yeah. I'm sure it'll be fine. Have you heard anything else about Bud?"

Bella insisted on filing a missing person's report a few days after Bud disappeared, even though I thought it was a waste of time. It's not the first time he's done this. But I guess she actually believed him when he said he'd changed this time.

I almost had too.

Sometimes it sucks being right.

A beat of silence passes then she murmurs, "I haven't heard anything about Bud. How 'bout you?"

"Nada," I reply, hating the disappointment which still manages to flood my system anytime we discuss the lack of update in regards to Bud's whereabouts. "But listen, since you called...I had a little issue with my landlord."

"Don't tell me--"

"I'm not getting kicked out, but..." I bite the inside of my cheek, bracing myself for the slew of curses I know are seconds from being hurled my way. "One of Bud's friends showed up and offered to watch Pix until Bud returns."

"You're joking, right?"

"It's not like you could take her, and--"

"Mia's gonna be pissed--"

"I know, but--"

"I get it," she mutters, though I can still hear the disappointment in her voice. "Seriously. I do. And you know we'd take her if we could, but with our rent agreement being locked in and the housing market going up, it's not like I can pick up and move to watch my ex's dog until he shows up again. But it isn't fair to expect you to put up with her, either," she adds, her frustration fizzling. "I'll, uh, I'll talk to Mia."

"She's going to hate me--"

"She's going to be disappointed, but she'll get over it. This isn't your fault. It's her dad's."

Yeah, no. She's definitely going to look at this like it's my fault, and part of me still feels like it is.

"I have the friend's number," I say, though I'm not sure who I'm reminding. "We'll set up a time so Mia can hang out with Pix or something."

"Good idea. I think Mia would like that."

"How's she doing?" I ask carefully.

"Struggling, obviously. But there isn't much I can do, you know? It sucks. As soon as Bud decides to start showing up again as a father, he disappears."

"It is weird," I mutter, unable to console her when we both know it's a moot point. It's like she said. The situation sucks. It's that simple. And so help me, when Bud decides to show up again, I'm going to rip him a new one for everything he's done. Because this? This isn't fair. For any of us. But especially for Mia.

"So when will you be dropping Mia off? Or will she be driving here on her own?" Mia just turned seventeen, and even though she has her license, Isabella and I agreed leaving her car at home might be the best idea, considering how Mia disappeared for two days the last time she stayed here. A picnic, it was not.

"I'll drop her off on Friday if that's okay?"

I look at the sunset calendar hanging on my wall. Other than the giant red circle looming a few weeks away, the dates are blank. "That'll work."

"And maybe call Bud's friend? See if you guys can meet up at the park so Mia has something to look forward to?"

"I can do that."

"Perfect. And thanks, Hadley," she adds. "I know this isn't easy on you."

"It isn't easy on any of us."

"Yeah, but still. I'll talk to you later, okay?"

"Sounds good. Bye."

After hanging up the phone, I tap the edge of it against my chin, staring blankly at the open manuscript on my computer. My attention shifts back to the calendar hanging on the wall.

There's no way I'm going to hit my deadline. And even though I'd like to use the excuse of Mia coming to stay with me as the catalyst, I know the real reason. And I hate it.

Shoving the thought aside, I pull up Fender's contact info and press call.

This should be interesting.

6

FENDER

The morning air is cool as Pixie and I walk down the sidewalk. Runners pass us by, though most cross to the other side of the street when they see Pixie lumbering toward them. She seems excited to be outside. Probably the Husky in her. It's like she craves exercise the same way I crave a certain something else.

I shake my head and shove the thought aside.

This is a good habit. Walks in the morning. And I need some new good habits. Good habits to replace the bad ones. I need them desperately.

My phone rings in my pocket, and I pull it out of my dark gray joggers, checking the name across the screen and groaning.

Sonny.

Which means someone spilled the beans to my brother, and he knows I'm not in rehab anymore. I'm not sure who. Could've been Milo or Jake since I'm staying with them. Possibly our dad, though he promised to keep it quiet. Honestly, it could've been Hawthorne for all I know. He saw me at SeaBird. He knows I'm back. But it doesn't matter. I can't talk to Gibson right now, anyway. I have too much shit and anger to sort through before crossing that bridge. And if I don't get a handle on said shit, I'll yell at him, blaming my biggest supporter for things that aren't his fault. It isn't fair to him. But ignoring his calls isn't exactly mending our relationship, either.

It isn't his fault I screwed up. It's mine. And owning up to my mistakes is the first step in recovering. All right, maybe not the first one, but still.

The call goes silent, and I start to shove it back in my pocket when the thing starts ringing again in my palm. It's a guitar riff from Broken Vows' first song. I can still remember Gibson playing it for the first time. Later, I tweaked a few notes and made it my own. Hell, I can still remember us recording it together. Afterward, I uploaded it to my cell and made it my ringtone, excitement buzzing in my veins as I forced the drummer of Broken Vows, Phoenix, to call me so we could hear it play. The memory leaves a bad taste in my mouth.

I should change it. My ringtone. But a part of me likes the burn. The reminder of how far I'd come, only to let it slip through my fingers.

Sonny's name flashes again, but I ignore the call and shove my phone into my pocket, picking up my speed until I'm full-on sprinting down the road. My chest heaves, my muscles tighten, and a soft sweat breaks out along the back of my neck, but I don't stop.

I'm not an idiot. I know I'm running from my past. My mistakes. My brother, who's never been anything but a badass who always had my best outcomes in mind. But I can't help it. The little voices inside my head won't shut up. The ones who tell me I'm not enough. That I screwed up. That I'll never be able to get back what I lost.

With ease, Pixie keeps up, her long pink tongue hanging

out from one side as she races beside me. Our feet pound against the pavement, and my lungs scream at me to slow down, but I refuse to give in. Not again. I'm not weak. I can't be. I refuse to be.

Don't be weak.

My phone rings a third time, and my chest tightens for a completely different reason, having nothing to do with exertion as I slow my pace and dig into my pocket again. A curse sits on the tip of my tongue as I slide my thumb across the screen, answering it blindly.

"Listen, I don't have time for this right now. I know I should've called, but--"

"Fender?" a quiet, feminine voice interrupts.

My brows pinch as I pull my cell away from my ear and look at the screen. "Hadley?"

"Yeah. Hi."

Shit.

I clear my throat and rub my hand over my face, Pixie's leash still looped around my wrist as I try to catch my breath. "Hey. Sorry. I, uh, I thought you were someone else."

"Oh." Pause. "Okay? Uh, let's try this again? Hi. This is Hadley."

My mouth quirks up with amusement, and my breathing starts to steady. "Hey."

"So...how's Pix?"

I look down at Pixie to find her looking up at me, practically grinning. "She's good."

"Good. You two are acclimating?"

My attention shifts to the quiet street, the drops of water still clinging to the grass from the sprinklers. The warm air filters through my lungs. I never would've experienced any of it if Pix hadn't woken me up at the asscrack of dawn.

With a ghost of a smile, I mutter, "We're doing all right."

"Good," she repeats. "So, I was wondering if maybe my

niece and I could meet you at the park or something next weekend? I know you might be busy and all, but…" Her voice trails off but leaves her desperation hanging in the air.

I don't blame her. Pixie's kind of a badass. I've only had her for a few days, and I'm already attached. I can only imagine how her niece must feel knowing someone else is watching her dog.

"I can meet you," I offer.

"You're sure? I don't want to be a burden."

"You're not a burden, Hadley. Just text me the time and place. I'll meet you there."

"Okay. Thank you, Fender."

The sound of my name on her lips makes my brows furrow. It's soft and sweet and laced with gratitude.

No one's grateful when I'm around.

I clear my throat and look down at the concrete beneath my worn Nikes. "You're welcome. See you then."

7

HADLEY

"**H**ey, Mia, we gotta go--"
"I'm hurrying!" my niece snaps through the closed bathroom door.

Isabella dropped her off yesterday. Within fourteen hours, she's gotten mad at me for snooping about her life, not having any food in the house, and--the issue I'd predicted--getting rid of Pixie.

So this? The fact she's taking her sweet time and is going to make us late for our little meet-up with Fender at the park? It's the icing on the cake.

I swear I'm going to strangle her.

The six years between us might feel like a lifetime to me when she's acting like a child, but in reality, it isn't much. I know this. But all I want is a little bit of respect, and I feel like it's the *one* thing she's unwilling to give. Not to mention the constant bickering getting on my nerves. It's like we're siblings. But we aren't. And when you combine the closeness in age along with the polar opposite personalities, we're like oil and water. Oil and water who are supposed to be at the park in––I look at my phone––thirty seconds, even though it's a ten-minute drive from here.

My annoyance spikes.

"You're going for a run, Mia," I remind her, my voice sickly sweet. "It's not like you need your makeup to look perfect––"

She wrenches the door open. "Says the girl who basically lives in pajamas."

"Perk of being an author," I volley back. "You ready to go?"

"Yup."

She grabs a black athletic jacket from the bathroom counter and slides her arms into it, leaving the zipper open to reveal her toned stomach and hot pink sports bra. The girl's fit; I'll give her that much. She must've gotten it from her mom's side because my curvy figure wouldn't be caught dead in something so revealing. And yes, I'm blaming the genes and not my addiction to chocolate or the fact I hate running with every fiber of my being. So sue me.

I follow behind her and grab my keys before we make our way to my car. She doesn't say a word. Other than when we're arguing, she hasn't really said much since Isabella dropped her off yesterday. The only evidence I've had proving she hasn't turned into a mute is the one-word answers I've been gifted with any time I ask her a question.

"How's school going?"

"Fine."

"Have you decided which college you want to attend?"

"Nope."

"Totally get that. Which ones are you considering?"

"I'm gonna shower."

Okay, the last one was three words, but you get my point. Chatty, she is not.

In silence, we drive to the park, my gaze darting toward

her in the passenger seat every few minutes. I pull into the parking lot next to a giant grassy field with a dark asphalt bike path surrounding it.

Mia's expression is hard, her eyes sharp as she scans the area.

"So?" she demands.

"Let me call him."

"This wouldn't have been an issue if you hadn't gotten rid of her."

Oh, look. More than three words.

I sigh and pull up Fender's contact information, pushing the call button. As it rings, I watch an old car that has definitely seen better days pull into the parking lot. A gruff Fender answers, "Just got here. Sorry."

"You're fine. I'm in the white Camry."

"I see it. I'll be right there."

Sure enough, the rusted black sedan's driver-side door creaks open to reveal a sexy Fender who looks as droolworthy as I remember. My attention shoots to Mia beside me, and her lips part in surprise. I don't know why I'm curious to see her reaction. Maybe to prove I'm not insane for thinking the guy's good-looking, but I'm not disappointed.

"*That's* Dad's friend?" she asks.

"Apparently."

She gulps.

"I know, right? Remember you're underage––"

Her neck snaps toward me. "Ew."

"Just sayin'," I start, but she cuts me off by shoving open the passenger door and unfolding herself from my car, slamming it behind her.

Puffing out my cheeks, I do the same, the warm morning air grounding me as I lock the car and head to Fender and Pixie.

"You're the niece?" Fender asks Mia as she approaches them.

She smiles sweetly and replies, "The one and only," as she squats down and scratches Pixie's ears. The dog wiggles its massive butt back and forth excitedly.

Without waiting for an invitation, she takes the black leather leash from Fender's grip, pushes to her feet, and announces, "We're going for a run. Be back in an hour."

"An hour?" Fender chokes out.

"Yup. Come on, Pix." Mia takes off running down the black asphalt path, and Pixie follows behind.

He looks at me with wide eyes. "She seems...nice?"

"She's something," I mutter under my breath. My gaze stays glued to my niece and her favorite creature on the planet as they shrink in the distance. A soft sigh escapes me.

An hour. I have an hour to talk to a stranger. Okay, maybe *stranger* is a harsh term. I glance over at him, trying to be inconspicuous. Acquaintance? Yeah. That's more fitting, I guess. Doesn't change the fact I have an hour to kill with the guy.

Which is juuuust great for my introverted brain.

Thanks a lot, Mia.

"Soooo," I start, dragging out the word as I fold my arms and peek over at the guy beside me. Again. His stubbled jaw and soft blonde wavy hair are a sexy combination. Effortless somehow. Like he woke up looking this good.

Of course, he did.

"Kind of assumed you meant a little kid when you said niece," he notes, tilting his head toward the receding girl in question. "How old are you, anyway?"

"Not *that* old," I counter. "And rude."

He chuckles, looking sheepish. "I wasn't trying to be. But she must look old for her age, and you must look hella young for it. There can't be what? More than three years between you two?"

"Six, actually. I was an oops baby, and so was Mia. I guess we're kindred spirits on that front, but I'm pretty sure it's the only thing we have in common."

He rocks back on his heels and tucks his hands into his pockets as he tears his gaze away from the horizon and turns to me. "Noted."

"Thanks for meeting us, though. It means a lot to Mia."

"No problem. How's she doing?"

"Mia?" My face scrunches, surprised by his curiosity.

"Yeah. With her dad missing and all..." His voice trails off, leaving me the uncomfortable task of filling the silence with a truth far too heavy for a Saturday morning. To be fair, we have an hour to kill, and it's not like we have anything else to talk about.

"Honestly? Not so great. Or at least, I'm assuming, since she hasn't been talking much to...*anyone*?" I realize aloud. "She and her mom are in a fight because she got caught sneaking out of her house the night before she was supposed to stay with me. So now, her phone's been taken away, and she's stuck with one of her least favorite people on the planet with no outside communication."

"Least favorite?" he prods, those navy molten depths wreaking havoc on my insides as he studies me curiously.

I tuck my hair behind my ear and fold my arms. "Something like that. Although it's hard not to be her least favorite person when we're so close in age, and her lack of respect is infuriating. It doesn't help that we rarely see each other unless her dad's on a bender, and her mom needs someone to keep an eye on her, even though Mia's adamant she can take care of herself. Which I would believe if it weren't for how freaking irresponsible she is sometimes. I swear. She's taking right after her father, and we all know how he turned out.

And then, I have to figure out how to balance being the aunt, the friend, and the responsible adult without overstepping my bounds while shouldering the blame every time I fall short." I take a deep breath, surprised by my own bout of word vomit I just spilled all over an innocent Saturday morning conversation as I puff out my cheeks and mutter, "It's…exhausting."

"Sounds exhausting," he notes, his expression unreadable.

"You have no idea." I shake my head. "Especially when I never signed up for it in the first place."

His forehead wrinkles, finally showing a crack in his cool demeanor. He cocks his head to one side and faces me fully. "You sound a little resentful."

I jerk back. "Excuse me?"

"You're right." Raising his hands in defense, his poker face slipping back into place, he offers, "I shouldn't have said anything."

"Well, you did."

"You're right," he repeats and rubs his hand down his face, his shoulders hunching with defeat. He digs into his pocket and pulls out a brown bag of M&M's, popping a small handful into his mouth. I watch in fascination as he chews slowly and offers some to me.

"Want some?"

"No."

"Okay." He sighs, clearly uncomfortable.

"Why do you think I'm resentful?" I demand. I shouldn't be offended. I'm the one who word vomited on the guy, spilling my entire relationship with my niece in a two-minute monologue which probably *does* make me sound like a callous bitch toward my own flesh and blood. And maybe I am.

But he wasn't there for the nights when Bella would show up on my doorstep with a sullen Mia, having come straight from Bud's because my brother had forgotten about the drop-off and wasn't home. He wasn't there when the phone would ring at two in the morning, and I'd have to bail out Bud from jail for peeing on a police car while drunk off his ass, or when the bar would call me, begging me to come get my brother who'd passed out in the men's bathroom.

The memories flash through my mind one after the other, and a cold realization hits me square in the chest.

None of those situations were Mia's fault.

But if she and Bud are two peas in a pod, which is pretty freaking clear to see, is it so wrong for me *not* to want her going down the same path? To feel like it's my responsibility to guide her toward a different one? Is it so wrong?

Tongue in cheek, Fender looks over at me again, silently debating whether or not he wants to say whatever's rolling around in his handsome head.

"Say it," I snap.

"You remind me of my brother, I guess."

"Your brother?"

"Yeah. Sonny. He likes to take his role of big brother very seriously. Like you with the aunt role," he clarifies. "Sometimes, it's nice. Other times, all I need is a friend, but he's too busy babysitting me and being *responsible* to notice."

"So you're saying I *should* be the friend?"

"I'm saying she already has a mom who's disciplining her. Maybe she could use someone who simply listens and lets her figure her shit out on her own."

I lick my lips but stay quiet as his words rattle inside of me. Jarring, but in a way which––shockingly––isn't uncomfortable. Because he makes a good point. She's going through a lot. We all are. And just because my brother isn't here to parent her doesn't mean I should have to fill his shoes.

Whoa.

I shouldn't be surprised by the realization, but I am.

"I'll keep that in mind," I answer, my voice crackly. I clear my throat and add, "So your brother… Are you two close?"

"We used to be."

"Used to?"

"He still wants to be," he clarifies.

"And you don't?"

"I, uh…" He squeezes the back of his neck, his gaze hazy as if lost in his own thoughts. "I need some space. It isn't his fault or anything. But with our pasts and how everything went down over the last few months, I think it's better for me to take a step back and figure out some shit on my own."

Even though he's speaking cryptically, I can feel where he's coming from. I don't need the details, and I'm not about to pressure him to give me any, especially when we barely know each other, but it's clear he needs a friend. Not a fixer. Someone who listens.

Just like Mia.

With a subtle nod, I say, "Well, if you ever need a listening ear, I'm more than happy to practice listening with you. Ya know, since apparently, I need to work on that particular skill for Mia's sake. We could practice, and I could kill two birds with one stone and all."

He throws his head back and laughs. "Noted."

But he doesn't say anything else, and I can tell it's time to change the subject. For now, anyway.

"So, what do you do?" I ask.

His smile turns stiff and slides off his face entirely.

I grimace and add, "I'm sorry, I didn't know--"

"That I'm a minefield like your niece?"

I bite my lip but stay quiet.

"It's fine," he adds. "And I'm a musician. Or at least, I used to be."

"Used to be?"

"Yeah."

My mouth ticks up before smoothing to a look of indif-ference.

He gave me a one-word answer.

He and Mia *are* alike.

"You don't play anymore?" I confirm.

He leans against the hood of his car, staring blankly in front of him. "I, uh, I guess I'm taking a break from it."

"Hmm," I hum, joining him on the chipped paint. The metal is warm against my thighs yet still causes a shiver to race up my spine, but I ignore it, too focused on the man beside me to care. "Well, if you ever decide to stop taking a break, I'd love to hear you play."

"You like music?" he asks, glancing toward me and tossing another few pieces of candy-covered chocolate into his mouth.

"I like everything."

"Oh?"

"Mm-hmm."

"Like what?" he prods.

"Like...everything?" I answer with a light laugh. "I'm a writer. Pretty sure it's in our DNA to want to experience a little bit of everything and find little puzzle pieces we can click together. Ya know what I mean? Even if it's watching or reading or living vicariously through strangers, which, let's be honest, is how I prefer it. I'm a sucker for a good story."

"And you think I'm a good story?" He quirks his brow.

My smile widens, and I couldn't hold it back if I tried. "Actually? Yeah. Tall, blonde, handsome, wounded singer with brother issues who shows up on girl's doorstep and has a hero mentality, a chip on his shoulder, and a penchant for saving dogs from evil landlords? I'd read that book."

His laugh makes my stomach tighten as he stands back up, tucks the small bag of M&M's back into his pocket, and tilts his head toward the swingset. "Good to know. Care to join me?"

I follow his lead and sit on the black rubber swing beside him a few seconds later. The metal digs into my thighs, but I ignore the discomfort and use my feet to create some momentum. Pumping my legs back and forth, my hair tangles in the wind. I don't care, though. I like this. This energy. It's refreshing. Not carefree, exactly, but...poignant. Exhilarating. Something to distract me from Bud's disappearance, and I desperately need a distraction. Honestly, I'm starting to wonder if the mysterious man beside me needs one too.

8
FENDER

"Shit," I seethe, taking in the M&M wrappers scattered along my bedroom floor. I'd left Pixie here for thirty minutes, tops, and this is what I found.

Near the bed, Pixie's massive body heaves as she pukes up a dark brown, putrid sludge, and my stomach rolls. My nose wrinkles, and I dig my phone out of my pocket and Google dogs and chocolate. The combination isn't promising. My panic spikes as I pull up Hadley's information and press call. I haven't talked to her since the park, but it isn't because I haven't wanted to. If anything, it's because I *have* wanted to. And I shouldn't want things like that. Connections like that. I could see it in her eyes. She felt it too. The pull. But I've learned the hard way how dangerous a pull can be, and I don't plan on responding to it anytime soon.

But Pixie puking her guts out is a different story, and Hadley has a right to know.

How could I be so damn stupid? The bag was on my nightstand. I'd been eating them this morning before I left.

You're a fucking idiot, Fender!

I scrub my hand over my face, unsure what the hell I'm supposed to do in this situation when Hadley's quiet feminine voice filters through the speaker.

"Hello?" Her tone is hushed and raspy, as if she already knows I fucked up.

"Pixie got into chocolate."

"Wait, what?"

"Pixie got into chocolate," I repeat.

She sniffles. "H-how much chocolate?"

I look around the wrapper-covered floor, my skin paling. She must've found the stash in my closet too.

"A lot of chocolate," I tell her.

"We, uh,"––another sniffle––"we need to get her to a vet. I don't know who she usually goes to, but––"

"Probably the one by Bud's place. I remember driving past it every day when I crashed on his couch."

"I'll meet you there," she murmurs.

As I go to hang up, she adds, "And Fen?"

"Yeah?"

"This isn't your fault, okay?"

With a self-deprecating laugh, I squeeze my hand into a fist and search for Pixie's leash, not bothering to hide the disdain in my voice as I reply, "Sure, it isn't. See you in fifteen."

HADLEY'S WHITE CAMRY IS IN THE LOT, AND I PULL IN NEXT TO it, shoving my car into park. Pixie's massive, at least 120 pounds, but I cradle her in my arms as if she's a child, ignoring the putrid scent clinging to her breath as we head into the vet's office.

When Hadley sees us, she points to Pixie and tells the vet tech near the receptionist desk, "That's her."

The guy can't weigh more than the dog in my arms and is wearing blue scrubs and white Nikes as he waves me to a back hallway. "Follow me."

We head to an exam room but don't have to wait long when someone appears in a white coat with the name Dr. Grover scrawled above the right pocket on his chest.

"So, I heard this girl got into some chocolate," he confirms, examining Pixie in my arms.

I nod and force myself to set her down but keep my hand on her head, unable to stop myself from touching her, though I'm not sure if it's for her benefit or mine. I feel like shit because she feels like shit, and it's all my fault.

"Do you know how long it's been since she ate it?" he prods.

I look down at Pixie and attempt to do the math in my head. "Thirty to forty-five minutes, I think?"

"Has she vomited or had any diarrhea?"

"Both." I scratch behind her ear, surprised by the fear coursing through my veins. I've barely had her for more than a few weeks, but the idea of her dying because I left chocolate out kills me.

You're such a screw-up, Fen.

Dr. Grover squats down and studies her carefully. "We're going to take her back and see what we can do to get the toxins out of her system."

"Thank you," I return.

Dr. Grover slips a baby blue slip-knot leash over Pixie's head since I couldn't find mine in my rush to get here. He urges her to follow him into the back room. And because she's the most obedient dog in the world, she listens without hesitation, though her head hangs low and her steps are slow as if each tiny movement is exhausting.

As the door swings closed behind them, I collapse onto the maroon vinyl cushioned bench in the exam room.

With my elbows on my knees, I rest my head in my hands and let the silence and unknown eat me alive.

"She's going to be okay," Hadley murmurs a few minutes later. I can feel her sit down beside me, though I don't bother to look at her. I can't. I'm too ashamed. She trusted me with Pixie, and I let her down.

"You don't know that," I mumble. "You don't know if she's going to be all right."

"I was talking to the vet tech before you got here. He said this happens more than you'd think, and as long as the dog gets here in time, they're usually able to treat them without any issues. It helps that Pixie's massive and would've had to eat a ton of chocolate for it to really affect her. I think she'll be fine, Fen."

"But if I hadn't--"

"Stop," she orders, grabbing my knee and squeezing roughly with her tiny hands. I drop my arms to my sides and look over at her. Her eyes are bloodshot and drained.

"Look, I'm sorry--"

"I'm not crying because of Pixie, although it *does* feel like her incident is the icing on top of a crap cake..." Her voice cracks, then trails off, and she rubs beneath her red-rimmed eyes.

"What happened, Hadley?"

"The police called. Apparently, they found some evidence which may or may not relate to Bud."

"What kind of evidence?"

She shakes her head. "I don't know. They won't tell me. Which is frustrating. Because I feel like...if I just had all of the puzzle pieces, I could make them fit, ya know? His disappearance. Where he is. Why he hasn't come home yet. I need the stupid puzzle pieces, and they won't give them to me. It's...frustrating." She shakes her head again as if to stop herself from falling into the same little loop of unanswered questions she's been drowning in since Bud first disappeared. She tucks her hair behind her ear and lets out a slow breath. "I don't want to talk about it. I want to focus on Pixie's situation. Something I can potentially have control over."

Pixie.

The knife in my gut twists.

"Yeah, well, I'm sorry I added more to your plate," I grunt, another wave of guilt flooding my system. "If something happens––"

"We'll deal with it."

"You trusted me," I remind her.

"And so far, you've been doing a great job. This one situation doesn't change anything. It's chocolate. It happens."

"Doesn't make me feel any less guilty."

"Well, it should." She leans closer, her glasses framing her baby blue eyes contrasting with her dark lashes and dark hair like a lighthouse on a stormy night. Captivating. And enough to pull me from my guilt. For a minute, anyway.

"You did nothing wrong," she says. "I promise."

My phone rings in the otherwise silent room, and I dig it out of my pocket, grateful for the distraction. My forehead wrinkles as I take in the unfamiliar number. I look at Hadley, remembering my manners, and I start to tuck it back into my pocket.

"Who is it?" she asks.

"I don't recognize the number."

Reading my thoughts as if they're her own, she suggests, "You should answer it."

"You sure? I don't want to be rude––"

"Yeah. We're just waiting for Pixie anyway."

I nod and slide my thumb across the screen, answering the call hesitantly. "Hello?"

"Fen?"

"Who is this?"

"This is Hawthorne."

Pinching the bridge of my nose, I hang my head. "Now isn't really a good time."

"I have a show for you."

I flinch back. "Excuse me?"

"SeaBird. Friday night. You're playing."

With a dry laugh, my emotions finally catch up to me. "Me and what band?"

"You *are* the band. For now, anyway. Bring an acoustic guitar and a few covers. If you have any songs you've written yourself, bring those too."

"Hawthorne--"

"You have the talent, Fen. I'm not gonna let you waste it."

"Wait," I bark before he has a chance to hang up.

"Yeah?" he answers, his voice impatient.

"Let me think about it."

With a sigh, Hawthorne says, "If I let you think about it, you're gonna overthink about it, and you're gonna say no--"

"I won't say no. I..." I suck my cheeks between my teeth and bite down. Not enough to cause any real damage, but enough pressure to make me hurt. To confirm I'm not dreaming this shit up. That I'm really on the phone with Hawthorne, and he's giving me another shot, even though I'm not entirely sure I want it. "Let me think about it."

"I don't care what it takes, Fender. I'm going to get you back on a stage, even if I have to call Gibson--"

"Leave Sonny out of this," I seethe.

Silence.

Hadley's spine straightens beside me, but she doesn't budge as she picks at her cuticles like they're the most fascinating thing in the world.

Desperate, I dig into my pocket for my packet of M&M's, but it's empty.

I must've forgotten to grab another bag, one Pix hadn't managed to rip into, when I'd rushed out the door with her.

Shit.

My knee bounces up and down, and I scrub my hand over my face, an apology on the tip of my tongue for snapping at him, though I can't make myself say it. Because I *do* want Hawthorne to leave Sonny out of this. It's my life. My future. My music.

Mine.

"Why?" Hawthorne asks a few seconds later. His tone is less demanding and more empathic this time. Like he wants to understand. Like he wants to help. There's only one problem. I don't know what he can do.

"I need to do this on my own."

"But you're not on your own, Fen," he returns gently. "You have family and friends who want to help you––"

"I gotta go."

"Call me by tomorrow with your answer, or I reach out to Sonny."

The call ends, and my fingers tighten around my phone in a death grip. I tap it against my chin, barely refraining from throwing it against the wall.

"What was that about?" Hadley asks.

"A guy with a lot of pull in the music industry. Hawthorne," I clarify. "He wants me to play a show."

"And I sense you don't want me to congratulate you?"

I snort. "I guess not."

"You don't want to play?" She squeezes my thigh again, and for some reason, it grounds me. Her touch. The warmth from her tiny palm. I stare at the back of her hand on my lap but stay quiet.

"You can talk to me, you know. As a friend," she murmurs, and it's surprising how much I could use one right now. A friend.

I think it's normal. To feel alone. The rehab facility hooked me up with a sponsor, but we didn't exactly click, so I told him I wasn't interested in keeping in contact once I was released. And because I'd checked myself into the facility voluntarily, the guy didn't really have a leg to stand on. We haven't spoken since.

I know I have Milo and Jake, though. Even River, Gibson, Stoker, and Phoenix would be here in a second if I ever needed them. But right now, when I'm trying to figure out the new me, reaching out to them feels forced. Like they're waiting for the other shoe to drop. For me to fail again. For me to screw up. And I don't blame them. I have failed. Spectacularly. Over and over again. Not to mention they have their own lives now. They don't need my shit. Not right now. Not until I prove I can do this without them.

But Hadley? She doesn't know about the baggage I carry. The baggage I was forcing my friends to carry with me. And for some reason, it's refreshing. The knowledge that the new me is the only me she's met. Maybe she can bring a fresh perspective. One I can't see because of my tainted past.

Licking my bottom lip, I tap my hand against my jeans. Remembering the M&M's are missing, I settle back into the cushioned seat. "It's complicated."

"We've got time. And honestly? With everything going on, I could most definitely use the distraction."

I chuckle dryly, deciding to let out a bit of the pressure which has managed to build in my chest over the past few weeks. "I'm scared to play again."

"Why?"

Another dry chuckle vibrates up my throat. "Let's just say I didn't make the best decisions when I started playing music professionally. The pressure. The desire to please everyone. The drive to push forward. To be perfect. To live up to my dad's name. It was a lot."

"Your dad's name?" she asks.

"Donny Hayes."

"The rockstar?" Her eyes widen with disbelief behind her black-rimmed glasses.

I laugh a little harder this time. "The one and only."

"Your dad is Donny Hayes?"

"I believe we already covered that part."

"I know, it's... Wow. I had no idea."

"Yeah."

"I can't even imagine that type of pressure."

She has no clue.

"It's a lot," I admit.

"But you love it? Playing?"

"I used to."

She tilts her head to one side. "Used to?"

"Now, I'm starting to wonder if I loved the music or the high from the audience. I haven't played since..." I scratch the scruff of my jaw. "I haven't played in a while. Not since my band fell apart."

"What happened?" she prods.

I shake my head, my lips pressing into a thin line. Such a simple question. Two words. If only I knew the answer. One that wasn't a convoluted mess of regret and mistakes, all of them made by me.

She frowns. "You don't have to tell me--"

"I screwed up," I mutter.

The compassion in her gaze is too much. I feel like I might suffocate from it.

"I think you should try playing again."

"You do?"

She nods. "Even if it's only for closure. You *not* playing-- not knowing what the trigger is for your *why* behind your love of music--it has to be killing you. Isn't it?"

61

"Maybe," I reply, my hands itching at my sides. I wipe them on my jeans.

"Then, you should play. Even if it's your final show, and you never pick up an instrument again. I think you should still do it."

Curious, I glance up at her, tearing my gaze from the linoleum floor to the crystal blue irises staring back at me. "Yeah?"

"Yeah."

"Would you want to come?" I ask.

Her eyes widen. "Me?"

"Yeah. You." My mouth tilts up as I take in her surprise at my offer. "I thought you said you could use the distraction."

She smiles, her cheeks stretching and turning pink all at once. "I'd love to, Fen."

The back door opens, and Dr. Grover steps into the white and gray exam room, interrupting us.

"Pixie's going to be okay," he starts. "We got all the chocolate out of her system, and she should be good as new by tomorrow. We'd like to keep her overnight as a precaution, but you should be able to pick her up in the morning."

"Thank you," I reply, relief flooding my system.

"Don't mention it. And, uh, we want you to know we've been thinking a lot about Bud. If you guys need anything, let us know."

Hadley nods, her expression tightening. She turns on her heel without another word.

I thank Dr. Grover for his help, pay the bill at the front desk, and rush out of the exam room to catch up to Hadley. She slows at the door, feeling my presence behind her but doesn't say a word as I push it open for her. The warm breeze causes her hair to tangle around her face almost instantly, and she dips her chin to her chest, shielding herself from it.

Or maybe she's shielding herself from *me*.

We make our way to the cars in silence. When we're standing by the vehicles, I ask, "You okay?"

She shakes her head and brushes beneath her nose with the back of her hand, avoiding my gaze.

My hands itch to grab her face and force her to look at me, but I restrain myself. Shoving them into my pockets, I lean against her driver's side door. Patient. Weary. And with the knowledge that if there were ever a time to walk on eggshells, it would be now.

"How did he know about Bud's disappearance?" I ask quietly.

Her straight, white teeth dig into her lower lip as she peeks up at me. Then she drops her gaze to the ground.

"Is everything all right?" I prod, hating how I already know the answer. Of course, it's not. Her brother's missing, and the police found new evidence or some shit. But I don't know what else to say or how I can make her feel better.

"Yeah," she lies. "It's just...a couple of weeks before you showed up, Isabella, Bud's ex, went to the police and filed a report. His disappearance was all over the news for a few days, which is probably why Dr. Grover knew about it. I don't think Bella wanted to admit Bud might've fallen off the wagon again, ya know? The investigation is still ongoing, but you know Bud, right? And even though the police found some other evidence like I mentioned earlier, it's not exactly comforting either way. There is no bright side. No silver lining right now. And I guess when Dr. Grover mentioned Bud, it was one more reminder of how my private life isn't so private. Not right now. And the lack of answers in the whole thing is..." She sucks her lips between her teeth, forming a white slash across her face as she shakes her head. "It's exhausting."

The tightness in her smile is pathetic at best as she peeks

up at me, but the fear in her shiny eyes kills me. The fear for her brother. She's been so adamant he's on a bender and will show up any day now, but her gaze? The way her lower lip trembles slightly as she forces the oxygen from her lungs? They tell a different story. She's scared. And I hate that she's scared.

"Dammit, Hads." I pull her into a hug without giving a shit whether or not it's appropriate. She needs it. "I'm sorry."

"It's fine." Her arms wrap around my waist and squeeze. Letting me go, she backs up, wiping beneath her nose with the back of her hand again as she forces another smile. "I just wish I knew whether or not my frustration is merited. I keep telling myself he's being a selfish prick, but a small voice wonders if it's really the case. And that's..." She shakes her head and rubs her hands up and down her crossed arms. "That's where it gets a little scary. My mind starts going haywire because I write thrillers for a living, and either A, I can't tone it back, and my imagination gets the best of me. Or B, I overcompensate by cursing out my brother for disappearing when I have absolutely no idea whether or not it's his fault. But no matter the circumstances, I can't write. I can't focus. I simply keep waiting. And the waiting is slowly killing me inside. So...yeah." An awkward laugh escapes her as she digs into her purse for her keys, avoiding my gaze like it's the plague. "I guess you could say I really do need the distraction."

"I'm happy I can help," I offer. "Look. I gotta make a call, but if you need anything, I'm..."

She peeks up at me again, pushing the car fob to unlock her door, prodding, "You're...?"

A fucking disaster who has no right to the woman in front of him.

I clear my throat and open her car door. "I'll see you around."

"At the show, right?"

I nod. "See you then."

My HANDS SHAKE AS I STARE AT MARTY'S CONTACT information from behind the wheel, my blood practically vibrating in my veins as my heart rate skyrockets. Mouth dry, I lick my lips and take a deep, barely-controlled breath and press the call button.

Hadley left almost thirty minutes ago, but I couldn't start my car. I couldn't shove away my guilt for being related to the one guy who might know where Bud is. But I also couldn't push aside the craving flooding my system as soon as his name filtered across my mind.

Martin Hayes.

Fifty percent brother.

One hundred percent asshole.

Shit.

It rings four times––I counted––and a familiar voice crackles through the speakers.

"Hello, Brother."

9
FENDER

"**D**addy Dearest says I'm not allowed to talk to you anymore," Marty tells me through the phone. I squeeze it a little tighter, threatening to crack the damn thing, but force myself to ease up on it.

"And I'd like to keep it that way," I grit out. "But I have a question to ask you before we go back to cutting ties."

"Cutting ties? Why would we want to cut ties? We're family, remember?"

"Cut the shit, Marty––"

"Lots of cutting talk, don't you think? Maybe I should tell Dad––"

"I just want to ask you a question," I bark. "And after everything you put me through, I think I deserve an answer."

"Everything I put you through?" He laughs. "That's rich––"

"Have you seen Bud?"

"Bud?" He laughs again. "You mean your drug buddy?"

"Says the guy who introduced us," I remind him. "When was the last time you saw him?"

He hesitates. Probably to piss me off, and I hate how it's working.

"Can't recall," he answers a few seconds later, his tone dismissive.

A headache threatens to crack my skull in two as I pinch the bridge of my nose and rest my head against the steering wheel. "Can you give me a ballpark estimate?"

"No can do, baby brother."

"He said he was quitting––"

"They all say they're quitting." I can hear the amusement in his voice. "Speaking of which, you sound stressed. I can give you some molly if you're––"

I end the call and chuck my phone onto the passenger seat, my chest heaving. I drive home like a bat out of hell, desperate for a fix while knowing the only one I'll be able to hit is currently swimming inside my brain.

I need my guitar.

And the pack of M&M's I have stashed in the kitchen.

It's been hours. Hours since Pixie got into the chocolate. Hours since I agreed to play in front of people again, even though I've refused to touch any piece of musical equipment since I woke up in a hospital from overdosing. Hours since I hung up the phone with my dealer. Hours since I've been sitting with my ass on the ground, my back pressed into the side of the bed, and my eyes glued to the black guitar case taunting me from the open closet door.

It feels like it's been a fucking lifetime.

I rub my hands against my jeans, puffing out my cheeks while trying not to lose my shit. Things had been getting better with Pix around. I guess I'd been so distracted by taking care of something else, I forgot I still didn't know how to take care of myself. Or maybe I'm giving myself too much credit. Maybe Pixie was taking care of me all along.

Or maybe it's the idea of Hadley getting even closer to me and everything I have to hide making me feel like I have bugs crawling beneath my skin.

I spoke with Marty for the first time in months. Maybe he's the one I can blame for the messed-up imagery and cravings thrumming through my veins.

With another deep breath, I hang my head in my hands when my phone rings from my nightstand. Blindly, I reach for it and slide my thumb across the screen, answering the call without bothering to see who's calling.

"Hello?" I grunt.

"Hey, Fen." Sonny's voice is familiar but weirdly foreign too. We haven't spoken since the hospital. Since I told him to take my place as the face of Broken Vows. Since I almost wrecked his relationship with Dove.

Feels like forever.

"Uh, hey," I reply. My voice sounds like I've swallowed razor blades. I clear it and lean my head against the edge of the bed.

I shouldn't have answered the phone.

"I heard you're home. How are you, man?"

My calloused palm scrubs against my face as I squeeze my eyes shut. "Fine. You?"

"We've been good. Things are…good. Miss you, though."

"Yeah." I sigh and lift my chin toward the ceiling, ignoring the ache in my chest. "Miss you too."

"Saw you got a dog."

Confused, I cock my head and ask, "How? When?"

"Some paparazzi snapped a picture of you outside the house with one a few weeks ago."

I search my memories and realize it must've been taken

the first night I brought Pix home. I *knew* someone was following me.

At least I'm not going crazy.

"Didn't know I was still on their radar," I note dryly.

"Don't sound so surprised. People are anxious to hear you play again."

I scoff but stay quiet.

"You gonna meet up with us?" he asks. "We only have a couple more shows, but you should join. I'll get you a plane ticket--"

"I think I'm gonna pass."

He hesitates. And even from across the world, I'm pretty sure I can hear the wheels churning in his head as he processes my comment. Too bad I don't give a shit. Not right now. Not when I feel like my world is spinning out of control. I shouldn't have called Marty. I knew he wouldn't answer my questions about Bud. It was stupid. *I* was stupid.

"Fen--"

"Seriously. I'm fine. But I gotta go. I'll talk to you later--"

"You haven't been answering my calls," Sonny interrupts.

"I've been busy."

"Too busy to talk to your older brother?"

I shake my head even though he can't see me. I hate this guilty feeling and how it's all I feel anytime I talk to Sonny. He was my confidante. My sage big brother. My fucking hero. And now I'm pissed at him, even though I know he doesn't deserve my fury. I'm angry. And I'm hurt. I feel like I've been forgotten, despite knowing it isn't fair. I'm not being pushed away. I'm *pulling* away. It's on me. Not him. But it's like I'm watching the entire situation--my entire life-- through a looking glass, unable to control the outcome or the resentment or any other single action which could change the fact that I'm frustrated. Not with Gibson, but with myself.

I need more time. And while I take the time for myself, it only fans Sonny's concern. So, where does it leave me?

Fucked.

"Listen," he continues, "I'm not trying to make you feel guilty or anything. I know you're working through shit, but we miss you. You should come out--"

"I gotta go." I click the end button before I can stop myself and lean my head against the side of the bed. The seconds tick by slowly, picking up their pace like droplets of water during a storm when I find myself on my feet with my hand wrapped around the neck of the guitar and my skin slick with sweat. Pacing the bedroom, my grip tightening, I let the lyrics wash over me. Ones I've never dared to say out loud or even put on paper until they're pounding inside my skull with a palpable urgency.

Collapsing onto my bed, I cradle the guitar in my lap and play.

HADLEY

I haven't been out in forever. Which I guess makes sense since I'm an introverted author who lives in pajamas, but still. There's a buzzing beneath my skin as I pull SeaBird's door open. The place has good reviews, most mentioning the vibrant atmosphere and claiming fame through being the home of the up-and-coming band, Broken Vows. I couldn't help myself. I looked them up. And there's a reason SeaBird claims them. They're good. Like, really good.

And not only their new stuff but their old stuff too. The stuff Fender sang.

His voice? Damn, it's like honey. Sweet, earthy, unique. But it sticks with you long after the music ends, and I can't help humming along to it, even though it's only playing in my head as I find a seat at the back of the bar.

The place is crowded, lined with tables and booths along with a long bar at the back and a stage tucked to the left where a single barstool and microphone stand are set up. A song plays in the background, barely making a dent in the noise from the excited customers crowding the stage. Something in my gut tells me it isn't usually this busy, but what do I know? Maybe I'm the only one fascinated by the singer who disappeared from Broken Vows right after they caught their big break.

Part of me wants to ask why he left the band or if he has any intention of returning, but the other part of me doesn't want to broach the subject. We're just… Hell, I don't even know what we are. Friends? Acquaintances? Honestly, I have no idea. But one thing's for sure. I *have* been distracted. And my fascination with the elusive Fender Hayes is the only thing getting me through the day lately. Not that I'd ever admit it out loud.

I shake off the thought and take a seat at the clean bartop.

A gorgeous bartender with her hair in a high slicked-back ponytail approaches. "Hey. What can I get ya?"

"A glass of red wine, please."

Her perfectly plucked brow arches. "No preferences?"

"Nope. Whatever you have that doesn't cost an arm and a leg would be great."

With a smile, she dips her chin. "Coming right up."

She sets a glass in front of me a few minutes later and asks, "So. You here to see Fender play?"

I drag my attention from the empty stage and back to her. "How could you tell?"

"Because I haven't seen you in here before, and you keep staring at the stage as if you're waiting for a certain someone to take it."

A blush creeps into my cheeks. I reach for the glass of wine and bring it to my lips.

"Were you a fan of Broken Vows?" she asks.

"Not until Fender invited me to watch him play tonight. I'm kind of a recluse and didn't know about them."

"You know Fen?" She tilts her head to the side and assesses me with new interest. "Like, personally?"

I take another sip from my glass. "Yes?"

"Interesting. I didn't know he was seeing anyone."

"Oh, we're not..." My voice trails off, leaving my words hanging in the air.

"Gotcha," the bartender replies a few seconds later, though she doesn't exactly look convinced. "So, I assume you haven't known him very long since you weren't aware of his connection to Broken Vows. Am I right?"

"Yeah, we just met a few weeks ago."

"Interesting. And...how's he been doing?" she prods. Not with any malice or overbearing interest which would make a normal person feel uncomfortable, but with an honest curiosity reminding me of a good friend or even a Mama Bear.

Interesting.

"He's good, I think," I tell her.

Her eyes narrow in disbelief. "Yeah?"

I nod, hating how I'm beginning to second guess myself when under her scrutiny. "I think so?"

Another pause. "Well, good. Good for him. I'm glad he has someone to talk to," she decides.

Someone to talk to? My brow quirks. Why would he need someone to talk to? Or better yet, why would a random bartender who obviously knows Fender quite well be grateful he has someone to talk to? The questions continue building, but I shake them off and take another sip of wine.

I'm not sure why, but I feel like I'm missing something. A vital piece of information. One which would finally connect all the dots that are Fender Hayes and show me the real him instead of the acquaintance I've gotten to know over the past few encounters. Unfortunately, I'm not that lucky and am still as lost as ever. Hell, more so.

"Not sure I'd say Fender has opened up to me, but he

knows he can," I explain. "Or at least I think he does. So... there's that. Right?"

"Right."

She gets back to work while the bustle from the crowd grows more and more restless as the next few minutes crawl by at a snail's pace.

A few minutes later, a man in a fitted gray suit settles onto the barstool next to mine.

The bartender almost squeals when she sees him, leaning over the countertop to press a quick kiss on his lips. "Hey, babe! How's he doing?"

"Refuses to get on stage without his dog," the stranger replies, his mouth curving up with amusement. "*That's* how he's doing, Sammie."

Dog? My ears perk, but I keep my gaze glued to what little red liquid is left in my cup.

Be. Inconspicuous. Hadley!

"It's a good thing my dad owns the bar and wouldn't care," Sammie, the bartender, returns. "How's he doing otherwise?"

"He's..." I catch the man raking his fingers through his hair from the corner of my eye. "I guess we'll have to wait and see."

"I guess so. But he better hurry. The crowd's getting restless."

"Yeah. I don't know what he's waiting on."

"Maybe his new friend can help," Sammie offers, turning her attention to me.

Crap!

"Hawthorne, this is... I'm sorry. I didn't catch your name," she adds with a light blush.

Forcing a smile, I twist in my seat to face the guy fully while pretending I most definitely wasn't eavesdropping on their previous conversation. Nope. Not me. I was just minding my own beeswax.

"I'm Hadley. Hi."

"Hi." Sammie smiles and turns back to Hawthorne, shooting him a look I can't quite decipher.

With his massive hand outstretched, he says, "Like my girlfriend said, I'm Hawthorne. Nice to meet you."

"Nice to meet you too. I'm Hadley," I repeat with another awkward smile as I shake his hand.

"So, Hadley. You know Fen?"

He says it like I belong to some inside club, eyeing me with interest.

"Um…yes?"

"And? How is he?" he prods.

I laugh, déjà vu hitting me square in the chest. I toss Sammie a knowing look. "I see whatcha did there."

"And I'm not even sorry about it," she volleys back and heads toward the opposite end of the bar to help another customer.

"So?" Hawthorne's attention shifts from me to the empty stage. "How is he?" he repeats.

"He's fine, I guess?"

"Just fine?"

I let out a huff, surprised by my overprotective self who wants to ask why he needs to know but bite my tongue then explain. "Okay. I think he's going through some things, but he's processing it the best he can. Better?"

Hawthorne's chin dips as the lights on the stage flicker on, and Fender approaches the stage with Pixie right beside him. No leash. I don't know why, but the sight makes me smile. Like they're a team.

Clearing his throat, Fender heads toward the mic on stiff legs, looking uncomfortable yet still sexy as hell in a black T-shirt and dark jeans hugging his thighs. If I didn't know any better, I'd said this is his first show. He looks nervous. A little jittery. He's refusing to maintain eye contact with anyone. It's adorable and a little nerve-wracking at the same time. I want to climb on stage and give the guy a hug, but I wipe my palms against my jeans to restrain myself.

For now, anyway.

"Hey," he starts, his voice like warm honey. "Uh, I guess I'm gonna play you guys a song." His attention somehow finds me in the crowd, making me want to squirm on my barstool as I force myself to hold his gaze for another second, making my heart skip a beat. A soft smile flickers across his features, hinting at the confident rockstar everyone in this bar knows him to be. But the look quickly disappears. Hell, if I'd have blinked, I would've missed it. I'm glad I didn't. Because that look? His ghost of a smile? It could keep a girl warm in the middle of a freaking blizzard.

With another quick glance my way, he takes a seat on the barstool and cradles an old, beat-up acoustic guitar in his lap.

Pixie plops down onto the stage, spreading out and yawning as if settling in for a long night as Fender plucks the first notes from the strings of his guitar.

It's hypnotic. Watching him up there. As if the rest of the world doesn't matter. As if it all floats away. As if the soft, smooth notes sounding nothing like the harsher, more adren-aline-filled songs from Broken Vows are a lullaby. Something to soothe while casting a melancholic spell over the crowd.

He closes his eyes and leans closer to the mic, the same honey voice rolling over me. And that's what does me in.

The sadness.

The mention of mistakes. Of sorrow. Of wanting to turn back time, only to acknowledge it isn't possible, and your mistakes somehow gifted someone their dream. And how you can't get it back. How it's *selfish* to take it back. So you'll bear the weight of it all. Alone.

He's mourning.

For his previous life.

And it kills me.

As he hits the final notes of the song, he looks up at me again. His smile is pained. Hell, it's tortured, but I keep my butt planted where it is, forcing myself to stay seated as I mouth, "Amazing," back at him.

He chuckles, the sound low and throaty before muttering into the microphone, "Enough sad shit, yeah? Let's play something a little more upbeat."

The opening notes of "I Kissed A Girl and I Liked It" by Katy Perry ring throughout the bar, pulling laughter from the audience, and he dives right into the first verse. Pixie falls asleep on the stage, either used to Fender's playing or meant to be on stage as his sidekick even though it's a new role for both of them, until two more songs are played.

Someone in the crowd yells at him to take his shirt off, and a few people request Broken Vows' hits, but he doesn't acknowledge any of them. He simply plays. Just to play. Some are original songs, others are covers. But one thing's clear. He was made to be up there. To entertain. To sing. To make people feel in a way only music can.

And he's rocking it.

A little while later, he wipes his damp forehead with the back of his hand and checks the time on his phone, tucking it back into the front pocket of his jeans. Like we've witnessed a solid jam session in our friend's basement instead of a mini-concert in the middle of a crowded bar.

Not gonna lie. It's hot as hell.

"All right, guys. My voice hasn't had to sing this much in months, so I think we're gonna call it a night. Thanks for showing up, though. You, uh, you definitely know how to make a guy feel welcome." With a little wave of his hand and a final nod to a group of people in a booth near the front of the stage, he pats his leg and calls Pixie's name. She follows behind him, ready to go wherever he leads her.

And even though I know he'll probably come over to say hi to me in a minute, I already miss seeing him up on the stage.

Clearly, he belongs there.

FENDER

"**Y**ou killed it!" Maddie practically screeches. I approach the booth where all my friends insisted on sitting when they found out I'd be performing, and she pulls me into a massive bear hug.

Since Sammie's dating Hawthorne, and he's the one who set up the performance, Sammie spilled the beans to my friends. She knew they'd want to be here to support me. I'm not mad she told them. I should be excited they're here. But it feels weird. Like I'd disappoint them if I didn't put on a Broken Vows show instead of a Fender Hayes show. Like, if I can't live up to the guy they think I am––the party guy––I won't be worth it.

And I know it isn't true. In my gut, I know they love me and want me to be happy. I know they could see me spiraling and wanted me to get help. I know they liked me before the drugs. Before I felt the need to always put on a happy face.

But knowing something in your head and feeling it in your gut are two different things. The latter will take some time, I guess.

Jake and his girlfriend, Evie, each take their turns

congratulating me, and Milo slaps me on the back and says, "Good to have you back, Fen."

I squeeze the back of my neck, caught between the old Fen and the new one. Because being onstage? It felt good. I felt like myself again. It's a problem, though, isn't it? Or maybe it's not a problem. Maybe it's okay to be me. Just…the new and improved version. If I can help it.

"Yeah. It's, uh good to be back, I guess."

"Your new stuff. You write it?" he prods.

I nod.

"It's good. Different," he clarifies. "But really good."

"Yeah, Sonny better watch out. I have a feeling you're gonna give him a run for his money," Jake adds.

With a snort, I shake my head. "There's a reason I left Sonny to write the music for Broken Vows, man––"

"Yeah, so you could keep all the gems tucked away for a rainy day," Maddie teases.

I throw my head back and laugh, surprising myself as well as the rest of the group. "I dunno about that, but I'm glad you guys liked it. I'm gonna go say hi to a friend. I'll meet you guys back at the house."

"Sure thing," Jake returns.

Maddie adds, "Do you want us to take Pix?"

"My shadow?" I look down at Pixie. Her tail is wagging back and forth as she sits right next to my feet, completely oblivious to the sea of people or how many are probably dying to ask if they can touch her. "Nah. I'll keep her with me. Thanks, though."

"Aw, come on. Let us take her home so I can feed her the bacon I saved from breakfast this morning," Maddie begs. "I gotta make her love me more than she loves you."

Milo laughs and tugs his girlfriend closer to him. "Should I be jealous, babe?"

"All I'm saying is if your friend ever decides to breed Pix

when he gets back, I'm here for it. We'll leave it at that," Maddie replies.

With another laugh, I shove aside the reminder of Pixie's owner, for more reasons than one, and say, "You and me both. I'll see you guys at home."

"See ya!"

The place is crowded, and I weave between people, waving at the fans who tell me how excited they are to have me back while ignoring the people who ask where I've been over the past few months and why I'm not in Broken Vows anymore.

I can feel Hadley watching me. Watching me juggle the questions and compliments like a seasoned pro. I wish I could read her mind and know what she's thinking. If she's impressed. Disappointed. If she can see how exhausted I am from the few mentions of Sonny taking over Broken Vows, or if she thinks I'm overrated and didn't like my performance. I hope that isn't the case, because when I was up there? I played for me, sure, but the person who got me to sit down, to strum the first note was *her*. It was because of our conversation at the vet's office. It's because I wanted to know the *why* behind my love of music. And while I was up on the stage, I think I found my answer. It's not the drugs. It's not the high from having everyone's eyes on you. Okay, maybe a little, but not entirely. It's the energy. The pull. The connection. And holy shit, did I feel connected to Hadley as I sang. More than I've ever felt with anyone in my entire life.

Her mouth lifts in a soft smile as I finally break through the last line of people and plop down in the barstool next to hers.

"Sorry it took so long," I start.

"Don't apologize." She steps off her barstool and squats down, scratching Pixie's head in greeting. The girl's short but has curves any guy would drool over, and right now, I can see straight down her top.

Down, boy.

I clear my throat and look at the rim of her empty wine glass instead. There isn't a lip stain marring it. I don't know why it surprises me. It shouldn't. She isn't one for lipstick. I shouldn't have noticed that particular quirk either, but... I shake my head and stare at the rows of glasses and alcohol lining the back wall, attempting to get my head on straight.

Keep it together, man.

Just because I played a good show doesn't mean I can or *should* jump into bed with Hadley. Sure, sex after a good performance is a great way to get off. But embarrassing myself when I'm not able to finish because of my addiction to drugs isn't exactly going to end the night on a high note.

Pixie lays on the concrete floor beneath our feet to get comfortable as Hadley stands and slides onto the barstool next to mine, oblivious to the fact I was most definitely picturing her naked a few seconds ago.

"I had no idea I was hanging out with the cool kid," she tells me, her smile shy. "Did you know there were a pair of girls over here a few minutes ago who were gushing about your abs and were sorely disappointed when you didn't take off your shirt on stage tonight?"

I hide my smirk behind my hand but don't bother to deny it. Those were some good times.

"You know, if I was your girlfriend, I'd be jealous," she teases, her naturally red lips tugging into a wider smile, and it shoots straight to my groin.

Calm the hell down, Fen, I remind myself. *It's only the high from playing. Nothing more.*

"Dating a musician has its pros and cons," I agree while flagging down Sammie from behind the bar. When she sees me, she lifts her forefinger, telling me to give her a second, and goes back to filling a mug full of amber liquid.

"Pros and cons, huh?" Hadley asks. "Like paparazzi and strangers asking you to take off your shirt so they can see your abs?"

"Something like that."

"So, tell me. Would those be in the pro category or con?" With her elbow on the counter, and her chin resting in her hand, she gives me her full attention, clearly as curious about me as I am about her.

"Paparazzi, con. Strangers wanting to see your abs?" I don't bother to hide my grin as I casually look her up and down. "Pro."

She rolls her eyes. "For you, maybe. For your hypothetical girlfriend? Debatable."

"All right, what do you think would be a pro?"

"If I were the rockstar or the girlfriend?" she asks.

"Both."

"All right. As for rockstar, I think being able to connect with so many people, to touch them with your talent, and to have them listen to what you're trying to say is pretty incredible."

"Says the author," I point out.

She laughs and tucks her hair behind her ear, a soft blush creeping onto her cheeks. It's adorable. My hands itch to reach out and run my finger against the light color to see if it'll darken, but I restrain myself.

"Touché," she concedes. "I love reading reviews and hearing what people think about my stories. The criticism, not so much, but the ones where they talk about how they couldn't put the book down or why they named one of their children after my characters?" She shakes her head as if in disbelief. "It's something else."

"Yeah," I admit. "It really is."

"So there ya go. There's a pro for being a rockstar and/or an author. The pro for being a rockstar's girlfriend, however..." She taps her finger against her chin without bothering to hide the fact she's checking me out. Shamelessly. "Being able to take you home at night knowing every other female––and some males––would be going out of their minds with jealousy over you being mine."

"That's a turn-on, huh?"

"Definitely. We all want what we can't have, Fender Hayes. But knowing you have something or some*one* others covet?" She quirks her brow. "Yeah. It's a turn-on."

"I'll keep it in mind."

"I'm sure you will." She laughs. "Now, you tell me. What's the pro of being a rockstar's girlfriend?"

"You really wanna know?"

She grins, playing along. "Yes."

I lean closer, unable to help myself as I whisper against her ear, "We're great at keeping rhythm."

"Oh, really?"

"Yeah." I lean a little closer, her soft fruity scent tickling my nostrils and making me hard. "We also know how to find *just* the right note to make a girl sing."

Her breathless laughter fans itself against my cheek as she turns her head and peeks up at me. "Is that right?"

"Mm-hmm," I hum, though it comes out as more of a growl.

This is a bad idea.

And it's not like this can go anywhere. Not if I want to stay sober.

The reminder hits harder than a sledgehammer, and I clear my throat, shoving aside the high from being on stage so I won't do something I'll regret.

I reach for the glass of water Sammie must've placed in front of me while I was busy flirting with Hadley. She

84

watches me guzzle half the glass. The wheels are clearly turning in her pretty little head, and I'm aching to know what she's thinking about or if it involves me finding *just* the right note to make her sing.

But I don't ask her.

Even skirting around this subject is dangerous territory, but I can't help myself. She's too damn tantalizing.

"Interesting," Hadley returns as I set the glass back onto the counter, though I don't miss the way her baby blues zero in on my mouth.

Bad idea, Fen.

Flirting is one thing, but crossing that line? It's a bad idea. An *impossible* idea. It's a line I refuse to cross if I have any hope of staying clean.

And I *need* to stay clean.

I turn away from her and stare, once again, at the wall in front of me littered with an assortment of alcohol in fancy bottles. Anything to distract me from the girl beside me. "So, what'd you think? Other than the fans ogling me."

"I think you're good, Fen. Like, *really* good." The sincerity in her voice calls to me like a siren, and I turn to her again. The softness of her smile. The openness in her gaze. The way her red, pouty lips form my name.

Beautiful.

"She's right. You did good up there," a low voice interrupts. I turn to find Hawthorne on my opposite side.

With a tight smile, I reply, "Oh. Hey. Thanks."

"How'd it feel?"

Like coming home with a side of ticking time bomb, I think to myself but reply, "Good."

"Good. The first song. Was it your own work?"

I nod.

"And you haven't signed with anyone?" he prods.

"What are you saying?"

"You know what I'm saying, Fender. I want to get you in the studio. Under your own name if you're still adamant about keeping your distance from Broken Vows for now. What do you think?"

I scan his face, searching for the part where he says he's lying, and I'll never make it in this business. But I don't find anything except hope and confidence.

"I think you're insane for even offering," I counter when the silence is too charged.

"Why?"

"Because..." my voice trails off. I don't know what he expects me to say. I don't want to be offered a music deal because he feels guilty. I don't want Daddy Dearest to pull any more strings like he did the first time. I don't want to screw up and succumb to my addiction again.

I don't want a lot of things, and I can use each and every one of them as an excuse as to why Hawthorne's offer is insane. Why I'd be a fool to think he was serious, or this won't wind up exploding in my face if I take it.

"You have the spark, Fender," he continues. "Maybe it's genetic, and you can blame your father for your talent, but you and Sonny have it out the ass, whether you're playing together or apart. I'd be a fool if I didn't push you to become the best musician you can be."

He's saying everything I want to hear. But when something sounds too good to be true, it usually is. And hope's a dangerous thing. Especially for a guy like me.

Scrubbing my hand over my face, I remind him, "I'm a loose cannon. You said so yourself at this very bar not so long ago."

"Yeah. But I think we both know you aren't the same man I met the first night."

"You sure?" I challenge.

His stone-cold gaze could make a grown man cower, but I keep my head held high and meet it with cool indifference.

"I'll send you the papers tomorrow morning. If you want to get a second opinion, I can send them to your father, too, but I'll let you decide on that front."

"Who said I'm interested?" I argue.

"I know you like to pretend you're a dime a dozen, Fen, but I recognize a diamond when I see it. It's only a matter of time before every other label, manager, and producer starts knocking down your door. You have what it takes. And if you can keep your addiction under control, you'll make it to the top."

"What about Broken Vows?"

"What about them?"

"You signed them––"

"And I'll continue to represent them to the best of my ability because I believe they *also* have what it takes in this industry. But so do you. It's not an either-or scenario, Fen. You both have talent with and without each other. I get why you'd want to take a new path after everything you've been through. There's no shame in it. But you shouldn't discount your talent, pretending you rode on Broken Vows' coattails or some shit. Yeah, they're successful without you. They were successful with you too. But guess what, Fen? You've got what it takes to be successful without them, as well. It's time you start believing it. And if you decide to take anything away from tonight, it's exactly that. You've got what it takes."

Hadley's warm hand slips onto my knee, and she squeezes softly as if to say she agrees with him. I don't know why, but the touch grounds me, nudging me to believe something I would've laughed at if it weren't for her silent encouragement. I look down at her hand and soak up the warmth like a ray of sunshine. It feels good. Calming somehow. And it takes everything inside of me not to lean closer and let her wrap her arms around my chest. To feel her warm breath against the shell of my ear as she tells me what the hell I should do right now.

"I'll email you the contract in the morning," Hawthorne adds. "Do you want me to cc your father?"

"Hawthorne," I warn.

"Stop holding yourself back out of fear and answer the question, Fender."

I grit my teeth but mutter, "Let me think about it."

His chin dips. "Fine." Turning to Hadley, he adds, "It was good to meet you, Hadley. Keep this guy in line, yeah?"

"Pretty sure he can handle himself, but it was nice to meet you too." The warmth from her hand against my knee disappears when she waves to Hawthorne as he pushes himself up and walks out the door.

When we're somewhat alone, I challenge, "You've met?"

She shrugs. "Sammie introduced us when I said you invited me to the show tonight. I think he's worried about you."

My lips pull into a thin line.

"Want to talk about why?" she asks.

The truth about my past hangs on the tip of my tongue, but I swallow it back and follow her movement from seconds ago, shrugging while reaching for the refilled water glass Sammie must've replaced as I was busy losing my mind. After a few long pulls of liquid, I set it back down and mutter, "I gotta get out of here. Want to go for a walk?"

Pixie's tail hits the barstool leg beneath me, thumping excitedly, as she registers the word "walk" with enthusiasm.

Hadley laughs when she catches Pixie's response and gets to her feet. "I think a walk is a great idea."

HADLEY

"So...any more news about Bud?" Fender asks. The night is quiet. Peaceful. One or two cars pass every few minutes, but otherwise, only the sound of our shoes scuffing against the sidewalk guides us on our walk.

But I like it. The quiet. The opportunity to simply breathe for a few minutes instead of attempting to deal with all the daily stressors attacking me lately.

And it was nice. Until Fender decided to bring up the cause of my anxiety.

I shake my head and fold my arms despite the warm breeze. "Nothing yet."

"How's Mia?" he prods.

"About as good as you can expect with her father still missing. Isabella's trying to convince her to apply to a few colleges, but they're both pretty distracted with everything going on. And I have no idea if she'll be able to bring her GPA up enough to be accepted where her mom wants her to go, So...yeah."

"That's rough."

"It is," I agree. "Do you mind if we change the subject?" I

smile tightly, shocked by the onslaught of tears threatening to fall. I swallow them back and add, "It's been nice. Tonight. Not having to worry about things. I'd love it if I could keep the escape going for a little longer, ya know?"

"I'm sorry––"

"Don't apologize. It isn't your fault."

"I mean, I *did* ask," he replies. The streetlight casts a shadow, highlighting his smirk while causing butterflies to take up residence in my lower gut.

I laugh lightly and nudge his arm with my shoulder. "And I appreciate it. I just don't…" I take another deep breath. "I don't have the answers I'm wanting right now. But I *would* love for you to tell me why you're so hesitant to take Hawthorne's proposal."

He groans and drops his head back to look up at the night sky. "It's complicated."

"I kind of already figured that part out."

"What did he talk to you about anyway?" Fen asks.

"I already told you. He wanted to know how you're doing."

Another groan escapes him. "Of course, he did."

"Wanna tell me why?"

"It's complicated," he repeats, the same amused smirk etched into his features.

"Again, kind of figured that part out," I tease. "But I get it. I won't pry, but I will say this."

He stops and looks at me, his curiosity tainting the air around us until it feels almost electric.

"Go on," he encourages.

"I think you were made to be on a stage. It was the first time I'd seen you smile in… Well, let's just say it was a rare treat. You looked alive up there." I can still picture him on the stage with his guitar in his lap. The glaring lights bouncing off his handsome features. The way his forehead would wrinkle when he'd pluck out a complicated set of notes. The way he'd close his eyes and lose himself in the lyrics. It was beautiful. Absolutely breathtaking. I swallow thickly and clarify, "Well, maybe you weren't smiling in the beginning, but it's like you weren't numb anymore. You allowed yourself to *feel* up there. The good, the bad, and the ugly. I think that's important."

He stays quiet as if letting my assessment settle over him. He hooks his thumbs into his front pockets and mutters, "Being numb is safe."

"True. But without pain or sadness, there's no exhilaration or happiness. And isn't that what we're all searching for?"

His mouth tugs up at the side, amused. "Maybe. So what you're saying is, feeling––even if it's the shitty stuff––is still better than being numb?"

"That's exactly what I'm saying. And your lyrics? Your voice? They made me *feel*. And I think it's a gift worth sharing. I think *I've* been numb. I've been avoiding my writing. My niece. My brother and his situation. Everything. It's a coping mechanism. Something protecting us from breaking. But I think"––I blink slowly, surprised by my own findings––"it's okay for us to be broken sometimes. As long as we have someone to help put us back together."

I don't know why I do it. Why I give into the pull I've felt since the moment I first met Fender. Why I do something so freaking stupid and reckless. But I can't help myself. I want to *feel*. And after my little declaration, it's clear he makes me feel more than I've ever felt in my entire life.

My breathing is shallow as I rise onto my tiptoes and brush my lips against his. He doesn't move. Doesn't hold me. Doesn't pull me closer. Hell, he barely moves a muscle as I press my hands to his chest to balance myself, gliding my tongue along the seam of his lips. It's soft. Gentle. Hesitant because, let's be honest, the guy's a gorgeous rock god who's most definitely out of my league, and I just made a move on him.

I'm making a move on Fender Hayes.

What the hell am I doing?

And like a rubber band, he snaps.

The heat of his palms is scalding as he grabs my hips, pulling me against his hot erection and sliding his hands to my ass, squeezing hard enough to leave bruises through my dark jeans.

I love it.

Holy shit, I *love* it.

The demand in his touch. The heat from his groin against my stomach. The way his teeth dig into my lower lip as he sucks it into his mouth. I love it all. I open my mouth wide, and he dives inside, practically swallowing me whole, and a groan claws its way up his throat. Tortured. Guttural. And so freaking sexy, I can feel it vibrating against my core.

Until he pulls away.

Resting his forehead against mine, his eyes squeezed shut, he growls, "Stop."

My breathing is staggered. "W-what's wrong?"

"This is a mistake."

My heart plummets into my stomach as I pry my eyelids open. "W-what did you say?"

Pushing himself away from me and leaving a couple feet of distance between us, he lets out a slow, deep breath and repeats, "This is a mistake."

"Kissing me?" I choke out.

His Adam's apple bobs up and down in his throat as he swallows thickly. "Yeah. All of it."

"Why? No offense, but I could *feel* how into it you were." My gaze drops to the outline of his very hard cock straining against his pants.

His eyes harden, and his jaw ticks. "It isn't about that."

"Then what's it about?"

"It's…"

"Let me guess. *Complicated?*" I snap. I shouldn't be frustrated, but I am. I'm embarrassed. Hurt. I've been rejected by a guy. A guy I like. A guy I thought I connected with, but apparently, I'm an idiot. Shame floods my cheeks, but I stand my ground and lift my chin, staring up at him while demanding an explanation. Because this? This yo-yo feeling I have in the pit of my stomach? It freaking sucks.

"Tell me," I push.

"Yeah, okay?" he spits. "It's fucking complicated, and I don't need you to psychoanalyze me or tell me why I should or shouldn't feel a certain way."

"So what *do* you need? Huh?"

"I need you to leave it. Can you do that? Can you leave something alone without the need to fix it, or write a better ending, or make it fit inside your head like a puzzle piece? Just…leave it."

With my hands in the air, I turn on my heel and mutter, "Fine. I'm leaving it."

And even though it kills me inside, I do.

13

FENDER

"It's good to have you back, man," Ashton, another SeaBird employee, says, slapping me on the shoulder. "Good luck tonight."

With a tight smile, I nod. "Thanks. We'll see how it goes."

I signed Hawthorne's contract. Not because I didn't feel the need to shit my pants as I read it, but because Hadley was right about one thing. I definitely *felt* every word while scanning the document. Elation. Anxiety. Fear. So much fear. But also pride. Because Hawthorne might be a lot of things, but he's honest. And if he thinks I can do this and have the talent to make it in this industry, I think I might too.

If I can keep my shit under control.

The memory of Hadley and our kiss a couple weeks ago haunts me like a ghost. But I haven't allowed myself to analyze it. To examine why I didn't crave heroin or molly or even a fucking cigarette when her lips touched mine. Why the only thing crossing my mind as she kissed me was how badly I wanted to pull her closer. To distract her from all of her problems. To push her over the edge and help turn off the chaotic thoughts running a mile a minute inside her pretty little head.

And that's when reality hit me. Sure, I wasn't thinking about drugs *at the time,* but who's to say the cravings wouldn't hit me ten seconds later? Sure, I was lost in her for a minute, but what happens when I cave? When we take things to the next level? When I'm inside her, and I lose my shit in the blink of an eye? What happens if I spiral out of control again?

I feel like I've been given another chance. A chance to take my life back. My career. I can't lose it all for a girl or an opportunity to get off.

And despite her needing a distraction, she deserves more.

It isn't fair.

With a small handful of M&M's in one hand and my guitar in the other, I climb onto the stage at SeaBird. Pixie lumbers beside me without a care in the world, and I scan the crowd, my attention shifting to the barstool Hadley sat on during my last performance. I hate how I notice she isn't here.

Not that she'd know I'd be performing. I didn't tell her, but it doesn't take away the sting from her absence, though I refuse to acknowledge why.

It shouldn't hurt.

So, why does it?

When I catch people staring at me, I dump the M&M's into my mouth and chew slowly, letting the chocolatey sweet candy melt in my mouth.

Focus, Fen.

Once I've swallowed, I clear my throat and reach for the microphone, adjusting the stand so I can sit on the barstool with my guitar in my lap. I greet the crowd, thank them for coming out tonight, and play a few songs for the audience.

The first ones go by in a haze, but as I play the final note at the end of the fourth song, I scan the bar again, refusing to acknowledge who I'm searching for or the disappointment which hits when I realize she *still* isn't here.

Of course, she isn't, dumbass.

Why would she be here?

She didn't know I was performing tonight.

And even if she did… I rejected her.

The hurt in her eyes flashes through my memory, but I shove it aside and continue scanning the crowd. Anything to keep from picturing Hadley's pouty red lips drooped into a frown when I pulled away from her all those weeks ago.

My attention catches on a pair of familiar faces, one of which is currently eye screwing the other while slipping a tiny bag of white pills into her palm. My eyes narrow.

"Thanks for coming out tonight, everyone," I announce into the microphone, my pulse pounding in my ears as I attempt to rein in my anger. "As I'm sure you can tell, my voice still needs a little endurance training, so I'm going to have to cut this short, but you guys are awesome. I'll be here next week."

The stairs creak beneath my weight as I step off the stage and head toward the bar where a certain underaged teenager is busy flirting with a guy twice her age.

"Am I interrupting something?" I ask, wedging myself between Hadley's niece and the asshole dumb enough to sell her something right under SeaBird's roof. If Chuck or Ashton saw this, the guy would be finished.

"Hey––" Mia starts, but her mouth snaps shut as she takes in my glare.

"Do you mind?" the asshat interrupts.

We've never really spoken, but I recognize him from some of Marty's parties. Gages in both ears, his hair slicked back, and his weak jaw ticking as he dares me to stick around instead of leaving him alone with the young girl beside him.

My fists clench at my side. "Actually, yes. I was about to take your friend home."

He scoffs. "Go finish your little show. The girl and I are leaving."

With a low chuckle, I lean closer to the asshat and say, "Do you want me to call the cops for propositioning a minor and selling her drugs, or do you want to walk out of here with your balls intact? Choice is yours."

Pixie growls beside me, her hackles raised as she holds her ground by my side.

He shifts to his left and looks at Mia again but avoids getting too close to Pix, obviously weighing the pros and cons of fighting for her but decides she isn't worth it.

As he gets to his feet while making sure to keep the barstool between him and my dog, I mutter, "That's what I thought."

"Sorry, Beautiful," he tells her. "Your buddy's right. I gotta go, but you know how to reach me––"

I step between them and cock my head to one side, daring him to stick around and see what happens. "Get the hell out of here."

He lifts his hands in surrender and walks out, leaving me with a very pissed-off Mia to handle.

"Thanks a lot, asshole," Mia seethes.

The slinky strap of her red top slips off her shoulder, and I glare at the exposed skin.

She follows my gaze but doesn't bother to slip it back into place as she challenges, "You're not my––"

"Yeah. I know. Now, walk with me to my car, or I'll call the cops on you myself."

"Oh, so the other guy can't take me home, but you can?"

I roll my eyes and grab her arm. "Don't lump me in with that asshole. We might not know each other well, Mia, but you're still a child. And if your aunt, let alone your mom or dad knew you were here——"

"Yeah, well, my dad isn't here, is he?" she spits, her dark-rimmed eyes narrowed into tiny slits.

I tug her toward the exit and catch Chuck, SeaBird's owner, staring at me with hard eyes.

"She's my friend's niece who happens to be underage. I'm taking her home," I explain as we slip past him. "Put my guitar and shit in the back. I'll grab it later."

He gives me a nod and asks, "Want me to call your friend and give her a heads up you're coming?"

"I'll take care of it. Thanks, though."

"Don't mention it. Make sure to grab her fake ID. We don't let minors in here. And good show tonight," Chuck adds. "You've still got it."

I don't comment as Mia wrenches herself away from my grasp and marches out of the bar like a sullen teenager... which is exactly what she is.

14
FENDER

W ith another slow breath, I dig for my keys in my pocket and unlock the door. Mia yanks the passenger door open, slamming it closed behind her. My beater groans in protest, but I bite back my annoyance and climb behind the steering wheel after letting Pixie into the back.

Mia doesn't acknowledge the poor beast, probably trying to prove a point.

She's pissed.

At me.

"I was fine, you know," she huffs as I pull onto the main street.

I stay quiet.

"It's not like I can't handle myself."

My lips pull into a thin line.

"And he was a harmless guy. Cute too. Helped me out with something. Besides, it's not like I'm saving myself or anything."

I bite my tongue, my fury boiling just beneath the surface.

"You had no right to intervene," she adds.

Probably not, I think to myself, but I don't say a word.

With another huff, she turns in her seat and faces me, giving me a glare that would make most men cower in fear. "You're not my dad."

Duh.

"Say something," she seethes.

"What do you want me to say?"

"I don't know. If you're going to act like my dad, I expect a lecture."

"Is your dad a lecturer?"

"You tell me since you apparently knew him so well."

"Why'd you go out tonight, Mia?" I ask on a sigh. "Were you actually wanting to go home with the guy?" I bite my tongue to keep from mentioning the drugs I know are still clasped tightly in her closed palm. Not yet.

"Maybe," she replies.

"Why? Your aunt says you're smart––"

She scoffs. "My aunt doesn't know shit about me."

Partially true, but the malice still surprises me.

"She knows you're hurting," I offer.

Another scoff, and she twists in the passenger seat and faces the passenger window, though I can still see her reflection. The hardness in her gaze. The hurt.

"Am I taking you to your mom's or Hadley's?" I ask.

She hesitates, twisting her fingers in her lap like they're a dirty dishrag, though I doubt she even notices she's doing it. "My mom's."

"Is your mom home?" I prod.

Her gaze shifts to her lap, and she stops fidgeting but nods jerkily.

"You sure?"

Another jerky nod.

I dig my phone out of my pocket. "Okay. Let me just check with––"

"Fine! Take me to my aunt's. It's not like she even noticed I'm missing anyway."

Doubtful, Mia. Very doubtful.

I take a left at the fork in the road. "So, why'd you sneak out?"

"Look. Can we not do this?"

"I thought you said you wanted a lecture," I quip.

She glares back at me. "Guess I changed my mind."

"Yeah. Well. Looks like we have fifteen minutes to chat, and since you were stupid enough to put yourself in a situation like that––and trust me, I've put myself in plenty of stupid situations, so I can see them from a mile away––it looks like we're going to address it."

Her upper lip curls. "You don't know me."

"You're right. I don't. But I do know what it's like to make a shitty decision. To *know* I'm making a shitty decision. An *unsafe* decision. But to do it anyway because I'm hurting, and I want to numb the pain."

"Says the guy in a rock band. I'm sure your life is *so* hard."

"Says the guy who used to get so doped up before every show he can barely remember any of them," I snap. "Everything I worked for, everything I wanted out of life was in the palm of my hand. And because of shitty decisions, *unsafe* decisions, I stopped caring about any of it until I lost it all. So tell me, Mia, why are you making shitty decisions when I know you're smart enough to know better?"

My bluntness sucks the animosity from her pretty features, leaving a broken girl beside me. She stays quiet because we both know I hit the nail on the head.

"Were you making shitty decisions like tonight before your dad disappeared?"

"Don't talk about my father," she warns, the spark returning to her sharp gaze.

"I knew your dad, Mia. He was a little older than me, but

we hung out in the same group of friends." My knuckles turn white against the steering wheel, and I glance at her. "They weren't *good* friends, Mia."

"What's your point?"

"My point is...if your dad was here––"

"Yeah? Well, he's not," she snaps. Her thick lashes flutter as she sniffles and crosses her arms again, digging her red painted fingernails into her arms.

"Is that why you're doing this?" I ask. "Thinking maybe if he knows you're making shitty decisions, he'll come back? He'll come back, and he'll tell you how reckless you're acting?"

She stays quiet, staring blankly out the passenger window for a solid minute before her soft voice filters through the otherwise silent car. "Do you want to know what he used to tell me?" She squeezes her eyes shut as if lost in the memory. "He always told me whenever I'm presented with a situation, and I don't know what to do, I should ask, what would Dad do? And I should do the opposite." Forcing her eyelids open, she turns to me and adds, "Pretty messed up, right?"

Yeah. Pretty messed up.

But I get where he's coming from. The streets are empty as I make another left, heading toward Hadley's place as the blinker's clicking sound breaks the silence.

"Your dad's a good guy, Mia. But when you've made so many shitty decisions and you've lied to yourself countless times, it's easy to distrust your gut. To second guess everything you do. Because you don't know if it'll lead you back down the shitty hole you've worked so hard to claw out of. I think Bud was trying hard to clean up his life. Probably around the same time he started seeing you more."

"Yeah? Well, look where it got him. He's missing––"

"And I have no doubt he's doing whatever he can to get back to you, despite whether or not you decide to screw up first. He wouldn't want you putting your safety at risk, and he sure as hell wouldn't want you taking whatever's in your left hand."

The blood drains from her face, and her grip tightens around the little bag I know is clutched inside.

"Did he know you were heading down the same path as him?"

She shakes her head, the movement subtle but just as poignant.

"Have you taken drugs before?" I ask.

Another subtle shake.

"You sure?"

Her chin dips slightly, though she refuses to meet my gaze.

"Do you wanna know how old I was when I tried that shit for the first time?"

Silence.

"Thirteen," I tell her. "My mom had left her stash lying on the coffee table in our trailer. I popped a pill while she was strung out on the couch, and she didn't even notice. Hell, maybe she didn't care in the first place. But let me tell you something, Mia. Once was all it took. One time." My throat goes dry at the memory. "One time for me to crave the numbness. The bliss of *not* caring. Of quieting the voices inside my head. One time for me to fuck myself up so bad, I lost everything in the long run. *Everything.*"

She peeks over at me, the light from the streetlight casting shadows along her young features. Hell, she's just a child. A child with the power to completely wreck her world if she can't channel her fire properly.

"Screwing up your life because you want to escape it or because you want to get the attention of someone who can make it better isn't going to fix things, Mia. Trust me. I've been down that path. I wouldn't wish it on my worst enemy."

Her lower lip quivers as the softness of her voice fills the front seat. "I can't sleep. I only wanted something to help me sleep."

"What is it?" I ask but shake my head. "Actually, don't answer that. It doesn't matter what's in the bag. Some people mess with drugs, and it doesn't affect them. Not in the long run. They can use it recreationally and not bat an eye when they decide it's time to quit and grow up. But it's not what happened to your dad. And it's not what happened to me. And don't get me started on the fact you were putting your safety in jeopardy when it came to that asshole. You didn't know the guy. You didn't know if he was going to force himself on you if you went home with him then changed your mind. You didn't know if he would slip you something to take advantage of you when you got to his place."

Again, her arms tighten around her as the scenarios filter through her mind. She sniffles and leans her head against the window, defeated. "I wasn't going to go home with him."

"It was still stupid, Mia. I know it. And I know you know it too. Your mom, your aunt, and your dad care about you. They want you to be happy. And making decisions that'll hurt you isn't going to bring your dad back."

Her eyes shine with unshed tears when she asks, "So what? What am I supposed to do?"

"Be you. The best version of Mia you can be. It's all your dad wants. And if you can't sleep? Talk to your mom. She'll take you to get a prescription or something. Or your aunt," I add. "She cares about you too."

"She hates my dad," Mia whispers, the words damn near killing me.

I shake my head. "She doesn't hate your dad, Mia."

"Yes, she does."

"No," I argue. "She hates that she *loves* your dad."

She looks at me. Really looks at me. As if, for the first

time ever, she's trying to understand her aunt's rocky relationship with her father instead of assuming shit.

"Why?" she whispers.

"It's hard loving an addict." I laugh and pull up to the curb in front of Hadley's place. "Trust me. I can barely stand myself most days."

"But you're not doing that stuff anymore..."

"Just because I stopped doesn't mean I'm not addicted. It's a constant battle, Mia. Constant. And it never eases up. It's why I'm begging you to let me flush the little bag down the toilet for you."

She opens her hand and looks down at the contents causing my pulse to ratchet.

"But if you're an addict, are you sure me handing this bag over to you is a good idea?" she asks quietly as if she finally understands how serious the shit in her hand is and how much she screwed up by asking for it in the first place.

My attention drops to her hand in her lap and the little clear bag with four tiny pills lying inside. I blink slowly and look back at Mia to find her staring at me hesitantly.

"I can't let you go inside with that bag, Mia. I can't let you walk down the same dark path your father took. You're better than that. Better than him. Better than me."

Her expression crumples, and her lower lip trembles, but she doesn't hand the bag to me as she breathes out, "I miss him."

"I'm sure he misses you too, Mia."

"I hate that I love him, too, you know. That I miss him and only want him to come home." Her voice cracks, and her eyes gather with tears. "To *not* choose drugs over me."

My heart fucking shatters.

"Mia--"

Her arms are around me before I even register what's

going on as she holds on for dear life, her tiny frame wracking with full-body sobs.

It isn't fair. Any of this. Bud was trying to clean up his life. It only gave his family a glimpse of who he could be without the weight of his addiction. It isn't fair he was too weak to keep from spiraling, and the people around him have to suffer the way they are. And it isn't fair he's not here to hold them and make them feel better.

Addiction's shit for an addict. But sometimes, when we're too close to it, I think we miss seeing how much it rips apart the people around us.

Like Mia.

And Hadley.

Gingerly, I rub my hand along Mia's back as Pixie puts her giant paws on the center console separating us, nuzzling her nose against Mia's long, wavy hair. Like she can't stand to see her in pain. Like she wants to help. To comfort her.

Ditto, Pix.

But I'm helpless. So damn helpless, it hurts.

"Why?" she cries against me. "Why would he choose drugs over me? Am I so terrible? I know we fought some-times, but––"

"Stop it, Mia. Those thoughts aren't going to help anyone. Your father did *not* choose drugs over you––"

"But where else could he be? What else could he be doing? H-he disappeared." She hiccups. "A-and I don't know if he's coming back."

"I know, Mia. I know." My head hangs, my defeat eating me from the inside out.

We continue sitting like this. Mia crying. Me feeling like shit for not being able to shoulder her pain on my own. Until a few minutes later, when the sobs have slowed, and only a hollow Mia remains.

"Come on," I murmur, untangling myself from her limp grasp. "Let's get you inside."

We walk up to Hadley's apartment, leaving Pixie tucked in the back of my car with the windows rolled down a crack.

I knock on Hadley's door.

As we wait for her to answer, I drop my voice low and ask, "Where are the pills?"

She hands them to me, her eyes still glassy and bloodshot. "Please don't tell Aunt Had––"

The door opens, and I tuck the plastic bag into my back pocket as Hadley shrieks, "Where the hell have you been?!"

15

HADLEY

"I'm so sorry," Mia starts, her long hair hanging in a wavy curtain to hide her face from my scrutiny.

Like she's ashamed.

The question is, is it because she was caught and had to be escorted home by freaking Fender? Or is it something else?

Still fuming, I shake my head, unwilling to give her an inch. Not right now. Not when I've been freaking out and debating whether or not to call the police for hours.

"Do you have any idea how terrified I've been?" I seethe, my teeth clenching. "I've been losing my mind––"

"Hey, Hads. Do you mind if we talk for a sec?" Fender interrupts.

Again, I shake my head, still trying to process the mess in front of me. I force myself to step aside and give them room to come into my apartment. But I don't say a word. I'm afraid if I do, I'll say something I'll regret, and even though Mia most definitely deserves whatever word vomit would come tumbling out, she's just a child.

A child who freaking snuck out and gave me a heart attack.

Without waiting for an invitation, Mia darts off to the second bedroom down the hall, disappearing through the crack in the door and closing it firmly behind her. Fender tucks his hands into his pockets and rocks back on his heels, letting the awkwardness of our current situation settle over us in the middle of my entryway.

Lovely.

He looks as good as I remember. It's not like it's been eons or anything since we last saw each other--since I kissed him and he rejected me. But still. Part of me had been hoping I'd imagined his strong arms and wounded gaze that called to me.

Nope.

Still as potent as ever.

Thankfully, I'm too pissed at my niece to focus on it.

"What are you doing here?" I demand.

"She was at SeaBird--"

"The *bar*?" I almost screech.

He shoves his hair away from his face, looking sheepish. "Uh, yeah. I was playing, and--"

"I'm seriously going to kill her." I take a step toward the hall, but Fender reaches out and grabs my arm.

"Stop. It isn't her fault."

"Not her fault?" I shrug out of his hold and fold my arms, begging him to change my mind. "How'd she get in?"

"Probably has a fake ID, but that's beside the point."

"Beside the point?" I almost screech--again. He grabs onto my arm a second time and tugs me into the hall outside my apartment in search of privacy.

"Listen. I know she scared the shit out of you. But right now?" He drops his voice low. "She doesn't need another lecture--"

"*Another* lecture?"

"She kind of already got one," he mutters, avoiding my gaze.

"From who? You?" I scoff, annoyed with both the conversation and the way I can't seem to find the willpower to shrug out of his hold. Apparently, I only have so much self-preservation, and my earlier retreat from his grasp was all I could muster for one night.

Great.

"She needs someone to listen, Hads. A friend. Someone to tell her everything is going to be okay." He looks down at me, my chest brushing against his as I realize how close we're standing. The touch of his hand around my arm causes goosebumps in its wake as he slides it down to my wrist before letting me go. And I hate how I miss it instantly. His touch. His warmth. The slight scratch of his calloused fingers against my bare skin. All of it.

"She misses her dad, Hads," he continues. His voice turns my stomach into knots. "She feels like he doesn't love her because he might've fallen off the wagon again."

My expression falls, and my anger morphs into absolute loss. The pain in my chest radiates to my extremities with the overwhelming need to hug her. To tell Mia how much her father adores her and everything is going to be all right, even when I have no idea whether or not it's true.

Peeking over my shoulder to my still cracked apartment door, I run my hands along my bare arms and mutter, "Well, shit."

"Yeah."

I suck my lips between my teeth, guilt slicing my insides as I replay our last conversation. I snapped at her. Nothing crazy. But I wasn't exactly warm and welcoming when Bella dropped her off. Then, when she refused to come out of her room to eat pizza, which I know is her favorite and is the sole reason why I'd ordered it, I said she was acting like a spoiled brat.

Which wasn't fair.

I should've been more sympathetic. More patient.

With a defeated sigh, I fold my arms and face Fender again. "Thanks. For bringing her home," I clarify. "She's been gone for hours and left her phone here, so I had no idea where to even start looking or how to contact her. I didn't know if I should call the police or if I should call Isabella even though I didn't want to stress her out or make Mia feel like I was tattling on her––"

"I get it. It's a mess."

"Yeah," I say on an exhale. "It really is."

"At least I realized I'm not the only one who's broken, so there's that, right?" he quips.

With a dry laugh, I roll my eyes and say, "Glad we could be of service. So…" I peek up at him, ignoring the way my blood heats. The way my hands itch to reach up and feel the scruff against his cheeks to see if it's as soft as I remember. "Do you think I should be the one to talk to her, though? Or should I give her some space? Maybe call her mom? I'm flying blind here."

"Like I know what I'm doing with a teenage girl."

"Well, you got her to apologize, which I'm pretty sure is a modern-day miracle."

He chuckles and squeezes the back of his neck. Looking adorable. And almost shy. I bite my lip to keep from grinning like a crazy person. Especially under these particular circumstances.

"Do you want to come in?" I offer, hooking my thumb over my shoulder toward the cracked door to my apartment.

"Nah, I should probably get going."

"Oh." My expression falls.

"It's not that I don't want to. It's just...Pixie's in the car, and it's late--"

"I get it," I rush out. "I guess I'll see you--"

"Can I ask you something?" he interrupts.

"Yeah, of course."

"Do you, uh," he hesitates. "Do you hate your brother?"

My eyes widen in surprise. "Bud?"

"Yeah--"

"Of course not."

"So, you love him?"

"He's my big brother. I love him more than just about anything."

"But if you had a choice. Would you still love him? Despite his addiction?"

I pause, the words rolling over me in his warm, honeyed voice as I take in his eyes. They're shining with a restrained curiosity making my stomach tighten, and they're filled with so much more than simple curiosity. There's a depth there. A need to hear my response. A vulnerability hinting at something more than Bud and me. Something else. Something more...personal.

After a few seconds, I murmur, "Yeah, Fen. I would love him no matter what." I reach for his hand hanging limply at his side and squeeze softly. "Do you want to know why?"

"Why?"

"Because his addiction doesn't make him who he is. He is who he is in spite of his addiction. That's why I love him."

With a subtle nod, he turns on his heel, heading toward the parking area but stops and turns back around.

"Hey, Hadley?"

"Yeah?"

"I have another show next week at SeaBird. Do you want to come?"

My smile is soft as I lean against the doorjamb and fold my arms. "I'd love to."

"See you then."

16

FENDER

s I walk to my car, my phone rings in my pocket, and I pull it out. It's an unknown number.

Cautiously, I answer it, bringing my phone to my ear when a familiar voice crackles through the speaker.

"Hey, brother."

My brows furrow, and I recheck the number to confirm I'm not going crazy. "Did you change your number, Marty?"

"Nah, but I am calling from my buddy's cell since I figured you wouldn't answer if I called from my own."

Of course, he did.

After folding myself into the car and starting the ignition, I scratch Pixie behind the ear while she attacks me with licks from the backseat. I let out a sigh and face the inevitable, knowing if I hang up on the asshole, he'll only call again. "What do you want, Marty?"

"I want to know why you didn't tell me about your little concert at SeaBird. First, the one where Hawthorne offered you a deal, and now tonight. Should I be offended?"

I pause as the hair along the back of my neck stands on end. "How'd you know about Hawthorne?"

"A little bird told me. Speaking of telling me things, I think you and I should have a little chat."

"We have nothing to talk about," I remind him. Hell, I'm reminding us both. But after tonight, and my conversation with Mia, I'm more determined than ever to stay clean. And in order to do it, I need to keep the hell away from Marty.

Shifting my cell to my other ear, I growl, "Does Dad know you're calling me?"

"Dad and I aren't exactly on speaking terms. Not after he cut me off. Although, from what I understand, you and Daddy Dearest aren't exactly on speaking terms, either."

He's right. I haven't spoken to Donny Hayes since I was released. I haven't really talked to anyone since I was released, but that's beside the point.

"What are you getting at?" I ask, exasperated.

"I'm just saying I have a feeling you'll keep this little conversation between you and me instead of running to Daddy Dearest. That's all."

"And on that note, I'm hanging up--"

"Wait." His tone is cold. Lethal. And brooks no argument.

And because his broken baby brother is curious, I wait for him to finish whatever the hell he wants to say.

"I want in."

Jerking the phone away from my ear, I look at the screen, convinced I've heard him wrong.

"In?" I ask. "On what?"

"The contract. I want to sign as your manager."

I scoff. "You're joking, right?"

"Listen, I have photos of you high as a kite. Video footage of you fucking--"

"I don't care."

"The press would eat this shit up. It would ruin you--"

"Let it ruin me," I spit, my upper lip curling. "I'm sick of my addiction holding me back from what I want. I'm clean.

I'm going to stay clean. And I'm not about to make another deal with a snake just because I have a shitty past. Sonny was right about you. You're bad news, Marty. And you need help. Lots of it. If you decide you need a good shrink or rehab center, let me know. I stayed at a great one in Utah. Talk to you later."

I click the end button, toss my phone in the cupholder, and dig out a fun-sized packet of M&M's from my pocket. The warm chocolate melts on my tongue but doesn't ground me the way I hope.

Breathe, I remind myself.

Sensing my trepidation, Pixie puts her paws on the center console and nuzzles me with her giant, scrunched nose. I lean into her, soaking up whatever comfort she's willing to give a sorry ass like me. Because I know I don't deserve it. Or at least, the past me didn't. But the new me? The one who told Marty to fuck off? He isn't a coward. Is he? I go over our conversation again, committing it to memory.

The moment I broke free from the asshole who's controlled me for years.

And it feels good.

Even when I know Marty's right.

He has a shit-ton of blackmail on me. Most of it, I can't even remember doing. From orgies with random women to falling and hitting my head, waking up in a pool of my own blood because I was too high out of my mind. Yeah, the blackmail he has is real classy shit that makes me look like an irresponsible asshole.

Because I *was* an irresponsible asshole.

I pinch the bridge of my nose as Pix licks the side of my hand, anxious to take away my pain or frustration. If only it were so easy. If any of Marty's blackmail gets out, it could ruin me. But I've already walked that path with him. I'm not about to sign my own death certificate by doing it again. I can't. Not because of my career, but because of my life. Literally. I know my triggers. What could make me spiral. And being close to Marty again? It's a one-way ticket to Hell, and I've already spent enough time clawing my way out of it.

But losing everything again? Because of shit from my past? Even when I'm determined to stay clean this time?

Fucking sucks.

Pix scoots closer until almost all of her massive body is in my lap, and only her hind legs are in the back row of seats. Like she knows I need something to hold onto. To keep me from losing my damn mind. As if she can feel my frustration. My fear. My desperation to keep everything from spiraling. Like she wants to prove I'm not alone. Like I was *never* alone.

I scratch behind her ear again. "I'm gonna stay clean, Pix. Not just for me. But for you."

I swear her big brown eyes are zeroing in on my soul as she looks up at me and cocks her head to one side. Then she shifts her gaze to Hadley's apartment.

"Yeah. I know. I'll be strong for her too. No matter what. Promise."

Another wave of determination floods my system, so I shove my car into drive and make my way home.

When I get there, I head to the bathroom, the damn little bag of pills burning a hole in my pocket. I need to get rid of them as soon as possible. While I'm still strong enough. While I can still hear Marty's voice in my head. While I can still see Mia's distraught face and Hadley's beautiful one.

But as I pull out the bag and open the tiny ziplock top, my hands shake, and my breathing turns shallow, the faces of everyone I care about fading into the background.

I should flush them.

I should flush them down the fucking toilet so it's not my own life swirling down the drain.

But I can't.

I'm frozen.

Paralyzed.

Unable to do a damn thing but memorize the shape of them. Their sharp little edges. The dull, chalky color. The weight is so small and inconsequential in my hand, but it still somehow manages to make my shoulders hunch from the pressure of holding them with the knowledge of how quickly they could tear my world apart.

My kryptonite.

I don't want to take them. Not right now. Not ever. But being determined enough to hold them in my hands and still say no makes me feel strong. Brave, somehow. Stupid too. I get that. I'm not a complete idiot. But holding the one thing capable of breaking you in your hand and being strong enough to say no? There's power in it. And when I've felt so damn weak my entire life, I like the power. The control. I like it more than I care to admit.

A quiet knock on the door makes me flinch. I open the medicine cabinet and shove the tiny bag inside the Advil bottle before I can talk myself out of it. Not because I plan on using them, but because I want to take the power back. To know these tiny pills can't control me. Not anymore.

"Fen?" Milo calls.

"One sec."

The cabinet door closes with a quiet click, and I clear my throat, wiping my sweaty palms against my jeans, opening the door to a concerned Milo.

"Yeah?" I ask.

He looks anxious as his gaze flicks from one of my eyes to the other.

Assessing.

Analyzing.

I know that look. He's worried I did something stupid.

And while he's not entirely wrong, it's not what he thinks. Not this time, anyway.

"There a problem?" I challenge.

"Just checking on you." He turns on his heel and heads toward his and Maddie's bedroom. He stops when he reaches the door and faces me again. "You know I'm here for you, right?"

His sincerity crushes me as I shove my hands into my front pockets, never more exhausted than in this moment. "Yeah, man. I know."

He nods. "Night, Fen."

"Goodnight."

17

FENDER

She's here.

She's late. But she's here.

I don't want to acknowledge why I'm having a physical response to the beauty at the bar. Or why my gaze kept shooting toward her during the set. But as soon as I saw Hadley, the vice around my chest eased, and I could finally let go, losing myself in the music, the energy, and the gorgeous writer who has no idea how sexy she is.

And apparently, I'm not the only one who's noticed. My brows furrow as I lean closer to the microphone and sing the final chorus, the crowd joining in. Then I slip the guitar strap from around my neck and jump off the stage.

Pixie decided to stay at home, finally being won over by Maddie and some bacon from breakfast, leaving me on my own. Which is fine. She deserves a night off from babysitting me. If only I could find the same reprieve.

However, right now? I'm not thinking about myself, or Hawthorne, or Marty and what he may or may not be planning to screw me over. Right now? I'm thinking about Hadley and why the hell this asshole is talking to her.

Jealousy licks at me as I approach Hadley and the stranger while refusing to acknowledge that I have no right to feel upset.

She isn't mine. I made it perfectly clear when I pushed her away a few weeks ago. So why do I care if she's talking to a guy or if she's touching his leg, and––

Crash.

A body slams against me, and I jerk back, shaking my head as the stranger slips me a note. Curious, I unfold the paper and find familiar handwriting scrawled across it. *Marty's* handwriting.

You sure you don't want to make a deal?

My pulse spikes as I scan the message a dozen times.

What did he do?

Ignoring the cacophony of fear and anxiety, I shove the note into my back pocket and close the last bit of distance between me and the bar.

The guy is leaning toward Hadley, whispering something in her ear as she thumbs the buttons on his white shirt, giggling softly. My fists tighten at my sides, the urge to beat the shit out of the bastard simmering right below the surface. The old me would've decked him without another thought. He was reckless. Selfish. Angry. My nostrils flare as I let out a slow breath and force my hands to unclench.

"Hey, Hadley," I greet her through gritted teeth.

"Hey, you!" She slips off the barstool, almost landing on her ass. I wrap my arm around her waist to keep her steady.

"I missed you!" With her arms twisting around my neck, she pulls me closer and runs her nose along the column of my throat. "You smell good. Mmm." The sound goes straight to my cock. "Why do you smell so good?"

"You okay, Hads?" I ask.

"Mm-hmm. Just dandy. How are you?"

"Doing good. Just finished." I try to pull her away so I can inspect her closer, but she keeps the vice grip around my neck like she isn't ready to let me go. Instead, she leans closer, leaving me to carry almost all of her body weight as she sinks into me even more. Giving in, I rub my hand up and down her back while she breathes me in deep.

"Seriously, Fen. You smell soooo good."

Her pert nipples brush against my chest through the thin layers of fabric separating us, but I try to ignore them. "Are you sure you're feeling okay?"

"Yup." She pops the 'p' at the end, smacking the sound like a piece of bubblegum in my ear.

With a low chuckle, I grab her wrists from around my neck and pull away again. This time, she lets me. I scan her face and glassy eyes.

Doing the same, she cups my cheek and runs her fingers along the scruff near my sideburns. "You have pretty eyes. And you kind of look like Jax Teller."

"Who?"

"Sons of Anarchy. You know. With the motorcycle. Do you have a motorcycle? You should totally get a motorcycle."

"How much have you had to drink tonight, Hads?"

She lifts her forefinger and thumb, leaving a smidge of space between the two. "Just a liiiiiitle bit. How's about you, Mr. Teller? How much have youuuu had to drink?"

I look for the guy who'd been chatting with her, but the asshole's missing. Turning to Sammie behind the bar, I yell, "Sam!"

As she flips a bottle of Jack into the air and catches it in her other hand, she answers, "Yeah?"

"How much did she have to drink?"

She continues mixing the Jack and Coke for another customer but replies, "One glass of wine. That's it."

"And the guy she was chatting with. Did you know him?"

"The guy?" She tilts her head to one side and thinks for a

second. "Nope. Never seen him before, or at least not that I remember. Why?"

"Would he have had a chance to slip her something?"

Sammie's concern ratchets up a few more notches as she scans a very strung-out Hadley from head to toe. "Shit. I try to watch out for that, but I didn't see anything––"

"Fuck," I mutter under my breath while keeping a firm grasp around Hadley's waist.

"Is she all right?" Sammie asks. "Do you want me to call an ambulance?"

"I'll take care of her. If you can get the video feed to me, that'd be great."

"You sure? I can call––"

"I think I already know who's to blame, Sam. And he isn't stupid enough to leave a trail. I've got it, though. Thanks."

With a frown, a concerned Sammie grabs Hadley's now empty glass of red wine from the bartop and watches us leave. But she doesn't say a word because she knows as well as I do now isn't the time for answers. Right now? I need to take care of Hads.

Shit!

18

FENDER

"We could take my car, ya know. Even though yours smells better. How can your car smell better than mine? Especially when it's so old." Hadley looks around the car, twisting in the front seat to look at the back. "Wait. Where's Pixie?"

"She's at my place."

"Oh. You would think having a dog would make your car smelly, but it doesn't. It smells good." She leans closer to me and takes a whiff. "No. It's you. You smell good. I wonder if you drove my car, would it start smelling good too? 'Cause if it would, I would give you full permission to drive my car whenever you want. And I mean whenever you want." She winks behind her slightly askew glasses.

My jaw tightens, along with my grip around the steering wheel.

I'm going to kill him.

With her elbows on the center console, she cradles her head in her hands, fully facing me. "Why are you mad?"

"I'm not mad."

"You look mad," she decides, staring at me openly before

124

whining, "Don't be mad. It's no fun being mad. You should be happy. I'm happy. Actually, I'm feeling pretty damn fantastic." With a loud snort, she covers her face and cackles.

My stomach clenches.

The asshole drugged her then disappeared. And combine it with the note in Marty's handwriting burning a hole through my pocket? Yeah. I'm seriously going to kill him. As soon as Hadley comes down from whatever she's on. I can't leave her. Not like this. Even though my blood is hot with rage, and I'd give anything to beat the shit out of Marty and anyone else who was involved with putting Hadley in this situation, I can't.

But the worst part is, it could've been so much worse. He could've taken her. The asshole at the bar, or the guy who slipped me the note, or even Marty himself. They could've taken her and raped her. And it would've been all my fault.

Fuck!

I slam my hand against the steering wheel, and Hadley flinches away from me.

With a slow, controlled breath, I force my grip to loosen around the steering wheel and glance at Hads, who seems to have already forgotten my little temper tantrum. Instead, she's staring at me again as if I'm the most interesting thing on the planet.

"You feeling anything else, Hads? Sick to your stomach? Dizzy? Anything?"

Her lips purse, and she squeezes her eyes shut, announcing, "Nope. I feel happy. Light. I should drink wine more often. I'll have to ask your little bartender friend what kind it is, though, 'cause I've never felt this good after only one glass. All warm and fuzzy inside with a side of let's have sex in the back seat. Ooooh, that sounds really good." She rests her head against the headrest and runs her hands up and down her thighs.

Shit. She's horny. They must've slipped her something to heighten physical touch and endorphins. Ecstasy, maybe? Hell, it could've been Marty's own messed-up concoction. There's a reason I liked buying from him. He knew how to create a good high or a good trip if I was ever in the mood for any psychedelics. But Hadley wasn't in the mood for anything. This wasn't her choice. He stole that from her.

I pull up to the curb in front of Hadley's apartment building and scrub my hand over my face. I should take her to the hospital. Just to make sure she's okay. Even though I know Marty will have a solid alibi and won't be charged with shit for what he did tonight. But what will going to the hospital do for Hadley? She was drugged. It isn't her fault. But will we be able to prove it? Or will she wind up arrested for something completely out of her control? I should know this. The rules and laws behind drug abuse. But I feel like I don't know shit, and whatever decision I come to could wind up ruining the girl in front of me. Indecision eats me up inside as I stare at her for another few seconds.

I turn the ignition back on, and her eyes snap open. "Where are you going?"

"We're going to the hospital."

"What? Why?"

"Because--"

She grabs my wrist and tugs it away from the key. "You know what? No. No, we're not going to the hospital. It sounds like a terrible idea--"

"Hadley--"

"Come inside with me. Please? I feel really good, and I want to *keep* feeling good, and the hospital will make me feel like poop, and I don't want to feel like poop. Can we please--"

"You've been drugged--"

She smashes her finger against my lips. "Hush. I feel fine. Great, actually. Just come inside--"

Grabbing her wrist, I pull her finger away from my mouth and warn, "Hadley."

"Come inside. We'll snuggle. You'll like it."

"Hadley, you don't understand. I need to make sure you aren't having an allergic reaction, or that he didn't slip you too much, or--"

The hinges on my car squeal in protest as she shoves the passenger door open and stumbles into the warm, night air. "I'm not going to the hospital. I feel fine. Great," she repeats, "and I don't want to waste this feeling or this night by being poked and prodded. Wait. Being poked sounds pretty nice"--she winks--"but not in the hospital, and not by a bunch of doctors. I'm going inside, and there isn't a thing you can do or say to change my mind."

And with that, she flips her hair over her shoulder and walks a zigzag line toward her building.

Like a stone, the guilt from the situation feels heavy in my gut. As I watch Hadley make a fool out of herself, my phone rings. Sonny's name flashes across the screen, and I squeeze my phone tight, threatening to break the glass. I don't have time for him. Not right now. I shove it back into my pocket, turn the car off again, and race to catch up with Hadley.

I can't leave her alone.

She stumbles a bit, her legs wobbly, so I wrap my arm around her waist and let her lean into me. And I hate how good it feels. Her curves meld against my side, and her fruity scent teases my nostrils, so I hold my breath to keep from leaning closer. It doesn't stop her from nuzzling against my neck and breathing deep, though.

"Seriously, Fender." She squeezes me against her as I dig into her purse and search for her keys. When I find them, I shove the door open and guide her inside. Like a curvy monkey, she clings to me, her hands sliding up and down my body while making my blood rush south.

Not. The. Time.

When her fingers slide past the waistband of my jeans, I grab her wrist and force her back a few steps.

"You should get some sleep," I tell her.

"Okay. But only if you put me to bed."

Digging deep for strength, I tug her down the hall and open the first door on the left to find it's a bathroom.

"Wrong door." She laughs. "But nice try. What's behind door number two?" she adds, using her best show host impression, which makes me wonder if she chose the wrong profession. I shouldn't find her amusing right now. Not when everything is so messed up. But I can't help it. I roll my eyes and keep moving forward.

When we reach her bedroom at the end of the hall, the door bounces against the back wall as I shove it open and tug Hadley toward the four-poster bed tucked in the corner. It's covered in a black and white floral comforter and has a dozen pillows placed along the headboard. It would be annoying as shit to make every morning but probably feels like clouds when she's sleeping at night. I don't know why, but the sight makes my mouth tilt up before disappearing.

"Come on, Hads. Let's get you in bed."

She turns in my arms and faces me, running her hands along my chest and taking in every contour of my torso. "I couldn't agree more. You should join me."

Again, I grab her wrist, desperate for an ounce of self-control. "That's a bad idea, Hads."

"Why?"

"Because you aren't *you* right now."

"Who says? I feel like me. Only happier. And hornier." Her big, doe eyes peek up at me from behind her dark frames. "You should kiss me now."

"I'm not going to kiss you, Hads."

"Why not?"

"Because it's a bad idea, and you're not you right now," I repeat.

"Like that matters. I was *me* the last time we kissed, and what did you do? You rejected me."

The callousness in her voice makes me pause. After our last conversation when I dropped Mia off, I'd assumed she'd forgiven me for screwing up, but, apparently, I couldn't have been more wrong.

I step closer and tuck her hair behind her ear, my touch gentle and unsure while praying she isn't too far gone to see my sincerity. "Hads, I didn't reject you––"

"Yes, you did." She jerks away from me but keeps her feet planted, causing our chests to brush against each other as she tilts her chin up in defiance. "I made a move, and you rejected me. Yet here I am––again––and what do you do? You reject me." Her lower lip quivers as she holds my gaze, trying to stay strong, but I can see her wavering. "Why do you keep rejecting me, Fender Hayes?" She tugs at the hem of her shirt, pulling the black top over her head, then dropping it at our feet. "Is this not what you want? Am I not skinny enough?" She grabs her round, supple breasts through her bra and stands on her tiptoes, closing a bit of the distance between our heights. "Not tall enough? Not blonde enough?" She flicks her long, dark hair over one shoulder. "Is it the glasses? Do you hate these glasses? Fine. I'll take them off. I'll––"

I capture her wrists again, but she doesn't stop fighting me as she goes to rip off the glasses. They've only heightened her appeal since the first night we met. Using my stature and weight, I push her into the wall and pin her hands above her head.

Our breathing is ragged as I order, "Look at me, Hadley."

She shakes her head back and forth but squeezes her thighs together while her bra-covered tits press against my chest.

"Look. At. Me."

"No. I can't look at you and see disgust. I can't look at you and see indifference. I can't--"

"There isn't a single inch of you that isn't perfect, okay?"

She laughs but doesn't bother to look at me, staring blankly at the wall opposite us instead. "Sure, there isn't."

"I'm serious--"

"I just threw myself at you, and you said no. If I were so *perfect*, that wouldn't be the case, now would it?"

My muscles tighten with frustration, the heat from her bare body practically branding me through my clothes. "You have no fucking clue what you're talking about."

"Tell me. Tell me what I'm talking about. Tell me why I'm not the girl for you, or why you can't be my distraction, or me your distraction, or why it feels so good when you're pressed against me like this." Her voice trembles, and she takes a deep breath through her parted lips. "You feel so good, Fen. Why do you feel so good? I think I can taste your smell. Is it possible to taste a smell? 'Cause I think I can. I could smell you in your car, and I can smell you now. But I'm mad at you, which makes me not want to like your smell or how you feel against me, but honestly? I can't get enough of it. You should keep touching me."

She isn't making sense, which only feeds my frustration and guilt. There's no reasoning with her. Not when she's like this.

My grip loosens around her wrists, but she doesn't pull herself free from me. If anything, she melts into me more.

"You should get some sleep," I murmur.

"But it hurts."

"I'm hurting you?" I let her go instantly.

"No. My...down there. It hurts. I...I need some friction." She squeezes her thighs together again, and her hips shift toward me like a damn homing beacon. "Something. Please."

"It's the drugs."

"Drugs?"

"The guy at the bar, Hads. He drugged you," I remind her. "I told you in the car––"

"What guy?"

"There was a guy at the bar," I repeat. "You were talking to him. He slipped you something. Something making you feel the way you do."

"Happy and horny?" she asks. I watch her hands slide down her bare stomach, unbutton the top button of her dark jeans, and disappear into her underwear.

Shiiiit.

"You should kiss me, Fen," she begs, tilting her head up until those damn pouty lips are only a few inches from mine. I could lean down––

I tilt my head back and stare up at the ceiling. Her lips brush against the column of my throat.

Fucking. Hell.

With her hands pressed against my chest to balance herself, she rises onto her tiptoes and nibbles the sensitive skin right below my ear. "You taste good too."

"I'm not going to sleep with you, Hadley. This isn't you. This is the drugs."

"Will you at least make me feel better?"

"Hads––"

"Just a kiss," she begs. "It's all I want. A simple." Her lips press against my throat again. "Little." She moves up to my jaw beneath my ear, sucking softly. The feeling shoots straight to my cock. She pulls away and whispers, "Kiss."

The air is electric, pulsing between us as I look down at her, all doe-eyed and pouty lips. But the weird part? I'm not craving the high from whatever was slipped into her drink. I'm only craving her.

Hadley.

Her taste.

Her scent.

The feel of her round hips in the palms of my hands. Just to see if she feels the same as I remember.

I'm so screwed.

"Hads," I murmur, but she shakes her head and tangles her fingers along the short hair at the back of my scalp, pulling me closer.

And because I'm weak and broken––and apparently trading one addiction for another––I let her.

The kiss is soft at first. A little unsure. Like now that she has me, she doesn't know what to do with me. And neither do I. I'm frozen in shock and self-control. If I give in, I'm afraid I won't be able to stop. But I also can't pull away. Not when her tongue glides along the seam of my lips, and she gets bolder, tugging at the hair on the back of my neck with a bit more force. I open my mouth and give in, kissing her back.

She tastes like cherries. Not the fake, maraschino bullshit, but the real kind. Tart. Fruity. The perfect distraction on a hot day when your sweat is dripping down your back and your muscles ache from running outside.

And fuck me. I'm aching.

For her.

She's like a damn buffet, and I'm expected to have enough self-control to only sneak a taste? It's impossible. I want her. I want her so damn much.

She's on something, I remind myself.

But she wasn't on something when she kissed me for the first time.

And she wanted me then.

Why wouldn't she want me now?

My guilt rears its ugly head as her hand slips down my torso, finding my jeans and rubbing my throbbing erection through the thick material. My hips thrust on their own, and it takes every last ounce of self-discipline I can find to grab her wrist and pull her away from me.

"Stop, Hads."

"I want you, Fender. I want all of you––"

"You don't know what you're saying––"

"I know exactly what I'm saying," she argues. "So, I'm on something. So, I like the way I feel when you're touching me. But what's going on in here?" She taps her short, trimmed fingernail against her temple. "It's still me. It's still *my* wants. *My* needs. And I need you to touch me. I'm begging you, Fen––"

The taste of her kiss is the most addictive thing I've ever been exposed to as I silence her with my mouth. Because I can't take it anymore. Her begging. The slight tremble in her voice. The heat in her gaze. If the woman wants to torture me, she's doing a bang-up job. When her teeth dig into my lower lip, I shove myself away from her. Again. As if she's my own brand of narcotics. Because it's exactly what she is.

Sweat clings to my forehead, my self-control only taking me so far as her back hits the wall with a soft thump. I might not be able to control myself, but I can control her. *If* I can find a way to give her what she wants without compromising myself in the process.

"Lay on the bed," I growl.

She hesitates. But only for a second. Her curiosity spurs her forward.

With her gaze glued to mine, she slips past me, and the soft mattress compresses under her weight as she waits for my next order.

"I'm not going to touch you when you're like this," I tell her.

"But––"

The panic-stricken look passing across her face makes my mouth twitch.

So. Damn. Sexy.

"Let's compromise, yeah?"

Her brows furrow. "What kind of compromise?"

"You ever touch yourself, Hads?"

A light blush spreads out along her cheeks and down her throat to her almost bare chest. "Maybe."

"Good. I'm going to leave so you can get rid of the sweet ache on your own, okay?"

"That's not a compromise." Pushing herself onto her knees, she crawls closer to the edge of the bed, her breasts practically spilling out of her black, lacy bra while managing to be a guy's wet dream.

My wet dream.

My stiff cock weeps at the sight, but I keep my feet firmly planted. She reaches toward me and grabs my wrist while balancing herself on the edge of the bed.

On her knees.

Kill me now.

I look at her tiny hand wrapped around my wrist, refusing to meet her glassy stare that can see right through me.

"Not sure what else you'd like me to do," I admit.

"I want you to help me––"

"I already told you it's not going to happen."

"Okay. Maybe not touch me, but…stay," she pleads.

My fists clench at my sides as her desperation rolls over me. "I can't stay, Hads."

"I need you––"

"What you need is sleep."

"And I promise I'll go straight to bed afterward. *If* you stay."

"Hadley…"

"Please? I don't want to be alone. And looking at you…" The tip of her pink tongue darts out between her lips, threatening to kill me where I stand.

Stay strong, Fen, I remind myself.

"This is a bad idea," I warn her.

"You don't have to touch me––"

"Then, you don't need me to stay."

"Maybe I could use my favorite inspiration…in the flesh," she whispers, her gaze flicking to mine as her cheeks flush a brighter shade of pink.

Does she mean I've been her inspiration in the past?

A low groan slips out of me. "Hadley…"

"Stay," she begs. "Watch."

"I'm not going to watch."

"But you'll stay?" she challenges.

Tongue in cheek, I squeeze the back of my neck and drop my chin to my chest, staring at the outline of my throbbing erection instead of the gorgeous woman on her knees in front of me.

It's official. I've died and gone to Hell because I'm pretty sure this is the most artful form of torture ever created.

"I've already compromised enough," she reminds me. "I don't get your hands on me. I don't get your mouth. Your…" her gaze drops to my jeans, and her breath hitches. "Stay. Please? This hurts. It's painful now. Like a mosquito bite or something. It needs to be…scratched."

"So scratch it, Hadley," I tell her.

Her grip tightens on my wrist, refusing to let me go. "Only if you stay."

Fuck me. This girl owns me. We haven't even slept together, but she owns me. Completely. The look in her eyes.

135

KELSIE RAE

The need. The desperation. The desire. And I believe her. She wants this. Not because of the drugs. Not entirely, anyway. But because she likes me. Because we've connected before tonight. Before someone slipped something in her drink. Before she showed up to watch me play. She wants me for *me*, the same way I'm so desperate to claim her for her. The girl with the quirky glasses. The girl who doesn't see how damn desirable she really is. The girl who fucking owns me.

"Fine," I concede, causing a shy smile to spread across her flushed face. "But if you change your mind and want me to leave, just say the word, and I'll go––"

"But I don't want––"

"I know, Hads." My mouth curves up with amusement at the desperation in her voice. "I know you don't want me to go. I'll stay. But I want you to stop torturing us both and touch yourself."

So I can get the hell out of here and rub one out in your bathroom.

"But I want you––"

"And maybe we can take the next step when you aren't still on something. But for tonight, we need you to ride this out, and since you're refusing to sleep until you scratch your itch, this'll have to do."

She chews her lower lip, holding my gaze while weighing her options. "But you'll stay? You'll watch?"

"You mean I'll let you torture me while I keep my distance?"

She nods, her innocent smile turning downright sinful.

Again, my cock twitches as if it has a mind of its own, straining against my jeans for the wet dream in front of me.

I shift back on my heels. "Yeah, Hads. I'll stay."

"Promise?"

I groan and scrub my hand over my face. "You're playing with fire, baby girl."

"Will you watch, Fen?" she begs, her tongue darting out between those damn pouty lips. "Will you watch me?"

"Hads," I warn.

"Please?"

I shake my head and turn around to face the wall. "This isn't you."

"If you keep saying that, I'm going to do this tomorrow when I'm sober."

A bark of laughter escapes me. "Is that a threat?"

"Maybe," she returns, growing bolder. More confident. It's sexy as hell.

I glance over my shoulder and order, "Lay down and slip off your jeans."

She smirks but does as she's told, apparently satisfied with my response. As the soft rustle of blankets quiets, I turn back to the wall and stare blankly in front of me.

"What next, Fen?" she whispers behind me.

"Are you still wearing your underwear?"

"Yes. It's a thong, in case you're wondering. Black. Lacy."

I groan and close my eyes. "I want you to feel yourself through your underwear and tell me if you're wet."

"So wet." I can hear her shuddering as she feels herself through the flimsy cotton of the thong she just described.

What I wouldn't give to tear the thing to shreds...

"Tell me, Fen. Tell me what you'd do to me if it were your hands on me instead of my own."

Resting my head against the wall, I take a slow, unsteady breath and squeeze my eyes shut even tighter. "I would spread your legs wide, Hads. I'd spread them wide and blow softly against the wet fabric."

She gasps.

"I'd nibble on the little divots between your thigh and your lips, sucking softly as you squirm beneath me."

A soft moan reverberates through the room, practically killing me.

"Then what, Fen?" she whispers.

"I'd pull your underwear aside and slip my finger into you. Pumping softly as you squeeze me tight."

Another gasp.

Fucking hell. I can't see her. I refuse to look, but I can picture it. Her writhing on the bed, her hair a tangled mess as she shakes her head from side to side. Her eyes squeezed shut. Her button nose scrunching. Her jaw slack.

The zipper digs into my dick as more blood rushes south, making me light-headed. I'm gonna come in my jeans, and I haven't even touched myself.

But she's touching herself, and it's all the motivation my dick needs.

I can hear her. The soft, wet noises behind me. The little moans. The staggered breaths.

It's the most erotic thing I've ever witnessed, and I'm not even watching.

"Keep going," she begs. "Keep going."

The neediness in her voice makes my legs tremble, and I brace my hand against the wall to keep from sliding to the ground––or worse––losing the last of my self-control and bringing to fruition everything I'm describing to her.

"Tell me," she whimpers.

"I'd add a second finger and crook them together, teasing the little bundle of nerves inside of you while licking your clit slowly with just enough pressure to drive you wild until your hips would buck off the mattress and your fingers would dig into my hair––"

"Shit, Fen," she breathes out, the soft wet sounds getting faster and faster as she fingers herself. "Please."

I palm myself through my jeans, the heat burning me alive as she moans my name.

"Fender…I'm coming. Shit, I'm coming, Fen."

My heart pounds against my ribcage as she finishes orgasming, my own just out of reach until I unbutton the top of my jeans, squeeze the head of my cock, and am ripped apart by wave after wave of fucking bliss.

Damn.

I came in my palm like a freaking sixteen-year-old, and I don't even care. Hands down, it's the hottest thing I've ever experienced, and I refuse to ruin the moment by calling whatever just happened a mistake, though I'm sure my self-loathing will be in full effect by tomorrow.

Our heavy breathing mingles together in the otherwise silent room. Her hushed voice finally breaks it. "You can turn around, Fen."

I gulp, reach for the tissue box on her nightstand, and wipe myself clean.

"Are you avoiding me?" she teases.

I scrub my clean hand over my face, wad the used tissue in my other hand, and glance over my shoulder.

With one leg straight and the other bent at the knee beneath the black and white comforter, she looks up at me with a soft smile capable of melting an iceberg.

"Hi."

A low chuckle vibrates through my chest, and I squeeze the back of my neck. "Hey."

"Will you snuggle me?"

Another laugh, louder this time, rises to the surface. "Snuggle you?"

"Yeah. I might not need sex anymore, but your touch still feels good. Please?"

"Hads––"

"Hold me," she whispers, her eyes glazed with vulnerability. I don't think it's from the drugs. I think it's from her. From what we just experienced. What we just did.

What we definitely shouldn't have done.

But I'm weak. Too weak to tell her no. To go home. To leave her alone even when I know it's what's best for her.

With my heart in my throat, I tell her, "Give me a sec."

The water is cool as I wash my hands and dry them while ignoring the voice inside my head telling me to get the hell out of here.

Once I'm finished, I climb into her bed and pull the covers over us before I can talk myself out of it. She cuddles into my side, her breathing soft and even against my chest until we both fall asleep.

19

FENDER

t's still early. Or late, depending on how you look at it. I'd guess maybe three in the morning, but I'm not sure. There isn't any light filtering in from the window, but my body feels like a livewire. Hadley is pressed against me, her breathing soft and shallow, tickling my neck as she nuzzles closer. Last night was...a mess. And even though she begged me to stay, I shouldn't have. I shouldn't have done that. I shouldn't have let her do that. Touch herself. Especially not in front of me. But I didn't know what else to do.

I was weak.

I look down at the woman curled against me.

I'm *still* weak.

Because I want to stay. I want to kiss her. To tell her I like her. To ask if she'd be willing to take a chance on a screw-up like me.

But would it be a mistake? Would it hurt her in the long run? I scrub my free hand over my face, unsure what to do. I didn't crave any drugs last night while I was with her, but who's to say I won't the next time? Will there be a next time?

She was drugged, for God's sake. Will she even remember what happened in the morning?

The haze from our little *encounter* is still making my logic clouded at best. It doesn't help that I can still feel her perfect tits pressed against my chest or the tiny wisps of her hair beneath my chin.

I need space. To think. To breathe without tasting her scent in the air. To give her a chance to change her mind. To get her head on straight.

So, even though it kills me, I slip my arm out from beneath her and keep my steps slow and steady as I exit her apartment, careful not to wake her up.

I tell myself it's because she needs her sleep. But I'm not an idiot. I know I'm a coward for refusing to face her. For letting her spend the rest of the early morning alone. To let her wake up in a cold bed instead of wrapped in my arms.

But allowing it would be a mistake.

And I'm tired of making mistakes.

THE DRIVE HOME IS SHORT AND DOES LITTLE TO CLEAR MY head as I pull up the driveway and park outside.

Darkness blankets the main living area, but the kitchen in the back of the house is bright. I step closer, exhaustion seeping from my pores when a familiar face peeks around the corner from the kitchen.

"Sonny?" I ask.

When he sees me, he rushes toward me but stops short as if he can't decide whether he wants to punch me or pull me into a hug.

"What are you doing here?" I ask numbly, stepping around him and heading into the kitchen.

His footsteps echo behind me as he demands, "Where the hell have you been? You haven't been answering my calls––"

"Phone's dead," I answer him. Or at least, I assume it is. It had been running on ten percent when I finished the show last night. And yeah, I ignored his call as I drove Hadley home afterward, but other than that? Nothing.

But I was a little preoccupied, so who knows?

"And your excuse before last night?" he challenges. "We've had one call, Fen. One. And I'm not stupid enough to believe you answered it on purpose."

"So, you thought showing up on my doorstep was the right way to go?" I challenge.

"I thought addressing shit instead of sweeping it under the rug was the right way to go. And since I'd already tried giving you space, but it didn't work for shit, I figured flying home to talk to you might do the trick."

"Yeah, well, I hate to disappoint you, but I'm not in the mood to talk right now."

"Tough shit. I'm done tiptoeing around you, Fen. We kept your secret. We wanted to give you space to get better, so you could come back to Broken Vows––"

"What are you doing here?" I interrupt.

He rubs his hand over the crown of his dark mop of hair, looking sheepish. "I told you I was worried about you."

"Why?"

He scrubs his hand over his face and mutters, "Sammie called. Told me about the girl getting drugged at the bar. I took the redeye. Just got in. She said she was worried about you––"

"Fucking Sammie," I grit out and pinch the bridge of my nose, reaching for a glass from the cabinet when what I really want is a shot of whiskey. "You guys need to learn to keep your noses out of my business."

He grabs my shoulder. "You're my brother, Fen. Your business is my business."

"No. It isn't," I argue, wrenching myself away from him and pointing to my chest. "My business is my business."

"Why are you acting this way?"

"Like what?"

He frowns. And I hate knowing I put it there. "Like you're mad to see me."

"I'm not mad," I start, sticking my tongue in my cheek as I search for the words to express what I'm feeling. The only problem is, I have no fucking clue. I set the glass back onto the counter. Exhausted.

"Then, what are you?" he prods. But he keeps his distance. Not for his sake, but for mine.

"I'm tired of everyone trying to fix my problems instead of letting me handle my shit on my own."

"I've *been* letting you handle your shit on your own, Fen, and look where it got you." He waves his hand at me.

"You mean in rehab?" I demand.

"Not what I meant."

"What did you mean?"

"I meant..." He heaves a frustrated sigh and looks up toward the ceiling as if to see if our raised voices have woken anyone else up. When only silence greets him, he continues. "I meant you pushing everyone away. You're not answering Dad's calls--"

"Oh, so now he's *Dad* to you?" I scoff. Donny Hayes and Sonny have never been close, and even that's an understatement. I was the one trying to mend my relationship--and Sonny's--with our dad. But Sonny didn't want anything to do with him. The bastard couldn't even stand to hear our father's name. And now, he's calling him *Dad*? It shouldn't piss me off, but it does. I shake my head as the realization hits me. It's the final straw that broke the camel's back. *My* back.

"You really are just taking my life, aren't you," I spit. It isn't a question. It doesn't need to be. And while I'm not in the mood to hash this shit out, I guess there's no time like the present.

"What the hell are you talking about?" he asks.

"I'm talking about *you*. I'm talking about why I haven't been answering your calls. Why I've been avoiding you. I'm jealous! I'm jealous because I messed up, and you get to ride off into the sunset with my dream, and all I can do is applaud your perseverance on your way out."

As if I've sucker-punched him, he jerks back and leans against the granite island. "*Your* dream? I thought Broken Vows was *our* dream."

I laugh dryly and shake my head back and forth. "It was until you decided to be the face of it."

"I wanted *us* to be the face of it," he argues. "It isn't my fault you refused to cut Marty out of your life and wound up overdosing––"

"Yeah, well, what do you want me to say? You were right? Fine, Sonny. You were right," I snarl, pacing the small kitchen like it's my own personal Hell, and there's no way to escape it. "Marty's an asshat who not only decided to put my life in danger but thought it would be funny to send me a message last night by spiking my friend's drink with something."

Stunned silence is the only thing greeting me as he blinks slowly and shakes his head, attempting to put together the pieces I've given him. "It was Marty? Are you sure?"

"Gave me a note and everything. He's pissed Dad cut off his funds and wants to get his revenge on me because of it."

Finally understanding, Gibson's upper lip curls in disgust as his frustration with me shifts to the other black sheep in the family. I don't know why it annoys me, but it does.

Because he hates Marty. And now, I feel like I'm just as bad as he is.

"That sonofabitch," Sonny grits out.

"Yup. Apparently, there's only one golden boy in the family, so congratulations. Glad I could help you claim the title." I'm not sure where my sarcasm is coming from, but frustration can only build for so long before it needs to be let loose, and it's no-holds-barred.

Pixie pads into the kitchen with a low growl when she sees the intruder across from me. She must've heard our raised voices. I call her over and scratch behind her ear while trying to rein in my annoyance and frustration and every other emotion simmering through my veins.

But being numb isn't exactly an option anymore, so I shove them aside and say, "It's okay, Pix. He's…" I look up at him, my nostrils flaring. "He's family."

She stalks closer to him, gives him a quick sniff, and lays down on the kitchen mat beneath the sink, satisfied he isn't a threat.

With a sigh, Gibson takes a seat at the barstool tucked beneath the gray granite countertop in the center of the kitchen and motions to the chair beside him. "Take a seat, Fen. I think we need to talk."

"I don't feel like talking."

"Yeah? Well, I flew all the way down here because I was worried about you——"

"It isn't your job to be worried about me."

"Then who's is it? Huh? Because you've never been one to take care of yourself——"

"I'm *trying* to take care of myself," I yell, finally losing the last of my restraint as I stomp closer to him and slap my palms against the counter, towering over my older brother so he'll finally see me. *Really* see me for the first time ever.

Not the happy-go-lucky teenager pretending he didn't

have a care in the world from when we first met. Not the sarcastic asshole who liked making jokes while we were on the road. But me. The weak, broken brother who's trying to be better despite the odds stacked against him. I force another breath into my lungs and add, "I'm trying to stay away from shit that'll hurt me. I'm trying to keep my head on straight. I'm trying to get my life back because it feels like it was ripped away from me by none other than my own flesh and blood."

Silence hangs over us like tree branches heavy with snow, and I'm afraid they'll snap at any second. But I don't know how to take back what I said or if I even want to. Because even though I haven't wanted to voice it aloud, the accusation has been filling every tiny crevice inside of me since the moment Dove and Gibson took the stage without me. And there's no going back. Not anymore.

"You think I ripped your life away?" he murmurs, his tone quiet but laced with disbelief.

I stay quiet and shake my head, pushing myself away from the counter to pace the kitchen again. I want to storm out. But I can't actually leave. I have nowhere else to go.

"Fen, I need you to listen to me. And I mean really listen to me."

I shake my head, my fury boiling just beneath the surface until I'm convinced I'll explode at any second.

Gibson pushes himself to his feet, grabs my arms, and halts my pacing––despite Pixie's warning growl––forcing me to look down at him. "I've already told you I want you back in Broken Vows––"

"There isn't a place for me in Broken Vows," I spit. "There isn't a place for me anywhere."

"You belong by my side. You're my brother––"

"Yeah, well, Marty's our brother too––"

"Marty's an ass who happens to share some of our DNA.

He is not my brother, and he sure as hell isn't yours, either. What he did to your friend? It's unacceptable. We'll call Dad and tell him—"

"And what's Dad going to do? Huh? There's no proof. No evidence. Dad already took away the one thing Marty cared about, which is making him even more desperate and unhinged than ever. The security footage will only show a random guy with his face covered by his dark hoodie. It'll be shit for the police to use because we both know how well Marty covers his tracks. So what am I going to do? I only know how to hurt the people I care about. I should just—"

"Stop it, Fen."

"No." I tug my arm from his grasp and march toward the front door. Pixie stays right by my side, but I force her to stay at the base of the stairs, and I slam the door behind me.

I gotta get out of here. And where I want to go? Well, the landlord wouldn't be too happy if I brought Pixie along.

~

I DON'T KNOW WHY I'M NOT STRONG ENOUGH TO GRAB A hotel or something, but I wind up on Hadley's doorstep. I shouldn't be here, but I also don't want to be anywhere else. Not when I know Marty could've hurt her last night. How he did hurt her. I need to know she's still okay.

Besides, the best sleep I've had in months was the few hours I spent in her arms. And after my conversation with Sonny and all the shit we stirred up? It's clear I shouldn't have left her bed.

My hands shake as I wipe my sweaty palms against my jeans before knocking softly against Hadley's door.

A few minutes later, it opens with a quiet squeak. Her eyes are tiny slits as she fights the glare from the hall light outside her door and covers her mouth with a yawn. She's wearing a baggy T-shirt that barely reaches her thighs but didn't bother to find her glasses, and her hair is a mess of tangles hanging around her shoulders. I'd laugh if she didn't look so damn beautiful it makes my chest ache.

"Where'd you go?" she asks a few seconds later, oblivious to my staring. Her voice is soft but crackly from sleep.

"Can I come in?"

With a few slow blinks followed by a slight nod, she steps aside, and I grab her hand, making sure to lock the door behind us. I climb back into her bed as if I never left it.

"You okay?" she murmurs once she's settled beside me.

My mouth itches to lean down and kiss the crown of her head, but I restrain myself. "We'll talk tomorrow."

She nuzzles closer to me but doesn't argue. She's too tired.

A few minutes later, her breathing steadies, and I know she's asleep. If only it were that easy to quiet my own racing thoughts.

But having Hadley beside me is a start, and I hate how I notice my softening muscles and the way her scent calms me. I hate how she affects me the way she does and how I showed up on her doorstep tonight. I hate how much I missed her. How much I still miss her even when she's in my arms because I'm counting down the days when she'll realize I'm not worth her time and will leave.

I squeeze her a little tighter, praying I'll be strong enough to keep her safe.

From Marty.

And from me.

20

HADLEY

The morning light filters through the window, casting a warm glow around my room. I roll over but freeze when I recognize a strong arm wrapped around my waist.

My eyelids feel heavy, but I blink away my exhaustion and twist around in Fender's grasp.

He's still asleep.

He looks peaceful like this. The constant worry lines etched into his skin have softened, and his hair is a mess. He's so freaking handsome, it almost hurts to look at him. Like I'm staring at the sun. Someone larger than life with no idea how to settle.

"Why are you staring?" he grunts, though he doesn't bother to open his eyes.

I grin. "Sorry. I think I'm still reeling."

The worry lines reappear, and he peels one lid open to look down at me. "About that––"

"Thank you," I interrupt. "For bringing me home. For keeping me safe."

"Hads…"

"I mean it." His scruff feels prickly against my hand as I palm his cheek. "I feel safe when I'm with you, Fen."

He shakes his head and pulls away, untangling his body from mine while leaving me cold and alone.

"Last night... I've been thinking about it a lot, and it can't happen again."

"The drugs? Yeah. I agree——"

"No, I meant..." He pauses, scrubbing his hand over his face roughly. "You and me."

Pushing up onto my elbows, I sit up, lean my back against the dark headboard, and bring my knees to my chest. "Why not?"

"The guy drugged you because of me, Hads."

"What? That's bullshit. Despite what you may like to believe, women are preyed upon every single day. And even though no one likes to acknowledge it, the truth is, anytime I leave my house, I know there's a risk of something happening to me. Every woman knows the risk. So, yeah. I went to the bar and should've paid better attention——"

"What happened to you wasn't your fault," he growls.

"Maybe not, but when you go for a swim in shark-infested waters, you'd still be smart to pay attention to your surroundings. That's on me."

"No, it's on me. Because that shark wouldn't have attacked you if it weren't for our...friendship."

The term stings, considering how desperate I was to jump his bones last night, but I let it slide and argue, "No offense, but you don't know——"

"Yes, I do. He was my brother's friend. The guy who drugged you," he clarifies. "Marty sent him to prove a point. To prove I have something to lose if I don't give him what he wants."

My lips part, but I choke back my gasp, doing my best to

hide my surprise with a look of indifference. "And what does he want?"

Sitting on the edge of the bed, Fender cradles his head in his hands, looking as defeated and broken as he did when he showed up on my doorstep early this morning.

"He heard about Hawthorne's deal. He wants to help with my music career."

"So?"

"So, he wants in on a piece of the pie," Fender grits out, looking over at me.

"And he thinks if he threatens me, you'll cave to his demands?" I clarify. "Is he delusional? It's like you just said; we're friends. You have lots of friends. What? He's going to threaten all of them? That's ridiculous."

Fender's expression stays blank, but I don't miss his hesitation to confirm my comment.

"It's ridiculous. Right?" I prod.

Silence.

"Fender, you can't let him control you. What's next? He threatens your roommates?"

"My roommates can handle themselves."

"And I can't?"

"You're different."

"How am I different?"

"You just are."

"How?" I demand. "You said so yourself; we're just friends––"

"Well, for one, I saw you masturbate last night," he offers. "Can't say I've seen my other friends do that."

"And you turned me down when I wanted it to be you instead of my fingers inside of me."

His nostrils flare. "You were drugged up, Hadley. What else did you expect me to do? Take advantage of you? I'm not that kind of guy."

"I know you're not, which is why I *wanted* to kiss you. It's why I kissed you the first time when I was sober, I might add, and you still pushed me away. So how am I different, Fen? You can't let your brother manipulate you because of a girl you don't even care about."

He twists on the bed until he faces me fully, his face a mixed concoction of surprise and outrage. "You think I don't care about you?"

"I don't know what to think. You watch me get off, snuggle with me until I fall asleep, and disappear. Then you show up on my doorstep a few hours later and ask to come inside. And now, when I think we're finally getting somewhere, you call me your *friend* and say what happened last night can't happen again. So, yeah, I'm not exactly sure what to think anymore. But I like you, okay? I like you for more than a *friend*, but I feel like you've already decided you're not interested--"

"You think I'm not interested?"

I roll my eyes, caught between frustration and amusement. I can't believe I even have to spell this out for the guy. "You've rejected me. *Twice.* And sure, I'll accept the whole *you were drugged up, and I didn't want to take advantage of you last night* argument, but what about now? If I leaned in to kiss you right now, would you push me away?"

His gaze drops to my lips before he looks away. "Of course, I would."

"So, how does it make me any different from your other friends?"

"Because I don't *want* to kiss my other friends, Hadley."

"But you said--"

"I'd push you away. I never said I don't *want* to kiss you. There's a difference."

My brows furrow. "How? Why?"

"Because…" His jaw ticks, but he doesn't finish his sentence.

"Because…what?"

"Because I can't give you what you want."

"And how do you know what I want?"

Frustrated, he blurts out, "I can't be intimate with you!"

What?

I bite my lip, more confused than ever. "Why?"

"I just can't."

"But last night––"

"I didn't touch you."

"I know, but––"

"I can't have sex without craving drugs, and I promised myself I wouldn't go down that road again or even get close to it. Yeah, last night didn't blow up in my face, but who's to say it won't the next time? I've already pushed the boundaries enough. Sorry to disappoint you, Hads, but I'm broken. I'm a sad, pathetic, broken man with an addiction that will never let me go."

My heart cracks. I scoot closer to him and grab his face, forcing him to look at me. "You're not sad or pathetic *or* broken, Fender."

He scoffs but leans into my touch and closes his eyes, giving me hope.

Maybe I'm not the only one who can feel what's growing between us.

"You're a human who's choosing to be stronger than his addiction," I tell him. "And it's something admirable. It's brave. Not only are you admitting your weakness out loud, you're owning up to it, facing it on a daily basis. That's huge, Fen. It's something my brother has struggled to do for decades. And yeah, maybe you should steer clear of sex for a while if you're afraid it'll push you over the edge, but it doesn't mean you can't be intimate with someone."

He scoffs again. Hell, I can almost taste his self-loathing as it taints the air around us. But I'm not about to give up. I'm not about to let him think he's doomed to live a life alone, all because he has a demon who refuses to let him go.

"We were intimate last night," I remind him. "We cuddled. You held me. That's intimate, and it's exactly what I needed."

He pries his eyelids open, his gaze shining with vulnerability and disappointment.

"And if it's all I can give you?" he asks, his voice quiet yet almost hopeful.

My heart feels like it's beating a million beats per minute as I lean closer and brush my lips against his. Softly. Like I'm afraid I'll startle him, and he'll run in the opposite direction if I'm not careful. And he might.

But he doesn't. He lets me kiss him. And what's more? He kisses me back, his lips melting beneath mine with a staggering intimacy. It's earth-shattering. It's more than a casual hook-up with a stranger. It's real and meaningful and so damn addictive I have to stop myself from straddling his lap in hopes of bringing us closer.

Because I do crave the closeness. But only with him.

With our foreheads still pressed together, I pull away from his expert mouth and whisper, "I'm not asking for your heart or your future, Fen. I'm asking for a chance. A chance to see if this can go where I think it can if you can let me in and trust me. Do you think you can give that to me?"

He cups my cheeks, the calluses from playing his guitar tickling my sensitive skin as he breathes me in. Like I'm a different kind of addiction, but one with the potential to be just as dangerous.

"And my brother?" His voice is low and throaty.

"Can go screw himself. I'm a big, strong girl. And he's a pathetic piece of shit if he thinks he can use me to get to you. You should call the police."

"And say what, exactly?" he asks. "My brother's trying to blackmail me into giving him money and access to my future without being able to give them any real evidence to prove it?"

He's got a point. But I hate seeing how worried he is. It isn't fair.

"I don't get it," I admit. "Why is he so invested in ruining you for money? Especially when his dad is the infamous rockstar, Donny Hayes. He's your brother."

"Half-brother," Fen clarifies. "He's also a jealous asshole who's pissed our dad cut him off because of his influence on me. Marty wants to get back at me for ruining his life, and he isn't afraid of taking what's important to me if it gets him what he wants."

My breath hitches as my gaze drops to his mouth, convinced I've heard him wrong. "Am I important to you, Fen?"

With a soft kiss to my forehead, he murmurs, "Yeah, Hads. I think you are. And it scares the shit out of me."

I smile even though he can't see me and rest my forehead against his chin, breathing deep. "We'll figure it out."

21

FENDER

"**B**agel and schmear, huh?" I note as Hadley glides the sharp, serrated knife through the blueberry bagel.

After our little chat, we rolled out of bed and took separate showers because I think she could tell I needed some space. I ran out to grab us some coffee, and she sat in front of her computer to work. When I got back with our much-needed caffeine, I asked if I could stick around for a while longer, and she agreed as long as she could get some work done. So, I hid in her bedroom, playing pointless games on my phone, which had been brought back to life thanks to her charger, before opening Reddit to learn about random shit.

And now? It's lunchtime, which apparently means bagel and schmear in this household.

"They're the best," she tells me.

"It's two in the afternoon."

"Even better," she quips, her dark glasses propped on her button nose. She looks relaxed. Happy. In her element. It's a stark contrast to the girl I brought home last night who was a bundle of energy looking to get laid.

After adding a large dollop of strawberry cream cheese, she takes a bite of the open-faced pastry and asks, "Want some?"

There's a small smudge of schmear at the corner of her mouth, so I grab her waist, pull her closer, and lick it off, almost groaning as the combination of Hadley and cream cheese explodes across my tastebuds. I don't know why I'm so open about kissing her. But after our conversation this morning, I feel like a weight's been lifted, my worries dissipating. Or at least some of them. She's right. I might not be able to give her sex anytime soon––if at all––but whatever's going on between us is still worth exploring. And if she's willing to put her heart on the line while I figure my shit out, even though she knows how messed up I am in the head, I'm too weak to tell her no. I'd be a fool if I did. Because she's perfect.

Freaking *perfect.*

She grins back at me and deepens the kiss. Pulling away, she runs the pad of her thumb along her bottom lip.

"I can't decide if you taste better than my favorite duo"–– she lifts her bagel in her opposite hand––"or if I'm still dreaming that you're actually here."

"I'm here," I assure her, though I'm still reeling myself. "And I do taste better than your favorite duo, but it's a close race."

She throws her head back and laughs, swaying toward the small white desk in the corner of her family room. "Touché. I still can't believe you came back last night."

"I'm sorry I woke you up after leaving in the first place."

"Yeah, so..." She takes a seat on a small swivel chair and turns toward me, balancing the bagel in one hand while eyeing me warily. "Are we gonna talk about it? I mean, I think I can figure out why you left, but why did you come back? Is everything okay?"

"Everything's fine," I lie. "Family stuff."

"Which part of the family?" she prods.

"Sonny this time. I haven't heard from Marty since the bar."

"Gotcha. How's Sonny doing, anyway? You haven't told me much about him."

"He's good. Or he was until I yelled at him last night."

"Is that what happened? Why you came back? Because you got into a fight with him?"

I grab the second half of her bagel off the cutting board and take a bite. "Maybe."

She quirks her brow.

I chew slowly while making my way toward her, dodging the beaten-up leather couch decorated with a dozen gray and white pillows, just like her bedroom. "It's also why I've been hiding away in your bedroom all day while you were working."

"Attempting to work," she clarifies and motions to her dark computer screen. "Not necessarily working. The words aren't flowing, ya know?"

"Is there a reason they aren't flowing?" I close the last bit of distance between us, shove the final bite of bagel into my mouth, and dig my thumbs into her shoulder blades, hoping it'll ease a bit of the tension which seems to build anytime her work is mentioned.

With a soft moan, she rolls her head forward and says, "I write thrillers, Fen. And the fact my brother's missing hits a little too close to home. I can't focus. I can't create a scene or a loophole or a clue leading to the next chapter. Anytime I even start going down that road, I...freeze." Her muscles tense beneath my hands, but I keep rolling my fingers in hopes of loosening them. "And it's not like my mind goes blank, either. I think it would be easier. Instead, every plot-line I start to weave together hits too close to home. It's like the story I keep imagining includes a body. A male body with a shaggy dog in need of a home, or he has a past with drugs and a daughter who needs her father. It won't stop. Any of it."

With a frown, I try to think of something to say, something to comfort her, but I come up empty. Because it sucks. And there isn't a solution. There isn't anything I can say to make her feel better or bring her brother back. At least, nothing in my control.

I squeeze her tense muscles again, digging my thumbs into the base of her skull and rubbing down her spine as I mutter, "I'm sorry, Hads."

"It's not your fault," she whispers, still defeated. "He's never been gone this long."

"Have you heard anything else from the police? Since they found the evidence…"

She shakes her head and turns around in her swivel chair. Wrapping her arms around my waist, she pulls me into her until her head is pressed against my stomach. Her hair is soft and silky as I run my fingers through it, still desperate to comfort her. To make everything okay, even when I know it isn't possible.

"They're keeping everything really quiet," she whispers. "Every time Isabella or I call for an update, all they say is," she drops her voice low, mimicking the male detective who's heading up the case. *"We're doing everything in our power to bring him home. Please let us do our job.* The problem is, I can't seem to do mine while he's missing, and my editor wants to kill me because of it."

I sigh and rub my hand up and down her back. "Is there anything I can do to help? Do you want me to leave so you can concentrate?"

"I want you to stay. I want you to stay, and I want you to kiss me."

"Hads," I warn her. "I don't want to distract you--"

My phone rings in my jeans, cutting me off, and I dig it out.

"Who is it?" Hadley asks.

"It's Hawthorne."

22

HADLEY

"Hello?" Fen answers the call with a tight jaw as he rests his hip on the edge of my desk.

The room is quiet, but I still can't hear what Hawthorne's saying on the other end. However, I have a feeling it has something to do with me because Fender's gaze darts my way a few seconds later.

He frowns and replies, "Yeah. She's okay."

Silence.

"Thanks, I'll, uh, I'll let her know."

More silence.

Fender sits on the edge of the desk, his spine ramrod straight. "Are you serious?"

The soft, low voice echoes from the speaker though I still can't make out what's being said.

"Yeah. I mean, I get it's a big opportunity, but––"

Silence.

"I know, but what about Broken Vows?"

Silence.

"I don't want you to do me any favors––"

He scrubs his hand over his face as Hawthorne says

162

something else.

"Yeah. I know," Fender replies.

Silence.

"Yeah. I know I need to talk to Sonny."

Silence.

"I know. I've been going through some shit."

More. Freaking. Silence.

"Yeah. I'll take care of it."

Seriously. This conversation is killing me. I scoot the swivel chair a few inches closer, torn between giving the guy some privacy and ripping the stupid phone from his hands so I can put it on speaker.

"For how long?" Fender's gaze shoots to me. "Yeah. Get me an extra plane ticket. What're the dates?"

Silence.

"All right. Yeah. We'll, uh, we'll be there."

He hangs up the phone but stays quiet, blowing out all the pent-up oxygen in his lungs as he stares blankly at the wall.

"So?" I ask.

"It was Hawthorne."

"You mentioned that." I smile and touch his knee. "What'd he say?"

"He was calling to see if you were all right. Sammie mentioned what happened last night, and he wanted to know if he could help with pressing charges."

"Which is a moot point since the guy disappeared."

"I'm still going to have Sammie and her dad send over the surveillance footage to the police, though I doubt anything will turn up."

"What else did he say?"

"He mentioned an opportunity."

"What kind of opportunity?"

"A charity concert."

"What kind of charity concert?" I prod, shoving him in

the shoulder while somehow amused and annoyed by his lack of transparency.

"It's for kids with cancer."

"That's really sweet."

"Yeah. He wants me to open for Eager Cane."

"Really?" My eyes widen in surprise. The band is huge. Like, top 100 huge. I touch his cheek and force him to look at me instead of getting lost in the floral painting hanging on the wall opposite of where we're sitting. "That's amazing, Fen."

He sucks his bottom lip into his mouth and nods. "Yeah. Just a one-time gig for now, but it's in LA."

"Yeah?"

"Yeah. He wants to fly me out to perform."

"That's...big, isn't it?"

I can see his hesitation, his fear, as he forces a smile and squeezes my knee. "Yeah, Hads. It's big."

"And? Are you nervous? Excited?"

"I'm..." He shakes his head, probably still trying to wrap his head around the situation. "I'm a lot of things."

"Like what?"

"Like...nervous. Yeah." He chuckles dryly. "Excited, maybe? Anxious, definitely. It feels weird that Hawthorne set up a few interviews with potential band members who aren't from Broken Vows, though, but I guess it's normal."

"It's exciting," I offer.

"Still weird. To be up on stage without Phoenix, Stoker, Sonny, or even Dove. But..." He shrugs his shoulders and tucks his hands into the front pockets of his jeans, looking lost. And alone. And not nearly as excited as the old Fender would've been if given the same opportunity. Then again, I didn't know him before. It's easy to see this is tearing him apart, and it's killing me.

"But what?" I ask.

"I dunno. I miss them, I guess. But I don't want to be handed anything because of the shit from my past. I'm nervous it's the only reason Hawthorne invited me to play instead of Broken Vows."

"I can understand that," I console, resting my head on his shoulder while savoring the heat from his palm against my thigh. "Did he say why?"

"No, but he assured me he isn't picking favorites, and he'll continue to represent each of his clients fairly. I guess he thinks this opportunity is the best fit for me personally."

I lift my head and look up at him. "I think you should trust him."

"Yeah. He also mentioned Broken Vows is back from their tour. "

"Which you knew because you showed up on my doorstep after talking to Sonny."

"Yeah. But I didn't know it was officially over. Not even when I saw him at my place. It makes me feel like a shitty brother."

"You're not a shitty brother," I tell him.

"Depends on how you look at it. Especially lately." He sighs. "As you know, Sonny and I aren't exactly on good terms. Not after I yelled at him yesterday and accused him of stealing my dream."

"I get that too," I admit.

"I gotta smooth things over with him."

I chew on the inside of my cheek. If anyone understands family drama, it's me. My relationship with Bud is far from perfect, but if I've learned anything since he went missing, it's not to take our time for granted. You never know when shit will hit the fan, and I'd give anything to hug my brother and tell him I love him. I have a feeling Sonny would, too, if the roles were reversed. But is it my place to tell Fender?

I finally murmur, "It's probably a good idea. To smooth things over with him," I clarify.

"Yeah. I don't know how, though. He's my brother. I love him. And I know he loves me. But...it's weird, I guess. Seeing how things played out. And I'm not saying he was in control of all of it, or any of it is his fault because it isn't. I know it's not. If anything, it's mine. But it still hurts. To feel like I was replaced. Like the band didn't need me. They needed a front runner, a singer, sure, but me particularly? Not really. I feel like I was...replaceable."

"Did any of them ever say you were replaceable?" I ask carefully.

He shakes his head.

"Have any of your bandmates tried calling?"

He nods.

"Have you talked to any of them?" I press.

He shakes his head again. "No. And that's on me. I know it is. But knowing it up here"--he taps the side of his head--"while feeling the opposite in here"--his hand moves to his chest right above his heart--"are two different things."

"I get that too. Maybe you should take a step back and analyze the *why* behind your conflicting perspectives."

He smiles, but it's laced with sadness and doesn't reach his eyes. "It's a little easier said than done."

"True. But I'm here to help if you need me, and I get how it can be difficult to analyze things like this. Because up here?" I mirror his movements from moments ago and cup the side of his head, running my fingers along his scalp until he leans into me and closes his eyes. "Is based on logic. And down here"--his heart beats against my palm, warming me--"is based on emotion. Both have merit. Both should be taken into account. But when they're at war with each other, it can be hard to analyze the situation without bias."

"True," he concedes. "You're further away from the situation. What do you think?"

I bite my lip, recognizing how carefully I have to tread while appreciating his desire to hear my insight. It means there's trust here. And I know Fender doesn't trust easily. So, I appreciate his trust. More than he'll ever understand.

"You sure you want to hear what I think?" I ask.

He nods, albeit subtly, as if he can't decide whether or not he's ready to hear the truth. As if maybe he already knows what I'm going to say, and he isn't sure he's going to appreciate hearing it out loud.

I lick my lips and murmur, "Maybe you aren't mad at them. Maybe you're mad at yourself, and you're taking the anger out on them. I think we both know we're responsible for our own actions, and while they probably could've handled a few things differently, shutting them out isn't fair. They want to be here for you. They want to show their support. You should try letting them."

He hangs his head and grabs my waist, nuzzling into my neck and seeking solace in my body in a way that makes me feel powerful. Strong. And I will be strong for the man in front of me. Hell, I'd go to war for him. I can feel it in my bones. And while the realization should be terrifying, it isn't. Because he deserves to feel that kind of protection. He's earned it.

"You're right, Hadley," he whispers against my heated flesh. "You're right. I'm going to fix things."

"Don't do it for me––"

"I'm not. I'm going to do it for myself. It's time I fight for what I want instead of letting the world around me decide what I deserve."

I smile and squeeze him a little tighter, raking my fingers through the back of his head and down his neck, tickling his sensitive skin as the tight muscles slowly melt beneath my touch.

After a few minutes of comfortable silence, he lifts his head. "Speaking of fighting for what I want. Would you like to accompany me? To the concert?"

"You want me to come?"

He nods.

"Then, yes, of course. I'd love to."

"Yeah?"

I nod. "Just tell me when, and I'll be there."

"Perfect."

23

FENDER

The last notes echo through the studio. I let them ring out and grin at the new bassist and drummer Hawthorne set me up with.

It's weird. Kind of feels like a first date or some shit, but they're talented musicians looking for a lead singer and guitarist, and I'm an okay lead singer and guitarist looking for a drummer and bassist.

Apparently, Hawthorne thinks it's a match made in heaven.

"That was great, man," Gunner tells me, spinning his drumstick between his tattooed fingers as his nose ring glints in the studio light. "I think we've got something."

"Me too," I answer.

"It was a little rough around the edges but not bad at all," Jess pipes up. He runs his hand over his shaved head and cracks his neck from side to side. "But I'm beat."

"Me too," I repeat, the exhaustion settling into my bones.

"Gunner and I were gonna hit up a party tonight since Hawthorne flew us in for this meeting. Do you know of any?"

My throat swells, and my palms grow sweaty as I register his words. "Any parties?"

"Yeah. You partied with one of my buddies while on tour with Broken Vows before..." Jess clears his throat, and Gunner's mouth snaps closed, realizing he's opened a massive can of worms.

"Before what?" I prod, unamused as I set my guitar into its case and fold my arms.

Jess lifts his hands, showing me his palms as if to prove he isn't a threat or some shit. "He didn't mean anything by it. He just meant...you know...since you used to like to party, we were wondering if you'd like to party tonight or something. You know, bonding time."

"I don't do that anymore."

"Really?"

"It's not my scene," I clarify.

They both nod but exchange glances as Jess pulls something from his dark leather pants. "No worries, man. We'll chill here. We don't need a party to bond and shit."

When I see the bag of white powder, my mouth waters, and my skin breaks out in a cold sweat. I can hear my heartbeat in my ears, and little black dots taint my vision as I zero in on it. Is there an elephant on my chest? I feel like there's an elephant on my chest. Like it's preventing my lungs from fully expanding, and the only way to get the damn beast off me is to reach out and––

The chair I'd been sitting in thuds against the ground as I shove to my feet and back away from Jess like he's holding a loaded gun pointed directly at me. The old me would've snorted it without any hesitation. I would've ridden the high and probably written a kickass song while I was at it. But I can't. I can't do this. I gulp down as much as I can and take another step back, clenching my fists at my sides.

That's another thing the old me would've done.

I would've beaten the shit out of this guy if he offended me. But right now, I feel like nothing more than a scared, pathetic piece of shit as a sweat breaks out along my brow.

"Dude, what's your problem?" Gunner asks.

"I said it's not my scene anymore."

"Yeah, man. We get it. Saw the news articles and shit. We'll keep it on the down-low. Not a big deal."

I shake my head. "Get out of the studio."

"What?"

"I said get the hell out of the studio. Now."

"Dude, it's only a little blow--"

"Now!" I yell. I feel like my chest is collapsing on itself as my entire body practically convulses. With anger. And need. So much fucking need I can't see straight. If Hawthorne were here, there's no way he'd put up with this shit. So, where the hell is he?

I look through the glass separating the recording area from the mixing booth, but it's empty.

Fucking empty.

"Listen," Gunner starts, but I storm out of the room without waiting.

The door bangs against the wall, jarring the pictures hanging on it, and I rip open the exit door, too, almost running into Hawthorne, who's talking on his cell.

He must've stepped out to take a call, but it does nothing to ease the itch beneath every inch of my skin. Like a thousand mosquito bites but worse.

It was right there.

I could've taken it, and no one would've known.

And I wanted to.

I wanted to try it.

To slip back into the oblivion that was my second home for years. Hell, it was my first home until it obliterated my life.

And I can't do it again.

"Let me call you back," Hawthorne murmurs into his cell. Hanging up, he grabs my shoulders and forces me to look at him. "What's wrong?"

"They brought blow into the studio!"

"Shit." He rubs his hand over his face and lifts his forefinger to me. "Stay here. I'll be right back."

"I'm not gonna work with them––"

"I said I'll be right back," he repeats and disappears into the studio. The warm night air only fans the heat in my veins, so I take a few slow breaths in and out.

Breathe, I remind myself, rubbing my hands from my forehead to my chin as I search my pockets for some freaking M&M's, even though I know they won't do shit. Not right now. Not when I know what two little walls are separating me from.

My encounter with Mia was different. Honestly, it was nothing compared to tonight. And I'm not sure why I was triggered in the studio when SeaBird felt like a walk in the park. Maybe it's because I always crave something when I play music. Sometimes it's worse than others, and today was a little rough, especially with my upcoming conversation with Broken Vows, but what happened in there? It was... worse somehow. And I can't shake the urge to march back in there and snort the little bag's contents up my nose.

But I can't.

My hands vibrate as I push aside the bag of M&M's and pull out my cell. With trembling fingers, I dial Hadley's number. She answers on the second ring.

"Hello?"

"Hadley?" I choke out.

"Fen? What's wrong?" The worry is clear in her voice and eases the vice around my chest. Not enough to breathe fully, but enough to allow *just* enough oxygen to enter my bloodstream.

"Hey," I breathe out. "Where are you?"

"I'm at home. Why?"

"I miss you."

"Miss you too. Are you okay? You sound…"

"Like I'm losing my mind?" I offer.

I can hear the smile in her voice as she murmurs, "Like you could use a hug. Do you want to come over?"

"Be there in ten."

24

FENDER

'm not entirely sure how I wind up on Hadley's welcome mat, my mind was a chaotic mess of regret during the entire drive, but the door opens before I have a chance to knock.

"Hawthorne called," she tells me. "I'm not sure how he got my number, but he knew you were hurting, so…" Her hair is a messy bun on top of her head as she wraps her arms around my neck and pulls me against her. My spine melts, and I tug her toward me.

She's so damn warm. So inviting. Like an anchor in my storm. My lungs expand as I breathe her in fully. Vanilla and blueberry. Probably from her lunchtime bagel.

Heaven.

"Missed you," I murmur.

"You too. Are you okay?"

I nod against her, tucking my head into the crook of her neck.

"You sure?"

Another nod, then I shake my head. "No. I'm not."

"Come in. Come sit down." She takes me with her, and we

both collapse onto the couch, a couple pillows falling to the floor when I pull her into my lap. With her knees on either side of my waist, we probably look like we're about to have sex. When in reality? I'm just trying not to break. She wraps her arms around my neck and tickles the back of my scalp. Her touch is soothing. Like a balm to my aching soul. I squeeze her a little tighter, melting into the cushions.

I'm not sure how long we sit there in silence when her quiet voice slices through it like a hot knife through butter. "Want to talk about it?"

"The new band members. They asked if I wanted to party, and..." I squeeze my eyes shut, the memory almost more than I can bear.

"And what did you say?"

"I told them to leave."

"Did they?"

I shake my head against her.

"So, what did you do?"

"I left instead."

Her fingers pause against my scalp, and she hugs me a little tighter and lets out a shuddered sigh of relief. "I'm proud of you, Fen."

"Bullshit," I curse against her soft skin.

Surprised, she tangles her fingers in my hair and pulls me away from her so she can look me in the eye. "Not bullshit. You said no. You were given an opportunity to slip back into a terrible habit, and you said no. It's something to be proud of."

"I almost didn't, though," I argue. "I almost screwed up again."

"But you didn't," she reminds me. "And that's huge, Fen. You're going to be given opportunities to mess up. We all are in life. It's what we do in those situations that makes us who we are. And you said no."

"But what if I can't say no next time?" My grip tightens around her like she's my life raft, and I'm caught in a never-ending hurricane.

"You will."

"How do you know?"

"Because you're the strongest person I know, Fen. I'm so proud of you."

"This is different, though. Harder."

"How?" she whispers. Without judgment. Simply a desire to understand. And she'll never know how much I appreciate it.

"This life," I explain. "The musician life. Going on tour again. The after-parties. There are opportunities to slip up every single fucking day." I squeeze my eyes shut and rest my forehead against hers. "I don't know if I'm disciplined enough to stay strong."

"You are," she promises me. "It's one step at a time. Today, you took a step in the right direction, and I've never been more proud."

"I feel like an idiot," I admit, still unable to pull myself away from her and look her in the eye. I'm too ashamed.

As if she can read my thoughts, she cups my cheeks and forces me to look at her. When my gaze meets hers, the disappointment I expect to see is absent, replaced with a determination I can almost feel as my own.

"You aren't an idiot. And I don't care how long it takes. I'll spend the rest of the night telling you this until you believe it. Now, did you talk to Hawthorne?"

I shake my head.

"Call him."

"I don't think I can talk to him right now."

"He wants to tell you something."

"I don't think I can hear it."

"Fen," she pleads. "Call him."

My phone vibrates beneath her thigh at that moment, and she lifts herself so I can retrieve it but settles onto my lap again.

When I see a text from Hawthorne, I almost roll my eyes and glance up at her.

Her smile is encouraging as she murmurs, "Read it."

With a sigh, I do.

Hawthorne: They're out. I'll find someone else to play with you at the charity concert. For now, focus on you and some new songs. We'll find a good fit. One who makes staying clean a priority. I'm sorry you were put in that position. We'll talk more tomorrow.

"Did you have something to do with this?" I ask Hadley.

"Not exactly. When he came back outside to talk to you, you'd already left, so he called me about what happened. I chewed his head off, and he apologized a bazillion times, saying he already fired them. I asked if he had any ideas on how to prevent this from happening again, and he agreed finding sober band members is a priority. Not just for you, but for me too. Especially with everything going on with Bud, you know?" She bites her trembling lip and sniffles quietly. "Hawthorne joked it would wind up helping his bank account in the long run, too, and I guess that's that."

"You stood up for me," I mutter.

"You're not in this alone, Fen. I'm here for you. And so is Hawthorne. Now, if you could stop pushing us away, that'd be great," she adds, her mouth curved up in amusement.

A breath of laughter escapes me as I lean into her palm, soaking up her warmth for another second. Maybe she's right. Maybe I should stop being a bastard who pushes away the people who care about him and should start embracing them. Because if today proved anything, it proved I can't do this alone. And I need to stop trying. Determination floods my system as I type my response to Hawthorne.

Me: Thx

I set my phone on the white-stained coffee table in the center of Hadley's family room and pull her close to me again. This time, I press my head against the swell of her breasts. Not because I want to have sex or anything, but because I need to feel close to her. To not feel alone. Her heartbeat is soft, but I can still hear it. The sound is my very own lullaby, and soon, my eyelids grow heavy.

"Come with me to bed," she suggests a few minutes later.

The worry must be clear in my gaze as she brushes her soft fingers against my jaw and shakes her head. "Not like that, Fen. Not if you're not ready. Just snuggles and maybe a kiss or two. You look about as exhausted as I feel. Let's get some rest."

It actually sounds pretty fantastic.

Except I want something more. I want her. Maybe not fully. I don't think I can handle it. But...something. I need her now more than ever.

She shifts to get off my lap, but I grab her upper thighs and keep her in place.

"What is it?" she asks.

"I want to be close to you."

Her smile softens. "You are close to me."

"I need more."

Her brows pinch for a split second when understanding blankets her features. She pushes my shirt up a few inches and drags her fingers along my abs, circling my belly button.

"You tell me to stop, and I stop."

"That's the problem, though," I groan and watch her delicate little hands rub against the skin above the hem of my jeans. "I don't think I have the self-discipline to stop."

"Pretty sure you've proved tonight you have more self-discipline than you give yourself credit for, but..." She leans closer and peppers kisses along my jaw.

"When I'm with you, it's debatable," I admit, hardening beneath her.

She grins against my chin. "Let me ask you something. Your reservations with intimacy aren't necessarily based on what base you get to. Am I right?"

I chuckle, caught between amusement over her curious exploration of my body, and my fear of relapsing after she's finished. But I asked for this, and I want it. I want it more than ever. "Something like that."

"Have you had sex since you stopped using?"

"You sure you wanna talk about our previous partners when you're sucking on my neck like that?"

I can feel her smile against my heated skin again. She bites and moves to the other side. "Just trying to understand your boundaries."

"All right. I had a girl go down on me before the craving got to be too much, so I left."

"Have you masturbated since?"

"Hads––"

"Hey, it's an innocent question," she teases, licking along my jawline then nibbling on my ear. My blood rushes to my groin, and it takes everything inside of me to keep from thrusting against her hand.

"No."

"Have you even orgasmed since you stopped using?"

"I did the other night. When you were drugged," I clarify.

Her jaw drops, and she peeks up at me. "You did?"

"Came like a twelve-year-old kid as I listened to you get off."

She laughs, the sound shooting straight to my chest and making me feel lighter than I could've ever imagined. Especially after a night like tonight.

"Best compliment I've ever had," she tells me, climbing off my lap and offering her hand. When I take it, she says, "But I think we should make it a little more fun this time, don't you?"

"What do you have in mind?"

Her straight white teeth dig into her lower lip. "Do you trust me?"

With a knot lodged in my throat, I dip my chin. "More than I'd like to admit."

"Good." She drags me down the hall and toward her bed. "I've decided there's one of two things you crave when on something. It's either A, the lack of control is what appeals to you because you don't have to overthink or over analyze the repercussions. You're able to simply feel. Or B, the drugs are appealing because they give you a safe space and an excuse to take control of what you want without overthinking or over-analyzing the repercussions. The question is, which does it do for you? The night I was drugged, I felt like I could take what I wanted, and it was quite appealing. I had courage, and while I won't be going down that road again as far as the actual drugs are concerned, I can see the appeal of having that power, that control, and I'm going to work on utilizing it when I'm *not* on something."

"Is that why you're being bossy right now?" I joke. But I'm not gonna lie. It's hot as hell.

Her mouth quirks up on one side, and she pushes against my chest hard enough for my ass to land on the bed behind me. "Maybe. What I want to know is the *why* behind your craving."

"I'm not sure," I admit. "I guess I haven't really thought about it."

"All right. Let's play a little game and see if we can come to any conclusions."

"What kind of game?" I ask.

"Lie back and put your hands behind your head. If you move them, I stop. We clear?"

"Hads…"

The warning in my voice makes her pause before she climbs next to me on the mattress and cups my cheek. "Let me preface all of this by saying if you're not ready, it's okay. But also, we aren't going to have sex tonight, and I think you could use the distraction."

"We aren't?" My throbbing erection says otherwise, but my head? It's fighting its own battle, and I think she can see it in my eyes.

With a soft smile, she leans down and presses a sweet, almost innocent kiss against my lips. But when I run my tongue along her bottom lip, she pulls away, running her fingers along the slight scruff of my jaw.

"I don't want to push you into anything you aren't ready for. But I do want to see you happy and to see you not so terrified of the things you can't control. A relationship is about push and pull. Give and take. I think you were so used to people taking things from you, you started to feel like the only time you could take anything for yourself was when you were on something. I want to give to you. Without any expectations on your end. I want you to sit back and enjoy. But if it feels like too much, and I've pegged the situation wrong, all you have to do is say stop, and I'll stop. No questions asked. Understand?"

There isn't pity in her gaze. No reservations. Simply…a desire to understand. To help. To accept. And it's the latter that pushes me forward. Lifting myself onto my elbows, I kiss her again, dragging my tongue across her bottom lip like I did a minute ago and sucking it into my mouth. She moans softly, her hand warm against my chest as she balances herself beside me.

When she pulls away a few seconds later, her eyes are glazed with lust but also hesitation. Like she knows this is pushing me, and she can't decide whether or not she should keep doing it.

"I trust you," I repeat.

She leans in again, her lips brushing against mine as if she's reluctant to end our kiss the same way I am. Because I feel safe when I'm lost in her lips. When I'm lost in her gaze. I don't feel so broken.

Moving up to the shell of my ear, she whispers, "I've got you, Fen."

Then, her lips trail down my neck, my scruff scratching her sensitive lips as she travels lower, lifting the hem of my shirt to drop kisses along my abs and lower stomach until she reaches my jeans. My muscles tighten with anticipation as the top button slips open and the zipper slides down a few inches.

"Lift your hips, baby," she urges.

I do as I'm told, and she shimmies them down to my knees, running her nose along the outline of my swollen cock through the black cotton of my boxers.

My shaft jumps in excitement, and she smiles, peeking up at me. As our gazes connect, she slips the head free from the waistband and drags her tongue along it, like it's a fucking ice cream cone. Fisting my hands into the cotton sheets, I watch her mouth wrap around me and take me deeper.

Hot. Slick. Heat.

"Shit, Hads," I groan, the feel of her mouth causing a pool of heat to spread through me. My eyes want to roll back in my head, but I force them to stay open, unable to miss the view of Hadley's mouth on me.

She continues her assault and picks up her pace, listening

to my breathing and soft groans as she sets the perfect rhythm to torture me.

And holy shit, it feels good. I want to tangle my fingers in her hair. To pull her closer. To come down her pretty little throat. But I restrain myself, letting her take the lead the way she was clearly made to.

With a soft pop, she licks me from base to tip a few minutes later while her hands massage the bottom of my shaft while giving her jaw a break.

"Say my name, Fen," she whispers. "Be here with me. Don't get lost in your own head. This isn't about getting off. It's about us connecting. We clear?"

Yeah, we're clear. Because I've never been so in the present in my entire life. So much so, I don't want to finish down her pretty little throat. Not anymore. Because when I do, it'll end. This moment. This feeling. And I'd give anything to have it last forever. Only me and her. In her bed. And hell, maybe Pix sleeping on the floor if I'm being picky, but that's it. And now that've we crossed the bridge from friendship to more, I don't ever want to look back.

Unable to help myself, I hook my hands beneath her armpits and hitch her up my body, desperate for her lips. Her soft skin and sexy curves are a stark contrast to the clothes covering her as I slam my mouth against hers and take what she's giving me.

"You're cheating," she teases in between kisses, letting me dive into her mouth like I was made to be there.

Rolling her onto her back, I cage her in on both sides with my arms and say, "No. I'm being present. I'm being *here*. With you. Just like you asked. There's a difference."

And there is. I've never felt this way about someone. It's always, how can I get my partner to orgasm as quickly as possible so I can follow? Even with Trish, we both knew what we were there for, and it wasn't to connect emotionally.

Honestly, I didn't even think it was possible for Trish to connect with someone after the shit she'd been through, and I was okay with it. Because I was broken too. But right now? I want to savor Hadley. I want to get lost in her. Her curves. Her eyes. The soft lilt in her voice as she gets closer and closer to coming.

I heard it last night, albeit softly, and I want to hear it again. Only this time, I want to be the one who pushes her over the edge.

"Lay back," I order.

"Fen--"

"Trust me."

She does as she's told, and I get her naked as fast as possible, diving into her most sensitive area until she's dripping on my tongue. Satisfied she'll finish quickly, I flip us over again and smack her ass.

"Put this ass in my face."

With a light laugh, she spins around as I lay onto my back with my head propped on her pillow. She straddles my face while putting my shaft an inch from her mouth.

"Sixty-nine-ing it, huh? That's the way you want to go?"

"There a problem with it?" I challenge, nipping at her inner thigh.

"I mean, my focus might not be on point with you--" Her words turn into a garbled mess as I grab her hips, tug her toward my mouth, lick her clit, then push my tongue into her sweet pussy.

"Shhhit," she moans.

I lift her up for a brief second and ask, "I need you to fall over the edge with me, Hads. Think you can do that for me?"

She nods and leans down to suck on my dick, her mouth as greedy as her pussy as she pushes her hips into me while massaging my balls with her hands.

The combination is an explosion of...everything. My skin

feels hot and tight. Her short, stilted breaths mingle with the echo of my own heartbeat in my ears. Her taste on my tongue and the feel of my cock pumping in and out of her mouth is the hottest thing I've ever experienced. Every nerve in my body is on full alert as we each race toward our completion.

And I lose it, my cum hitting the back of her throat as she continues sucking and moaning around me. She's right. Attempting to multitask isn't my strong suit, but she must not mind because Hadley screams my name a few seconds later. Her body pulses around my fingers as I suck her clit into my mouth while wave after wave of euphoria hits her.

Once she's finished, she collapses onto me, her muscles like Jell-O, so I roll her onto her side and flip around to match her angle. The pillows are still at the top of the bed, our feet resting on them as she slowly comes back down to earth.

"Ho. Ly. Shit." Her light laugh makes my chest tighten. I lift my arm, and she nuzzles into me. "That was…" She pauses and shakes her head, then rests her chin on my pec and looks up at me. "How are you?"

"I'm on the fucking moon."

With a soft smile, she prods, "I mean…how are you overall? Still okay?"

I press a slow kiss to her forehead and close my eyes, savoring the new high I experienced today. "Yeah, Hads. I'm more than okay. Thank you."

She cocks her head to one side. "For what?"

"For pushing me without…pushing me," I finish.

The same sweet smile greets me before she kisses my pec and settles against me. "Anytime."

"So what now?"

"Now?" She leans up and kisses me softly. "We sleep. Goodnight, Fen."

A quietness settles inside of me as I look down at her, surprised by the peace I feel when it was only noise and chaos earlier tonight. Yet here I am, in Hadley's bed, after being intimate.

My arm tightens around her. I lay my head down, not giving a shit our feet are where our heads should be, and close my tired eyes.

"Goodnight, Hads."

25

FENDER

My hands shake as I open the Broken Vows group text thread I'd been blocking since getting out of rehab. After tweaking the settings to allow messages to come through again, I type a quick note to the band.

Me: Hey. I heard you guys are back in town.

I hit send and tuck my phone in my pocket as Pixie sniffs a fire hydrant next to the sidewalk. With a gentle tug on the black leash, she goes back to walking, matching my pace while the knot in my stomach tightens.

My phone buzzes a few seconds later, and I pull it back out. I'm nervous. Why the hell am I nervous? I shouldn't be. It's Phoenix. And Stokes. Dove was added shortly after she sang with Sonny while I was on a bender, and of course, there's Sonny on the thread too. But I know these guys. They know me. All of me. The good. The bad. And the ugly. So much freaking *ugly*.

I suck my cheeks between my teeth and read the message.

Phoenix: Hey, man. Yeah, we flew in a few days ago. How you been? We've been trying to reach you.

Me: I know. Sorry I've been MIA. Would you guys want to meet up for lunch or something?

Stokes: I'm in. What time?

Phoenix: Me too. I'm good for whenever.

I wait a minute, giving Sonny a chance to respond to my text, but the conversation stays quiet.

We haven't spoken since my blowup. I think he and Dove found a place, and he's been keeping his distance from Milo, Maddie's, Jake's, and my house ever since. Not that I blame him. I was an ass.

When another text still refuses to come through, I slip the loop of Pixie's leash around my wrist and use both hands to type my response.

Me: Let's do one o'clock today. Sound good to everyone?

Dove: Is this a guys-only get-together? Or...? I'm good either way. Whatever you want, Fen. :)

My chest tightens as I read Dove's kind message. She's the sweetest girl. Kind. Patient. A little quiet, but so damn thoughtful. I don't blame Sonny for falling for her. But I do feel even more like shit for holding any animosity toward someone who wouldn't hurt a fly. I glance over at Pix, who's sniffing a small patch of weeds near the sidewalk, puff out my cheeks, and text back.

Me: You're part of the band, Dove. Of course, you're invited. Should we meet at the house?

Phoenix: Sure thing. We'll meet you there.

Stokes: I'll grab some pizza.

Dove: See you soon. :)

I don't miss the lack of response from Sonny, but I refuse to overthink it as I shove my phone back into my pocket and walk toward Hadley's place, where my car is still parked. It's time I face the music. And my brother. Even if it kills me.

"Oh. Hey, Fen!" Dove greets me in the kitchen at the house. Pixie pads toward her, sniffs Dove's black leggings, and deems her safe. Then, she runs up the stairs to visit Penny, Maddie and Milo's daughter. They've gotten close over the past few weeks, and I wouldn't be surprised if I come home to a new puppy one of these days they can call their own. I shake my head as I watch Pixie's massive butt wiggle back and forth as she makes her way to Penny's room. I can almost see her squeezing through the cracked door as I wipe my sweaty palms against my jeans and turn back to Dove.

"Hey, Dove." I head closer and pull her into a hug. The blonde pixie feels like a twig in my arms as she stands on her tiptoes and squeezes me tightly.

"I missed you," she murmurs. I can hear the sincerity in her voice. Hell, I can feel it in her embrace, and I'm surprised by how much I've missed her. The little sister I never had.

I close my eyes and squeeze her harder as the realization washes over me. "Missed you, too, Dovey."

"Thanks for texting today."

"Thanks for being patient while I got the balls to text," I return.

With a sweet smile and a soft laugh, she pats my chest and steps away from me. "I get it. I mean, I don't *get it* get it, but I get it."

"I get it," I reply.

She laughs again and rolls her eyes. "Good. I want you to know Gibson gets it too."

My smile falls as I squeeze the back of my neck and blow out a deep breath. "I shouldn't have said the things I did the other night."

"He may have mentioned a thing or two."

"Is he going to be at lunch?" I ask.

With a one-shouldered shrug, she says, "You should ask him yourself. He's upstairs."

"I thought you guys found a place?"

"We're still looking. We've been staying at Sammie's for now, so you could have some space."

"You guys didn't have to do that."

"We know." The same sweet smile greets me, and she lifts her chin toward the stairs. "He's in his old room. You should go say hi."

I force myself to nod, turn on my heel before I can talk myself out of it, and call over my shoulder, "I'll be down in a few."

"Take your time," she replies, watching me go.

Every step feels daunting as I head toward the second floor. My hand is raised and ready to knock on Sonny's door when the familiar strumming of a guitar seeps through the crack.

I pause and rest my forehead against the doorjamb,

listening to the song Gibson's working on as guilt eats away at my lower gut. I don't know what to say to him. I don't know how to make things better. And I don't know how to apologize while still expressing myself.

I learned in rehab bottling shit up isn't healthy and can lead to relapses. But airing out past mistakes and regrets didn't exactly feel helpful, either. Not when my brother won't talk to me anymore because of it. Yeah, I probably should've had more tact when I told him how I felt, but I was like a volcano. I just erupted, and there's no taking it back.

The wood casing digs into my forehead as I continue resting against it and close my eyes, listening to Sonny pluck at his guitar.

After a few minutes, Sonny calls, "I know you're there, Fen. Get your ass in here."

I roll my eyes but push open the door. Might as well get this over with.

On the floor with a guitar cradled to his chest sits Sonny. He lifts his chin toward the guitar stand next to his door where another red-lacquered acoustic guitar is resting and orders, "Help me out with this, would you?"

My hand flexes at my side as I grab the neck of the guitar and sit down beside him. But I don't say a word. I feel like my vocal cords are paralyzed. Like I couldn't use them if I tried. There's too much left unsaid, and most of it's on me.

He plays a string of chords, his brows furrowing. He shakes his head, oblivious to my inner turmoil. Or he's ignoring it. Regardless, a few seconds later, he looks up at me like everything's good between us and says, "This part. It doesn't sound right to me. What do you think?"

I replay the same string of chords, my face scrunching with concentration as I focus on something other than the mess I've made. "You're right. Something's off. Maybe try this." I pluck out a few more notes, changing the melody from C to C minor, then add a second variation which builds as the song goes on.

Sonny nods his approval and picks up where I left off. We continue going back and forth until another song is in the books. One sure to be a hit. Sonny stops strumming and looks at me. Really looks at me. Without malice or frustration. Simply an open sincerity I've been craving for months.

"You were right, Fen," he admits.

I glance at him as my lips press into a thin line.

"You were right. I didn't know I needed the spotlight until I met Dove. I didn't know I wanted to be up on a stage until I had a taste of it. When we first created Broken Vows, we agreed I would stay behind the scenes. It's what I thought I wanted. And then, when everything went down, I realized I wanted more from my career. I realized how much being onstage meant to me. But I want you to know I never wanted to take your place. I never looked at you like you were competition. I *still* don't look at you like you're competition," he clarifies. "You're my brother. We started this together, and I wanted to finish it together. But after talking with Dove, I guess I also understand why you might want to start fresh again. Why you might *need* a fresh start. Why you might feel like you aren't welcome, even though you are. The rest of the band and I would kill to have you back again. You were the face of Broken Vows, Fen."

I open my mouth to argue, but he cuts me off.

"Let me finish."

My mouth snaps shut, and I nod at him, urging him to continue.

"I'm sorry Dove and I may have inadvertently changed the face of Broken Vows while you were away. It doesn't mean the fans don't want you anymore, though. And it doesn't mean we can't change it again to fit all three of us. We're a team, Fen. We'll always be a team."

We're a team.

The words echo in my mind and combined with his apology and everything else he said, it makes me feel lighter somehow. Like we're going to be okay. No matter what I decide to do with my career. I'm not a burden or his little brother he feels obligated to look after. We're equals. Both in and out of the music industry. I didn't know how much I needed to hear it until now.

Mindlessly, I play another few chords on the guitar in my lap as I try to figure out what the hell I want out of life and my future with Broken Vows. I set the guitar aside on the carpet and release a slow breath.

"I appreciate that, Sonny. You have no idea how much. But I think you're right. When I was in rehab, I had a lot of time to analyze my surroundings and why I kept slipping." I glance up at him and swallow thickly as the memories from all the times I'd screwed up hit like a wrecking ball while knowing they're never going away. I can't erase them. They'll probably haunt me for the rest of my life, and there's nothing I can do about it except embrace my past mistakes and try to never make them again.

"I think I was using you as a crutch, Sonny," I admit. "I knew you'd always be there to pick me up again. I knew the band was always there to cover for me when I'd screw up. I think it was enabling me to continue spiraling. And while I appreciate your support and the way you guys are willing to let me back in with open arms, after taking a step back, I've realized I think I *do* need a fresh start. Even though it's been hard, I need to do this on my own. But I want you to know you're still my closest family. You're still my big brother. I gotta do this on my own."

He scans my face carefully, absorbing my expression the same way he's absorbed my words. Then he nods and slaps my back in a way that would be an asshole move if it weren't from my brother. "The door's always open with Broken Vows. The rest of the band agrees. But I get why you'd want to go on your own."

"Thanks, Son. You don't know how much it means to me."

"I'm here for you," he adds.

"I'm here for you too."

"And congrats on the charity concert," he continues. "You should've heard how jealous Stoker was when we found out."

I throw my head back and laugh. "Yeah. Sorry about that."

"Don't be. You deserve it. But don't be surprised if I call you every once in a while to see if you wanna do a crossover song or two."

The idea makes me grin. "Sounds good, man. I'm in."

"Good. So, where's your phone?"

I grimace and shift on my ass to pull it out. "Why?"

"You should call Dad." He motions to my cell.

"What?"

"Call Dad," he repeats.

"Right now?"

"The guys downstairs can wait for a few more minutes. He misses you."

With a quick look toward the half-open door, I let out another sigh and flip my phone into the air, but I don't unlock it as another wave of guilt washes through me. "Listen, about you and Dad reconnecting. I'm sorry about what I said the other night. I was wrong. And I think it's good. You and Dad. I shouldn't have been jealous."

"We wouldn't have reconnected if it weren't for you," he reminds me. "But you were right. Dad's changed. He's not the asshole I'd pegged him for, and I never would've given him another chance if you hadn't convinced me to. As for the jealousy bullshit? You gotta let it go. Dad misses you. He's been giving you space because he knows it's what you need, but I can't replace you, Fen. Not in Broken Vows, and not in

Dad's life, either. Call him." He pushes to his feet and heads toward the door. "And when you're finished, come downstairs and grab some pizza. The guys and Dove miss you too." He closes the door behind him, blanketing the room in silence. I unlock my phone and settle back against the side of Gibson's bed.

He's right. I need to stop ignoring all of my past relationships out of fear of rejection or disappointing them again. They're my family, blood or not.

Apparently, it's time to make a call.

HADLEY

The next few weeks go by in a blur. I've been preparing for Fender's concert, which includes clothes shopping and a salon appointment, but I haven't heard a word from the police as to whether or not they have any new information on Bud. It's disappointing, but I'm trying to stay distracted, and getting ready for my little trip with Fender has been an excellent one.

Things have been great between Fen and me. He even managed to smooth things over between him, Sonny, and his bandmates. And I've never seen him happier. We still haven't had sex. I think he's terrified to take the step, even though we've done everything else under the sun. But it's been good. We've still been intimate––both sexually and emotionally–– and I couldn't ask for anything more.

We spend our days at his place, thanks to Pixie and my insane landlord, but it's been nice. His roommates are great. Both Dove and Maddie are awesome, along with Jake's girl-friend, Evie. And even Mia's been hanging in there. She's hurting and anxious about the lack of information where her father's concerned, but Isabella found her a therapist, and she's been getting the help she needs. Well, that, and she's been taking extra runs with Pix after school ever since Isabella gave back her car keys.

Now, if only I could get these stupid nerves to stop assaulting my stomach as I curl my hair in the hotel room, that would be great. We flew out yesterday and spent the night in LA, getting ready for the charity concert.

Tonight's the night, and I'm kind of freaking out, though I have no idea why. It's not like I'm the one who has to be on stage or anything. Maybe it's because Maddie and Milo are watching Pixie at home, so Fender won't have his cheerleader on stage with him tonight. Or maybe it's the fact I know I'm going to be exposed to an entirely different side of Fender's life this evening. One I'm not quite sure I fit into. And I'm scared it'll rock the boat. Thankfully, Dove and Gibson will be with me to cheer him on, and I'm grateful for them. A familiar face or two is exactly what I need.

"You ready?" Fen calls through the closed door.

"Working on it."

The door opens a few inches, and I catch Fen smiling at me through the mirror.

"Damn, Hads. You look…" He steps inside and grabs my hips, pinning my back to his front as he checks out my reflection.

"Yes?" I prod.

With a soft, warm kiss to the side of my neck, he finishes, "Edible."

I laugh and put the straightener down, twisting in his arms. "You don't look so bad yourself." His soft gray T-shirt hugs his biceps and leaves his arms bare, showcasing Milo's fancy tattoo work, but he looks…edible. Fen was right. It's the perfect word choice.

I bite my lip then press a quick kiss to his mouth.

"You nervous?" I ask.

"Just trying to keep the right perspective."

"Any cravings?"

He's opened up to me over the past few weeks, giving me insight as to what his triggers are and when he would succumb to his addiction on tour. He's even given me warning signs to watch out for. Not that he needs a babysitter, but he recognizes his own weaknesses and knows I can be strong for him when he can't.

The responsibility is staggering, though. But so is his trust. And I won't ever break it. Even if it *is* a little intimidating. After all, Bud's my brother. I knew him before he fell down the rabbit hole of drugs and addiction. I knew him after. I saw how much it took its toll, whether he was on or off the wagon. It was a rollercoaster, and I'm not going to lie to myself and say I'm not terrified falling for Fender will lead me down the same path of heartbreak and disappointment.

One mistake. One slip up, and I'm gone. I'm not sure I can handle anything else. But it's a promise I've made to myself, one I've refused to admit to Fender. Not because I'm trying to keep it from him, but because I know he doesn't need the added pressure. I know he already puts too much of it on himself. And I know it'll only hurt him in the end if he realizes my feelings for him might be unconditional, but my self-preservation isn't.

I don't say any of it, though, as I turn around and continue doing my hair while carefully assessing his reflection in the mirror. He looks relatively calm. Not too jittery. Seems focused. Nervous but happy. He's okay.

"I haven't been craving anything but you," he quips, kissing my temple. "I'll let you finish getting ready. We should head over to the arena in twenty. Will you be ready by then?"

"Yup. Wouldn't miss it for the world."

THE DRIVE TAKES ABOUT FIFTEEN MINUTES. THE DRIVER Hawthorne sent to pick us up at our hotel is kind and tells us horror stories about driving in the middle of LA for the rich and famous before pulling up to the back of a massive outdoor arena.

There are cars already filling the lot, even though the concert isn't supposed to start for another few hours. My nerves shoot through the roof as I take in a few teenage girls carrying signs with Fender's name on them.

"You didn't tell me there were going to be this many people," I note as I smooth out my red crop top and dark jeans.

"I didn't know," he admits while eyeing the entrance already lined with fans waiting to get into the show and grab their seats. Thankfully, we're parked in front of a back entrance, but if they simply turn their heads and look our way, I'm pretty sure chaos would ensue.

I grab his hand and squeeze softly to distract him from the sea of people. "It's going to be awesome, Fen."

"We'll see," he mutters under his breath. "Let's get going, I guess." He climbs out of the backseat and offers his hand to help me up. Once I'm standing, he takes the guitar case from the trunk, and we walk inside, trying to be discreet so no paparazzi can catch us and start snapping pictures.

Which is weird. We're a couple of nobodies. Scratch that. I'm a nobody. Fender is obviously a *somebody*, which is made even clearer when a reporter spots us and calls, "Fender! Fender Hayes! Do you mind if I ask you a few questions?"

He tilts his head down and keeps walking, but I dig in my heels, making him slow a bit as I whisper in his ear. "You sure Hawthorne wouldn't want you to say anything?"

His nostrils flare, but he turns to the reporter and says, "Hey. What can I do for you?"

"I want to know where you've been and if you were planning on breaking up with Broken Vows from the beginning or if it was a recent development?"

With a death grip on my hand, Fender gives the reporter a tight smile, his gaze flicking from the crowd who, by some miracle, hasn't seen us yet and the guy in front of us. "Broken Vows is an incredible band full of great guys and an awesome girl," he clarifies, his smile turning genuine for a brief moment. "While we have split, I'm looking forward to continuing my relationship with them. In fact, we plan to collaborate on a few songs this upcoming year. Thanks so much--"

"Will you plan on taking your shirt off during the concert, Fender? I know it was your signature move."

He chuckles and lifts our laced hands, placing a kiss against the back of mine. "Not sure my girlfriend would like it, but I appreciate the interest. Have a good one."

He tugs me toward the back entrance, obviously finished with the short interview when a massive man with dark sunglasses and a permanently etched frown on his bulldog features stops us with crossed arms.

"Passes?" he barks.

Fender lifts the laminated pass hanging from a lanyard around his neck.

The security guard nods and turns to me. "Pass?"

My smile is tight as I do the same, lifting the pass for the guy to inspect.

Satisfied, he nods again and steps aside, allowing us entry while the reporter keeps peppering questions our way.

As we step inside and out of earshot, I look up at Fender with wide eyes. "Whoa."

His palm is warm as he presses it against my back and

leads me down a short hallway beneath the stage. "Yeah, I'm gonna kill Hawthorne."

"Why? You did good!"

"He should've at least given me a heads-up."

"Well, here's your chance to tell him. He's walking this way." My attention shifts to the tall, handsome guy wrapped in a fitted suit with Sammie on his arm who's talking to someone in a black T-shirt with a headset.

When he catches me looking at him, Hawthorne closes the last bit of distance between us and offers his hand for Fender to shake. "Hey, glad you guys made it here okay."

"Thanks for sending the driver to pick us up. It was thoughtful."

He chuckles, takes my hand, gives it a firm shake, and wraps his arm back around Sammie.

"Although you could've warned us about the size of this *little* charity event," Fender interrupts, but Hawthorne only laughs harder.

"If I had, would you have still come?"

"This isn't some small show――"

"I may have failed to mention the size of the stadium, and that's on me, but I didn't want you to back out because of nerves. That being said, there are plenty of other artists who would kill to be in your shoes tonight, and I don't think you should take it for granted. This is a good opportunity, Fender. Breathe."

Fender lets out a slow breath and shoves his hand through his wavy hair, pushing it away from his face while causing his bicep to bunch and flex. Damn, the man's good-looking, even when he's freaking out inside.

"Will there be any more reporters or anything?" he asks. "I feel like I was blindsided out there."

"They spoke to you?" Hawthorne returns.

Fender nods. "Asked where I went and if I was on bad

terms with Broken Vows. I said we were fine and plan on collaborating in the future."

"Good. Sounds like you handled it perfectly. Sorry I wasn't out there to help deter them from pouncing on you like a pack of wolves. I'd assumed keeping them from the back entrance would've been enough."

"Apparently, a few knew how to sneak through. And it's fine. I know you don't want me to lose my shit, but keeping me in the dark will do more harm than good."

"And from now on, I'll keep that in mind. I apologize."

Again, Fender nods, accepting Hawthorne's apology. Hawthorne guides us into the main area and introduces us to so many people it makes my head spin.

Seriously. This is crazy. There's a buzzing throughout backstage as people set up different instruments and test the lighting and sound system. It's insane. And so freaking cool, my fingers are itching to write all about it. If only I'd brought my computer.

A little while later, the crowd begins filtering into the stadium, and Fender gets ready to head onstage while I drink champagne from a flute surrounded by Dove and Sammie.

And the crazy part? I'm actually enjoying myself. When I said I was dating Fender as a distraction from my everyday life, I had no idea just how well it would suit me. But his friends? His family? They've welcomed me with open arms. I wouldn't change any of it for the world.

If only I'd known how quickly it would come crashing down.

27
FENDER

My hands are sweaty. I wipe them on my dark pants and grip my guitar. Hawthorne asked if I wanted to meet a few more potential band members before tonight's show since our first try had ended so poorly, but it felt wrong performing with strangers instead of my surrogate family. So, I asked them if they'd be willing to play with me for old time's sake during lunch when we'd all gotten together. Dove and Gibson loved the idea of me stealing Stoker and Phoenix for the night, but being up here without Dove and Sonny somehow feels wrong too. Like I'm stepping back in time instead of moving forward.

Stoker, the bassist, slaps me on the back as we wait to go on stage and asks, "Dude. You ready?"

"Not in the slightest," I admit, though a laugh catches in my throat. The old me would've said *fuck yeah*, popped a pill, and headed onstage with my guitar raised above my head and my shirt tucked into the back pocket of my jeans. But the new me? He's more honest. Which is terrifying as shit.

Stoker laughs too. "Same. This never gets old. Thanks for

having us play with you tonight, though. We've missed you, man."

Phoenix, the burly drummer who looks like a giant leprechaun, tosses his arm around my neck and pulls me into a hug, slapping my back roughly. "Yeah we have. You ready to debut your new song? That thing's the shit."

The oxygen burns my lungs as I breathe in deep and force myself to nod. "Yeah. Yeah, I think I'm ready."

"All right. Let's show 'em what you got."

The lights dim a few seconds later, and we all race onto the stage, settling into position as the lights flicker back on.

With sweaty palms, I play the intro to a new song. It still has a few kinks needing to be worked out, but it felt wrong playing anything else. And when I played it for the band at the house a few weeks ago, they agreed this was the one.

As my fingers pluck at the strings for a few more measures, Phoenix comes in with a slow pulsing beat, followed by Stoker on the bass. I search for Hadley in the crowd of people lining the side of the stage behind the curtains and find her surrounded by Gibson, Dove, Sammie, and Hawthorne. Her smile is soft and sweet as sugar as she holds my gaze. She'd opted for contacts instead of her usual quirky black glasses tonight and looks sexy as hell.

My tongue darts out, and I moisten my lips and let the lyrics flow through me.

I thought I was broken.
Lost.
Tossed aside in the trash.
But you turned me around
And looked past my past.
There's a future with us.
One I can taste.
Especially when I look at your sweet face

You put me together
We're a puzzle
Meant to be
And I know you can help fix me
Just stay with me
Stay with me

I sing the chorus, lost in my words, the rhythm, the lights, and the crowd, every emotion rolling through me like a thunderstorm. It gains momentum with each passing note until the last one rings through the air.

And then… Applause.

It's a high I know I'll never be able to replicate. One I'll always crave but is only magnified when I find Hadley grinning back at me with glassy eyes and so much pride, I almost feel like I deserve it.

She isn't ashamed. Or embarrassed to be mine. She's proud. And I think I could love her for it.

We play a few more songs, some belonging to Broken Vows while others are my own, before the final note of our short playlist rings out through the crowd.

After another round of applause, the lights dim, and we head offstage while another band takes their turn setting up.

But as I search for Hadley in the sea of chaos, I realize she's missing.

"Where is she?" I ask Sonny.

He shrugs and answers, "She had to take a call. I think she's…" He points to the back area of the building, and I beeline it toward the exit.

I just want to hold my girl.

28

HADLEY

I t was the text message sent to my phone that got to me. I'd had almost a dozen calls, all of which I'd ignored, but the text? Yeah. There's no ignoring it.

806.555.3239: This is Detective Burke. Please call me at your earliest convenience. It's important.

I push call and press my phone to my ear, chewing on a hangnail as I step out of Fender's line of sight on stage and search for somewhere quieter.

"Ms. Rutherford?" Detective Burke answers a few rings later.

"Hi. Yes. Hi," I repeat, feeling like a frazzled mess. "It's me. Hadley. I got your text––"

"We need you to come down to the station."

I plug my other ear with my finger, convinced I've heard him wrong as I dodge a few more people and step further away from the stage. "What? Why?"

"It'd be better if we could have this discussion in person."

"I'm out of town for the weekend. I'm sorry. I can swing by tomorrow or Monday if I need to--"

"I'm afraid this can't wait." The somberness in his voice makes the hair on my arms stand up, leaving goosebumps along my flesh.

Something's wrong.

Something is very *wrong.*

"What is it?" I whisper though I'm afraid part of me already knows. A small part I've been avoiding--burying-- for weeks. But I can't avoid it any longer. I can't run or hide or distract myself from this conversation or what it means, even if it's more than I can bear.

Please tell me everything's going to be okay, I plead to whatever higher power might be listening. *Please. I'm begging you--*

"I'm sorry, Ms. Rutherford," Detective Burke starts. My heart cracks as I brace myself against the wall. "But we found a body."

I cover my mouth and take a slow, unsteady breath. "A body?"

"Miss Hill"--*Isabella*--"is on her way to identify the body, but we believe it's Bud's."

My legs finally give out, and I crumple into a ball on the cool concrete floor as the tears gather in my eyes, cascading down my face without any signs of stopping. How can they when my brother's gone?

This can't be happening.

It can't *be.*

"A-are you sure?" My voice cracks, and I wipe my cheeks with the back of my hand. Maybe he's wrong. Maybe it isn't Bud. Maybe it's someone else. Someone who doesn't have a sister, or a daughter, or a dog, or--

"We can't be sure until Miss Hill confirms it, but there's a tattoo on his forearm which Miss Hill had initially described when she first reported Mr. Rutherford as missing."

No.

My vision is blurry from the onslaught of tears, so I close my eyes, but it only makes things worse. Because I can see his tattoo. It's etched into my mind. The swirling ink scrawled across Bud's forearm. He'd stopped by our parents' house the day after he'd gotten it. When it was still wrapped in Saran Wrap and looked bold but tender. He was so proud. So excited. It was for Mia's fifth birthday. He'd cleaned himself up for the first time in years and wanted to prove he could be the dad she needed. So, he got a job, saved up his money, then had his daughter's name tattooed along his forearm.

I remember it like it was yesterday. And no matter how low he was, he'd still save up his money every year to touch up her name on her birthday as a reminder to be who she needed. And even though he didn't always live up to his own expectations, he still tried. He was *always* trying.

And now, he's gone.

My body wracks with a sob, but I swallow it back.

Maybe I'm wrong. Maybe Isabella told Detective Burke to look for the wrong tattoo. Maybe he's mistaken. Maybe… maybe it's not Bud. I shake my head, trying to focus on being realistic while battling the desire to live in a stupid alternate reality where everything's fine instead of the dark, heart-wrenching reality threatening to swallow me whole.

"What tattoo?" I choke out. I need to hear it from him. That it's a dog or a cross or a skull or something that isn't his daughter's name. Something proving the body isn't my brother's. I'll take anything. Any hope. Any miracle––

"I'm sorry, Miss Rutherford, but it's his daughter's name. Mia."

Another sob wracks my body, and black dots line my vision as the truth hits me harder and faster than a baseball bat to the chest until I'm positive my ribs are broken, and I'll never breathe freely again.

No. No, no, no, no!

"If you could please come to the station at your earliest convenience."

"I'll be there as soon as I can," I choke out and end the call with my thumb.

The phone slips from my fingers, clattering to the ground as I cover my face and cry.

This can't be happening.

This can't be happening.

"Hadley?" Fender's voice rings out through the otherwise quiet area, but I don't look up. I'm afraid I won't be able to see him through my tears anyway. His footsteps pound against the floor as he makes his way toward me and drops to the ground, pulling me into his chest without waiting for an explanation.

"Sh...," he croons as his hand rubs up and down my back. "Sh... It's okay."

I shake my head against his chest, my body practically convulsing as my pain cuts through me like a dull spoon, leaving me hollow. It doesn't sting. It aches. It aches so deep, I feel like I can't breathe. Like I'm drowning. Like my lungs are refusing to work, and no matter how hard I try to calm down, it isn't possible.

There's too much pain.

I'm not sure how many minutes go by, but Fender picks me up in his arms and finds a coat closet to hide us away.

"He can't be gone," I cry, twisting the fabric of his gray T-shirt between my clenched fists. "He can't be."

"What happened, Hads?" he murmurs.

"The detective. Detective Burke," I clarify, barely able to speak past the lump lodged in my throat. "H-he...th-they found a body. They found a body, and the body has Mia's name on his forearm. It's the same place B-Bud had tattooed when M-Mia was little." I can't stop stuttering. I can't stop sobbing. I can't stop whimpering or making pathetic little noises in the back of my throat making me feel like I'm choking on my own pain. It's like my body isn't my own. Like I have no control over anything. Not myself. Not my surroundings. And not the outcome of my brother, who I spent years cursing for his addiction, only to find out he isn't missing because of a bender. He's missing because he's... he's...

My knuckles turn white as I cling to Fender, burrowing even closer and shoving my face into his neck, praying it'll ground me. That I'll wake up from this mess. That everything will be all right. That I'm dreaming, and none of this is real.

But it *is* real.

I know it.

I can feel it.

And it hurts more than anything I could've ever imagined.

I don't know how long we stay trapped in the coat closet. It could be hours. Hell, it feels like a lifetime. But there's one constant throughout the hell of it all. And it's Fen. Rubbing my back. Whispering apologies and promises everything will be okay.

And even though I don't believe him, I pray he's right.

Because this?

This pain?

This loss?

It's torture.

I've never been the strong one. But as I watched the girl of my dreams crumble in my arms, I learned what it means to show strength, and I vowed to burn down the world if it would protect her from this kind of devastation from ever happening again.

The next few weeks go by in a never-ending blur of heartbreak and tears.

Being questioned by the police. Being desperate for answers without having many. Planning a funeral. Dreading a funeral. Attending a funeral.

She moved in with me. Not officially. But when she told me she only sleeps when she's in my arms, I vowed to never let her sleep alone again.

And I've kept my promise.

Honestly, most of the time, she's sandwiched between Pixie and me in my bed, and I wouldn't have it any other way. If only it were under different circumstances.

The police had arrested a man named Troy McAdams a while back for assaulting his ex-girlfriend, who happens to be Jake's current girlfriend, Evie. After a month of interrogation and a plea bargain, the bastard finally admitted to his involvement in Bud's disappearance and where the body was hidden. Though he's adamant he wasn't involved in Bud's death, he did help the killer get rid of the body, which is why he knew exactly where the police could find it. After a few days of searching a forest on the edge of town, they found him in a shallow grave. He'd been beaten to death.

Apparently, Bud had asked a loan shark for some money. Where the money went, we may never know. Hadley assumes it was to feed his drug addiction, which only hurt her more.

And as for the loan shark? Troy McAdams told the police it was my motherfucking brother, Marty. He'd gotten over his own head with a loan shark and decided to spend his last dollar trying his own hand in the business in hopes of accruing enough interest from a few sorry bastards it would be enough to help him dig himself out of his own hole.

It's also why I think he approached me, trying to access my contract with Hawthorne so we could save his sorry ass with the money from it. Not that it matters. No one has seen him since shortly after Hadley was drugged.

I guess he was too busy running from the cops and the loan sharks who were after him.

I knew he was bad news, but I had no idea just how far he'd spiraled. But killing someone with his own two hands? Knowing someone who shares your blood is capable of something so reprehensible? It's a sobering realization. One I still can't wrap my head around.

He killed a father, a brother, a friend.

And now? Everyone else is left to pick up the pieces.

Thankfully, the police arrested Marty shortly after the body was found. He'd been hiding out in some low life's house, and they dragged him to jail.

And since Milo knows a few shady guys connected to the mob thanks to owning a tattoo shop, he asked Sonny and me if we wanted him to call in a favor.

It's a favor I probably should've prevented from being called in, but I couldn't help it. Not when everyone finally opened up about everything Marty had done to them.

Marty introduced me to drugs and not only encouraged me to continue down that shitty path, but he messed with my dosage one night in hopes of getting under Sonny's skin. It led to my overdose. I could've died, and he didn't even care.

He blackmailed Maddie into sleeping with him before Maddie started dating Milo in hopes of pissing off Gibson, too. Not that it worked. Milo was the one who loved her, not Sonny. But still.

Then, he blackmailed Maddie––again––when he found out she had a daughter. It screwed up her relationship with Milo even more. Marty convinced Maddie to lie to our dad and tell Donny Hayes Penny belonged to him so he could have access to Dad's bank account and help support his new baby girl.

And let's not forget how Marty threatened to blackmail me if I didn't give him access to my music career and funds. He even paid someone to drug Hadley, hoping to prove his point. If that isn't messed up, I don't know what is.

But the worst part? He murdered Bud and blackmailed Evie's ex into helping him cover his tracks.

It's unforgivable.

He's ruined so many lives.

So. Many. Lives.

It was time for retribution.

When my dad visited him a few weeks later, Marty was black and blue after being jumped in the jail yard. He's still alive and won't be eating out of a feeding tube. See? Sonny and I still showed him mercy. But at least he got an ounce of what he deserved.

He's officially behind bars, and while part of me feels like I should feel something close to regret or sadness or who the hell knows, all I feel is relief. If only he'd been put away before this, Hadley might still have her brother, and I'd still have my friend.

"You doing okay?" I ask Hadley as I step into our bedroom and rub a towel over my damp hair. Pixie needed to go outside earlier, but when I woke up to find Hadley still sleeping, I'd stepped down the hall, let Pixie outside, and took a shower, hoping Hadley would have a few more minutes of restful sleep. She needs it. But the bags under her eyes are still present. Just as dark as yesterday. Just as haunted. And I hate it. I can't fix it. I can't take away her pain or her fears. She has to learn how to handle them on her own.

Helpless, I watch her pull her messy hair into a bun on top of her head and paste a fake smile on her hollow features.

"I'm fine," she lies. "Sorry I didn't come to the show last night."

"Don't apologize." I throw the damp towel in the hamper and tug on a dark T-shirt from my closet.

Hadley shrugs one shoulder as if to say she can't help it. Apologizing. To me. To Isabella. Mia. No one should have to feel so much remorse or sadness. It guts me.

The fabric of my shirt she threw on last night slips down to reveal her soft, smooth skin as she sits cross-legged on my bed, watching me.

I step closer to her and kiss her shoulder. "How are you really doing, Hads?"

"Sad," is all she offers. "Where's Pixie?"

"Downstairs chewing on a bone."

She nods, though it feels mechanical somehow. Like she isn't doing it because she understands or has even grasped the comment, but because she's supposed to. "Oh. Gotcha."

"You sure you're all right?" I ask.

"Nightmare."

My expression falls. "Hads…"

"Tell me something good, will you? Distract me? How was the show last night?"

I want to dig deeper. To shake her and beg her to tell me how I can make her feel better, but I bite my tongue and snake my arms around her shoulders, pulling her into my chest so I can breathe her in.

When her body melts into mine, I answer, "The show was good."

"Tell me more," she pleads, her smile pathetic at best as she urges me on.

"Hawthorne was able to help me find a couple cool guys for the band. Ones without any drug habits," I clarify.

"Yeah?"

I nod. "Yeah. They're really good."

A genuine smile stretches across her face. "That's great, Fen. Really. I'm happy for you."

"Thanks." I stand up and bring her with me, keeping my arms snaked around her waist until her bare feet are on the ground. Then, I sway us back and forth, and she sighs, nuzzling into me. Like I'm her lifeline. The same way she's mine.

"Did you hear back from your editor?" I ask.

Her laugh is pathetic at best. She leans her forehead against my shoulder and sighs. "Yeah. Apparently, a murdered brother is a pretty good excuse for missing a deadline."

Shit.

I cringe but squeeze her a little tighter. "I'm sorry, Hads."

"Don't be. It's the truth. But yeah. They told me to take as long as I need. The problem is, my savings is all dried up, and my lease is coming up, and after helping my parents with the funeral costs, I have no idea how to afford--"

"What if you move in with me? Permanently."

She wipes under her bloodshot eyes and pulls away from me. Not enough to get out of my grasp but leaving us enough room so she can look at me. Really look at me.

"Fen..."

"I'm serious, Hads. Move in with me. Officially," I clarify with a smirk. It's no secret we've practically been living together for weeks, anyway.

She licks her lips, her gaze dropping to the ground. "I didn't tell you about my money issues to make you feel guilty--"

"I don't feel guilty." I lift her chin and force her to look at me. "Despite the shitty circumstances, I like having you here. I *love* having you here. I like taking care of you. I like spending time with you. And yeah, Hawthorne's chomping at the bit to get me back on tour, but you should move in with me."

"Here?"

I nod and drop a kiss to her forehead. "Yeah, babe. I love you."

With a watery smile, she wipes beneath her eyes again, trying to clean herself up when she has no idea how perfect she looks right now. Real. Raw. And a little broken like me.

"How can you love me?" she says through the same watery smile. But I can see the joy in her eyes, the need to believe me as she adds, "I'm a mess."

"You're a beautiful mess, babe. And an amazing person. Besides, you have a good reason."

"I don't want to talk about it," she chokes out, shoving down the memory of her brother the same way she has since the day after his funeral. I don't blame her. It sucks. And mourning is exhausting. She needs a distraction.

I squeeze her against me again and kiss the crown of her head. "You're *my* beautiful mess, Hads."

"Gee," she laughs. "Thanks."

"I mean it. Come here. Let me kiss you again."

She lifts her lips to mine, and I lean closer, kissing her. Tasting her. Craving her now more than ever.

It's funny.

It never gets old with Hadley. Kissing her. Her little whimpers. The way her knees go weak, and she leans into me.

Cupping her cheek, I tilt her head back a little more and dip my tongue into her mouth. The same whimper I'd been searching for vibrates up her throat as her hands slip around my waist as if her knees might give out at any second. Just like I predicted.

My erection presses into the soft swell of her stomach, and she moans, making me twitch against her. Her hands are unsure as she glides them up my shirt, lifting the cotton material up until my head pops out the other side.

"I wanna feel close to you," she begs. "Please."

"I'm here, Hads." Our clothes are strewn across the floor in five seconds flat before my hands are on her again. I swear, her curves mold perfectly against me, and I cup her heavy breasts, teasing her nipples until they're hard peaks as I guide her toward the bed.

My skin feels hot, and sweat clings to the back of my neck as I pump my cock in my hand and look down at the most beautiful creature I've ever seen.

She squirms under my gaze and chews on her lower lip, a

light blush spreading across her cheeks. Like she's shy. Innocent. Freaking adorable. And so damn perfect it hurts.

"You should stop staring and come kiss me," she murmurs, her tongue gliding across her bottom lip.

"You should let me make love to you."

The lust in her eyes softens, replaced with genuine affection. It makes my chest feel tight as she peeks up at me again through her red-rimmed lashes. "You sure you're ready? I don't want to push you."

"You've pushed me in more ways than I could've ever imagined, Hads. But only for the better. *Always* for the better." I climb onto the bed, bracing myself on either side of her and kissing her button nose. The heat from our bare bodies pressing together is like an inferno. And I love it. The heat. The way she feels against me. The light, shallow breaths skimming across my bare skin as she waits for me to take this to the next level.

A bead of sweat drips down my neck as I slide my hand between us and find her center hot and ready. Gently, I push my finger inside her, teasing her clit then massaging the little bundle of nerves inside her wet pussy. I drop my forehead to her shoulder. Shit. She's so tight. So wet. So ready.

With a moan, she grinds herself against my hand, desperate for more friction. More pressure. And while I know I could get her there with my fingers or mouth, I want it to be my cock pushing her over the edge this time.

I need it.

Again, I devour her mouth, tasting her and committing this moment to memory because it's one I want to remember for the rest of my life, and I've never been more ready to claim her as my own.

When she's a squirming mess beneath me, I murmur, "Let me grab a condom," and shift toward the nightstand.

Her thighs clench down on me, keeping my hand caught

between them as her greedy fingers tangle into my short hair and pull me closer.

"I'm on the pill, Fen. And right now, I don't think I can handle anything being between us."

My forehead wrinkles as I look down at her beneath me. "You sure?"

She nods and kisses me again, the muscles in her thighs relaxing as she opens up to me. "Never been more sure of anything in my life."

I settle between them and line myself up with her entrance, waiting for my addiction to crash into me at any second.

But it doesn't.

I don't need a pill, or a drink, or a powder, or a vial of anything. I only need her. More than I've needed anything else in my entire life.

As if she can read my mind, Hadley cups my cheeks and forces me to look at her. "I'm right here, Fen. Just like all the other times. You say the word, and we stop. No questions asked. We'll cuddle and watch *Dumb and Dumber* or something, okay? I'm here. And I love you——"

Her words catch in her throat, turning into a soft whimper as I push myself inside of her.

Shit, she feels good. All warm and wet and tight around me. With my forehead pressed to hers, I catch my breath and try to maintain an ounce of control so I don't split the woman in half with my need.

"You good?" I grunt.

She nods, peeking up at me as she catches her breath. "You?"

"You feel fucking fantastic."

Her laugh eases the vice around my throat. "Ditto."

"How do you want this? Soft and slow? Hard and fast?"

"Oo, you take orders now?"

"You know me; I aim to please."

Another laugh. "That, I believe. You should kiss me again."

I flick my tongue along the seam of her lips and kiss her deeper. And a few seconds later, our hips shift on their own, finding their rhythm. We start slowly, letting our frenzy build the same way our relationship has since we first met.

By the end, the headboard bangs against the wall keeping time with our heavy breathing, but it only adds to the adrenaline throbbing in my veins.

We come together a little later, our muscles spent and our chests rising and falling as Hadley draws random circles along my bare back. She's still pinned beneath me, but I'm not sure I could move even if I wanted to.

"Thanks for fixing me, Hadley," I murmur against her, my voice breaking the peaceful, quiet blanketing the room.

I can almost hear the smile in her voice when she whispers, "Thanks for letting me break, Fen."

My brows furrow, and I push my top half off her so I can look down and read her expression. "What?"

"It's a good thing. I promise." She tugs me down again, but I stay in my half-push-up position.

"I don't want to smother you," I argue.

"I like feeling your weight on me," she counters and grasps at my shoulders another time. "It makes me feel safe."

I collapse onto her, giving in, and ask, "What did you mean a second ago? Thanks for letting you break?"

"I just… I know I still have a long way to go, but I want you to know, if you hadn't been through everything you had, I don't think I would've been able to let you in. To let you see the ugly pieces of me. I think if you were anyone else, I would've pushed you away when I found out about Bud. But because you're you, and I know everything you've been through, I knew you'd let me break. And you'd be patient enough to put in the work to help me heal. I don't think anyone else would be willing to do it. To be with someone so broken." She sniffles and presses her lips to my shoulder. "I love you, Fen. I love you so much. So thank you for being broken when we first met. And thank you for being strong enough to let me in so I could put you back together again. So you could put *me* back together again. You really are amazing."

"Does that mean you'll move in with me?"

She laughs, causing her bare breasts to brush against my chest as she slides her hands up and down my back. It feels amazing.

"I'm not going anywhere, Fen," she promises.

"Well, I hope you go somewhere," I mention.

With her hands pressed against my chest, I do another half push-up to find her brow arching back at me.

"Excuse me?"

I bite my lip to keep from grinning at her. "You should get dressed. We need to buy you a laptop."

Her breath of laughter tickles my neck, and she pushes against my chest. Again. I roll over, taking her with me until our positions are reversed, and she's lying on top of me. Her long, dark hair is pushed over one shoulder--it must've fallen out of her messy bun while we were making love-- and hangs in a wavy curtain as she cocks her head to the side. "What?"

"I think it's time we get back on tour."

"What? When? "

"Three days sound soon enough?"

"Fen--"

"Hawthorne told me last night. After the show," I clarify. "You're gonna need a laptop so you can write while you come with me."

"Come with you?"

"Yeah."

"I thought you said you wanted us to move in together?"

"This would be our home base. For now. Until we decide to get our own place."

She shakes her head, dizzy from all the information I'm tossing her way as she asks, "And people are okay with it? Me just...tagging along?"

"I'm the head of the band, Hads. It's my music. My lyrics. And Hawthorne knows you. He knows what you mean to me. So, yeah. They're good with you tagging along."

"But what about my editor, and––"

"I told you to get ready so we can buy you a laptop," I remind her, smacking her ass. "You think I'm gonna let you give up on your dream so you can let me chase mine?"

With her lips pulled between her teeth, she shakes her head back and forth again, arguing, "What about Pix?"

"Pixie will be on stage with me for every concert unless you get bored and decide you want to write on the bus instead. Then, she'll go with you."

I can practically see her mind spinning as she processes everything I just threw at her. But the more I brainstorm, the more right this feels. She needs a distraction. She needs a fresh start. She needs a reason to get up in the morning, and this could be the perfect opportunity.

Digging her teeth into her lower lip, she mutters, "You're crazy. You know that, right?"

"I'm crazy about you." I kiss her forehead again. "Even when you're broken."

Her smile softens.

"Promise me something, though," I plead.

"What?"

"Promise you'll let me fix you the same you fixed me. Not today or tomorrow." I tuck her hair behind her ear, and she leans into my touch, closing her eyes and letting out a slow, shuddered breath. "But one day," I finish.

Blinking back tears, she nods against my palm. "I think you're already halfway there, Fen."

And even though it kills me to see her hurting, witnessing her watery smile gives me a spark of hope.

It's a start.

30

HADLEY

With my phone pressed between my shoulder and ear, I tell Isabella, "I know it's short notice, but with everything else going on, I think it would be good for me to have some space, ya know?"

"Trust me. I get it," she returns. "If I could run away, you know I would."

"I'm not running––"

"I know you're not. And I'm sorry. I didn't mean it that way. I'm still trying to find a new normal for Mia. She's going to miss you."

"I'm going to miss her too," I admit as I open the duffle bag and start packing a few of my things. We leave for Denver tomorrow night, but I figure staying ahead of the game and getting a few things done now might be a good idea.

"You know she's welcome to fly out and visit for a show or two," I add.

"Depends on how she handles the next few weeks. Despite the asshole being arrested, Mia hasn't been sleeping. She's in my bed most nights crying herself to sleep."

"Maybe a change of scenery will be good for her too." I hear the front door close. "Hey, I have to go. I'll call you later, okay?"

"Sounds good. And, Hads?"

I pause and turn toward the open bedroom door, distracted. "Yeah?"

"I really am happy for you."

My posture softens, my arms itching to give Isabella a hug even when I know it isn't possible. But I'm grateful. For her. For our friendship. It means a lot to me. And if anyone deserves happiness after the hell we've all been through, it's her and Mia.

"Thanks, Bells. Talk soon."

She says goodbye, and I hang up the phone, tossing it onto Fender's bed. *My* bed. Another smile stretches across my face. I can't believe we're moving in together. It's crazy. And amazing. I can't believe I'm so lucky to call Fender mine. I wasn't kidding when I said I couldn't do this without him.

I was so scared when we first started dating. Terrified he'd be just like my brother, and he'd relapse, fall into the wrong crowd again, and make a mistake. One he might not be able to come back from, and I'd be left alone. Again.

I didn't even recognize I was holding myself back from loving him until we made love for the first time, and he held me. It was perfect. Beautiful. Something to hold onto when I felt like breaking. Because I didn't have to be the strong one anymore. No. I have Fen.

I head to the bathroom and open the medicine cabinet, finding a giant bottle of Advil. The thing must've been purchased from Costco, so I untwist the cap, ready to pour a small handful of them into a ziplock for safekeeping when a tiny square bag clogs the container's opening.

Brows pinching, I stick my finger into the bottle and pull out the piece of plastic and realize exactly what it is.

No.

No, no, no, no.

My hand covers my mouth as I stare at the tiny white pills through the clear bag like they're a cancer.

Because they are.

Not literally, but they spread like one, infecting their host and those around them in a way I wouldn't wish on my greatest enemy.

I slide onto my ass and bring my knees to my chest, convinced I'm seeing things.

How?

When?

I thought he was better.

He promised.

I thought--

"Hey, Hads," Fen calls, his heavy footsteps bringing him into the bathroom where I'm caught lifelessly staring at the *one* thing with the ability to take Fender from me.

When he sees me with my ass on the cold tile, the tiny bag of pills splayed haphazardly next to me, he pauses.

"Hads--"

"I thought you'd stopped."

"What? I have!"

I look up at him, my gaze hardening. "Then where did these come from?"

His jaw works furiously as he crouches down beside me. "I can explain--"

I shake my head. "I don't want an explanation."

"Hads--"

"It's all Bud ever gave me. Explanations. He had an excuse for everything, Fender. Everything," I cry out, feeling like the ground is falling from beneath me. "And it might not've been what killed him, but in a way, it still was. Because if he hadn't met Marty, if he hadn't made a deal with the devil himself and gotten into debt in order to pay for his stupid addiction, he would still be here today. He'd be able to see Mia graduate. He'd be able to come over for Christmas dinner. He would be here if it weren't for *this*." I grab the bag of pills and shove them into Fender's chest.

"They aren't mine, Hadley."

I laugh, not bothering to wipe away the tears from spilling down my cheeks. "Bullshit."

"I'm serious, okay? I'd forgotten they were even in there. I confiscated them from Mia that one night. Remember? When I dropped her off at your place?" He grabs my face, his thumbs rubbing against my damp cheeks, desperate to wipe away my tears and my pain, but it's too late.

"You kept them for a reason, Fen. You might not want to believe it. Bud never wanted to believe it either, but you could've thrown them away. Instead, you tucked them into this bottle for a rainy day. And if you can't admit that, I don't know how you can expect me to stay. I'm not going to watch someone else I love succumb to this." I cover my mouth, dizzy as my world is torn apart. Again. "I thought you were stronger than that."

"Hads——"

I push myself to my feet and head back to Fender's bedroom, throwing the last few items strewn across the bed into my duffle bag and zipping it furiously. A piece of fabric catches in the zipper's teeth, but I yank at the tiny piece of metal even harder until it shuts fully.

Fender follows me, desperation painted across his stricken features as if I've cut him. But it isn't fair. Because he cut me first. He made me fall for him. He promised he was done with this. But if that were true, I wouldn't have found the damn plastic bag hidden away for safekeeping.

"Hadley," he pleads, his footsteps pounding behind me as I take the stairs two at a time.

I gotta get out of here.

"Please," he begs, reaching for my arm at the base of the steps and twisting me around until we're face to face. He looks so hurt. So broken. And I hate how I'm the one who's hurting him. But I can't stay, either. I can't go through this again. He has to see that.

"You're right," he rasps and puts himself between me and the front door, blocking my exit. "You're right. I should've tossed them. I should've gotten rid of them when I first confiscated them from Mia. I was weak. But I promise I'm telling the truth when I say I'm done. I don't even crave that shit anymore. Not like I used to. All I crave is you. All I *need* is you, Hadley. I need you so much. Please––"

"I gotta go, Fen." I go to squeeze past him, but he steps in my way.

"Don't leave. Please, Hads."

"I need to get out of here."

"What about the tour?"

"I'm not going on tour. Not anymore."

"Fine, I'll stay too. I'll stay, and we can work this out."

"I don't want you to stay, Fender," I snap. "I want you to go. I want you to leave me alone and let me go. Because this? This can't work. Not when it hits too close to home."

And I walk away, my heart breaking with every step.

HADLEY

"I'm going to miss this place," Mia says. She's sitting cross-legged on the bed in my spare room. The one she claimed as her own anytime Isabella would ask if I could watch her. It's funny. How far we've come. How much she doesn't hate me anymore. I still don't know what Fender said to her when he found her. I didn't feel like it was my place to pry, but whatever it was, it helped. It gave Mia the answers, comfort, determination––whatever it was––to finally let someone in. A lot of some*ones*, actually. And even though she's far from better and will probably have abandonment issues for potentially the rest of her life, she's trying.

For now, anyway.

And if I've learned anything from my time with Fender, it's trying is one of the first steps in getting the help you need and succeeding in fixing your problems.

If only it were enough to save my relationship with him.

Then again, part of me wonders if our relationship was doomed from the start.

I'd said I'd needed a distraction, not the baggage that came along with loving another person with an addiction.

Which is selfish, I know, but...it's hard. Loving someone with an addiction. Hell, it's almost impossible sometimes, but I think I could've handled it if it weren't for Bud. For everything he put me through. For everything he went through. And for his final decisions, which led him to the point of no return.

It's terrifying. That Fender could reach that point one day, and I'd be too in love with him to walk away.

But walking away wasn't exactly a picnic either. In fact, I've been miserable. So miserable, Isabella decided I needed another distraction. One in the form of a sullen teenager who needed something to do on a Friday night.

Which is why she's here, helping me pack up my two-bedroom apartment.

I found a little basement apartment. The rent is cheaper, and if I can get my butt into gear, what little savings I have left should be able to hold me over until I can get this damn book published.

Maybe.

Honestly, I feel like my writer's block has been worse than ever. I can't concentrate. I can't be creative. I can't think about plots or storylines or characters. All I can think about is Fender and how much I miss him. How much I want him to hold me. To feel his arms around me. To feel him deep inside me as we both fall over the edge, his whispered *I love you* washing over me.

I shake off the memories and look around the half-packed room.

There's still so much to do.

The edge of the bed is soft under my butt as I sit next to Mia and put my arm around her. "I'm going to miss this place too."

"It's weird. All the memories I have of this place." She looks around the room, and her mouth quirks up. "Usually of me wanting to run away because I was mad at you, but..."

"Har, har. I know I'm just your aunt, and we've had our own rocky past--"

"Because you like to hold the title over my head even though we're only six years apart instead of being a good friend, which is what I've needed most days," she reminds me, her tone dripping with sarcasm.

"Buuuut," I drag out the word, my gaze narrowing with faux annoyance. "I'm glad we were able to share those moments. And grow from them," I add. "Like you and your mom are. How are things going on that front, anyway?"

She rolls her eyes. "I might be *trying* to be better and more responsible, but I think my mom and I have a long way to go in the trust department. I..." She shoves her hair away from her face, looks down at her lap, and picks at some nonexistent lint on her yoga pants. "I'm not okay. I know it, and my mom knows it too. And having a daughter who's not okay must be rough for her, but I can't focus on making her happy when I can't even make myself happy, ya know? It's complicated."

"Sounds complicated," I admit. "Which reminds me...I need to talk to you about something as a friend as well as an aunt."

"Hads," she warns.

But I don't back down. I can't.

"Listen. I found some pills Fen mentioned belonged to you--"

"I don't need another lecture, Hadley." She rubs at her temples, still cross-legged on the bed, but I can see how close she is to getting up and walking away.

With my palm pressed to her knee, I keep my voice calm

and say, "Yeah, well, you're going to get one because I love you, and I don't want you to end up like your dad."

"Don't talk about him like that," she pleads. Her breathing is shallow, and her voice cracks like Pop Rocks. "He was a good guy!"

"I know he was, but he also had demons even *he* wasn't strong enough to battle, and I don't want you to pick up where he left off and––"

"I didn't take them, all right? I've never taken them. Fender intervened the *one* time I was even tempted. He told me how slippery the slope was and reminded me about stupid genetics and how it can influence our addictions. So, no, I won't be trying drugs. Ever. I'm even staying away from alcohol for the time being."

"Which you should because you're still a teenager," I remind her.

She rolls her eyes, blinking away the sheen from them, and wipes under her nose with the back of her hand. "Yeah. I know. Thanks for the reminder."

"What can I do to help? I can see you're struggling."

"Of course, I'm struggling. I miss my dad. I'm terrified of disappointing everyone. Of not getting into college and making my life better. I can't sleep. I can barely eat most days. It's like… as soon as he started being my dad again and showing up, he left me. No, he was *taken* from me by a selfish asshole who's rotting in prison. But even that doesn't feel like justice because it won't bring my dad home."

"Oh, Mia." I rub my hand up and down her back while feeling like she's bleeding out in front of me, and I have no way to stop it. I'd give anything to take away her pain. To make her feel better. And I hate how it isn't possible, and she'll have to fight this battle on her own. Sure, I can be there to support her along with her mom and therapist, but it takes time. So much time.

"Do you want to know the worst part?" she whispers. "Sometimes, I feel like it's all my fault."

"How can you say that, Mia? Of course, it isn't your fault. It had nothing to do with you. He had an addiction. That's all."

"What?" She pulls away from me and wipes the tears from her cheeks.

"The money he borrowed from Martin Hayes," I tell her. "He needed it to pay for his addiction."

With a look making me feel like I'm a crazy person, she argues, "No, he didn't. He gave it to my mom."

"What?"

"The money. He gave it to my mom before he disappeared. My mom was talking about college and how much it was going to cost for me to go to my dream school, if I even got in," she clarifies, her voice sounding strained and broken. "He said he'd find a way to help. Then, he wrote my mom a check a few weeks later. Mom didn't think much of it at the time. She was just grateful he was finally starting to show up in the dad department. But once that Troy guy mentioned the loan from Martin and why Dad disappeared because of it, she was able to piece things together."

"What?" I repeat. My mind feels like it's on black ice, and I'm spinning out of control.

"It's why I've been such a mess," Mia whispers. "Why I feel like it's my fault he's gone."

"Mia," I squeeze her tight against me. "It's not your fault, okay? It's not."

"I think it's a little debatable. He's gone. And it was all because I wanted to go to school."

"Sh…," I whisper. "That isn't true."

"It is, though."

I release a soft breath against the crown of her head as we both cry for her dad and his thoughtfulness. And for some reason, the truth is more telling, more poetic, and more bittersweet as I come to terms with the real reason why my brother isn't here anymore.

He didn't choose his addiction over his family.

He chose his family over his addiction.

And he really was stronger than I ever gave him credit for.

Which means… Could Fender be stronger too?

Was I too harsh?

Am I too late?

I let Mia go as the questions swirl around and around in my brain, leaving me more lost and confused than ever.

Mia's attention drops to her lap, oblivious to the mini-meltdown or how impactful this conversation has really been on me. I don't blame her, though. She has her own demons to deal with, and it's clear she's still fighting them.

"I know Dad wasn't perfect," she whispers, "but he was trying, wasn't he." It isn't a question. And now that I know why he really disappeared, I wouldn't argue with her anyway.

He *was* trying.

And I should've given him more credit.

"Yeah, Mia. He was trying."

She rests her head on my shoulder, staring blankly at the mirror hanging above the white dresser opposite the bed where we're still sitting. But she looks…empty. Broken. Torn to shreds and barely keeping it together with nothing but a few strings of determination. Ones I hope will hold firm until she can accept her father's sacrifice and how to move on without him.

When she catches me staring, she forces a smile and sits up fully. "So…enough emotional garbage."

"Mia--"

"Do you need any more help packing?" she interrupts.

Deciding to let it go, I lift my arms and motion to the

boxes scattered around the spare bedroom, not to mention the ones littering the kitchen, bathroom, and my bedroom. "Pick a room, any room."

And just like that, we get to work.

As beads of sweat drip down my neck and absorb into the back of my white T-shirt, I note the lack of light filtering through the family room window. It's late. I check my phone to see how long we've been working and whether or not I'm brave enough to call Fender and apologize or if I should do it face to face. Because if I've learned anything from my conversation with Mia, it's that I should stop assuming things. Especially someone's motivations behind their actions. And I plan on rectifying it as soon as possible...*if* Fender will give me the chance.

3 2

HADLEY

It feels weird being here, quieter somehow, but I lift my hand and force my knuckles against the hard door anyway. I didn't run over here after my talk with Mia. I wanted to clear my head and make sure I wasn't rushing into anything. But after missing Fender like crazy combined with the emotions of the last few days? It's clearer than ever. I need to see him. The only problem is, I have no idea whether or not he's on tour or if he even wants to talk to me after the way I left. And I wouldn't blame him either way.

He tried reaching out at first until...they stopped. His texts. His voicemails. And it only made me more insecure. And weak. For keeping my distance. For taking some time to myself to look at the situation from all angles, knowing if I go back, I'm all in. And I want to be all in with Fender more than anything else in the world.

I nibble on a hangnail and stare at the closed door for a few more seconds, doubt and indecision eating away at me before it creaks open to reveal the *other* Hayes brother.

"Hadley?"

"Hey," I murmur, my voice rusty from lack of use. Or hell,

maybe it's the nerves. I'm definitely stepping outside of my comfort zone for this, so it wouldn't surprise me. Still, I clear my throat and try again. "Mind if I come in?"

A cool, detached Gibson steps aside and invites me in with a small wave of his hand.

"Thanks. So…" I turn on my heel and take in the empty house from the entryway. "It's quiet in here."

"Maddie, Milo, and Penny moved out last weekend, and Jake still spends most of his time at Evie's. Riv and Reese are out promoting their new movie, so it's just me and Dove for now until we find a place we like."

With a jerky nod, I tuck my thumbs into the back pockets of my jeans and rock back on my heels. "Cool. So…have you talked to Fen lately?"

"About what?"

"Anything?" I offer. I can tell he's mad at me, and I guess I don't blame him. I was harsh with his brother. Too harsh. And even though I was hurting, it wasn't fair. That's on me.

"I told him to stop calling you. That you'd come around if and when you were ready."

"Oh." I bite the inside of my cheek, then force out, "So, I assume he told you about what happened?"

"Yeah. He screwed up, and you broke his heart without waiting for an explanation. That about sums it up, doesn't it?" He folds his arms, his eyes reminding me of a pissed-off falcon about ready to swoop down and eat me alive.

"I was wrong," I admit. "I lashed out, and it wasn't fair to Fender. He'd done nothing wrong. If he wanted to take the stupid drugs, he could've at any time, but he never did. I shouldn't have assumed––"

"I'm going to stop you right there," Gibson interrupts. "I'm not mad you yelled at him for keeping the drugs. You were right on that front. He might've been strong at that moment, but he won't always be strong. None of us are, and having any kind of temptation in the house would only wreck him in the long run."

Surprised and confused, I whisper, "Oh." I tuck my hair behind my ear but can't find the courage to look at him as I ask, "So why are you…?"

"Mad?" he finishes for me.

I nod but keep my attention on the polished hardwood floor beneath my sneakers. There are no Pixie or toddler footprints marring it, proving how quiet this house is without the people who make it a home. I fold my arms, feeling cold and so damn alone.

"I'm mad because you told my brother you love him, but you ran at the first sign of trouble," Gibson scolds. "Love is hard, Hadley. It's especially hard when you love someone like Fender. Trust me. I know. Putting up with his shit over the years hasn't exactly been a walk in the park. But he was *trying*. Actually, not only was he trying, but he was fucking killing it. He'd gotten his life back together, and he was being the strong one for *you*. When you were weak. When you needed a moment to breathe. To have someone hold you and tell you everything was going to be okay. He was there. He was the guy you needed him to be. And still, it wasn't enough. Because even though the table hadn't turned, and your roles weren't even reversed, you *still* threw it in his face, making him believe he wasn't worth the fight." He folds his arms and leans against the railing in the entryway. "That's bullshit."

"You're right. I was wrong, and I want to make it better." I sigh and press my fingers to my lips as everything I assumed and said to him during our last conversation rises to the surface, making me feel even shittier. "I need him, Gibson. I need him more than anything. Probably more than he needs me, in all honesty, but I guess I'm selfish like that."

Gibson's mouth quirks up on one side. "That's a load of

bullshit too. You have no idea how much he needs you. How much he's dying inside when you're not around." I sniffle, my heart cracking. "But I need you to promise me something, Hadley."

"What?" I whisper, sucking my lower lip into my mouth to keep it from quivering.

"Promise you won't run from him again. Not when he's putting you first. I know your brother messed you up. And I know loving someone who battles addiction isn't a walk in the park, but if he's willing to put you first, I need to know you're willing to put him first too. Even when it's scary. Even when you have to be the strong one. I need to know you'll be there for my brother the same way I know he'll be there for you."

"I promise."

His chin dips, and he hooks his thumb over his shoulder toward the kitchen. "Then, come in. My laptop's in the kitchen."

"Laptop?"

Gibson's smirk reminds me of Fender as he answers, "We have a plane ticket to buy."

33

FENDER

"You're on in five. You ready?" Hawthorne asks.

He doesn't usually tour with the band, but he had a meeting in Denver and figured he'd stop by. Not gonna lie. It's been nice to have him here. A familiar face.

Don't get me wrong. The new guys are great, and I like them a lot. But being on tour can be lonely. Like you're in a crowded room, yet have never felt more isolated or disconnected in your entire life. It's how I've felt every damn minute of every damn day since Hadley walked out.

Even with Pixie by my side, the world has felt bland. Like it's simply going through the motions. Like *I'm* just going through the motions. And I'm not sure how much longer I can take it.

"I asked if you're ready?" Hawthorne prods, reading my silence as anxiety when it couldn't be further from the truth.

I'm not anxious.

I'm numb.

And while it might've been what I'd craved before I met Hadley, ever since I fell for her, I realized it's the opposite of what I need, yet I'm drowning in it all the same.

I force myself to nod as I glance toward the restless audience a hundred feet away from between the stage curtains.

"You sure you're okay?" he asks again.

"Fine. Just tired," I lie. Although it isn't completely off base. I *am* tired. Bone tired. Not the kind of exhaustion you can fix with a solid nap, but one running deeper. More consuming.

I've been fighting this battle for what feels like a lifetime, and as soon as I could stand on my own and be strong, I was sucker-punched in the gut. My past sins caught up to me. Again. And there's no erasing it. No running from it.

I might've learned to accept my addiction and the constant battle it'll be for the rest of my life, but the truth is, I can't expect everyone else to accept it.

Especially not Hadley.

Not after everything she's been through.

Not after her brother, and *my* brother and…

I shove my fingers through my hair, grab my guitar from its case, and head onstage. The large platform is still dark, the blaring lights currently flipped off, but I need to do something. Anything. To keep my thoughts of Hadley at bay.

Pixie pads next to me onto the dark stage as the crowd starts cheering my name.

Fen-der! Fen-der!

And it feels good.

It does.

The rush. The anticipation. The fans who are here for me. To see me. To hear my lyrics. My guitar. It's heady.

But it doesn't hold a flame to what's at home for me. What I lost because I'm too hard to love. Because I'm a ticking time bomb who made a mistake. Not a big one. I know that. Even now, I look back on the moment when I put those stupid pills in the medicine cabinet instead of flushing them down the toilet. I hadn't wanted to take them. I had no intention of doing so. But I'd still messed up. And Hadley knew it. It's like I placed a tiny pebble at the top of a mountain without considering how much momentum it could gain if gravity took its hold on the damn thing.

That's where I was wrong.

I didn't consider gravity. I didn't consider Hadley or how she might react. I didn't consider my own strength and how I could potentially react on a hard day by keeping those stupid pills in my house. I didn't consider a lot of shit. And because of it, I lost everything.

The crowd continues chanting my name, anxious for me to play the first song even though the rest of the band is still offstage and the bright lights have yet to turn on. But I stay quiet, lost in my own head. In the memories of that night. In the potential of what could've been if I hadn't screwed up.

If I close my eyes, I can almost hear Hadley's quiet voice when she whispered she loved me after we had sex.

No. That shit wasn't sex.

It was more.

It was opening the door to our future and closing the door from our pasts. Or at least, it's what I'd thought. Somehow, my past caught up to me anyway. And there's nothing I can do to change it.

"Fen." The word is nothing but a whisper, and I'm not sure how it cuts through the crowd, but I hear it. The soft lilt. The breathy, strained syllable. I'd recognize it anywhere. It's been haunting me for weeks.

Her voice.

I turn around, convinced I'm going crazy, when a curvy brunette grabs my attention through the heavy black curtains hanging on the side of the large platform.

The guitar slips from my fingers, landing with a reverberating thud. Pixie's ears perk, and she searches for what spooked me. When she sees Hadley, Pixie races toward her,

her butt wiggling from side to side. With a grin, Hadley crouches down to greet the beast while my feet stay planted, positive I'm seeing things.

What the hell is she doing here?

She hates me.

I screwed up.

She shouldn't be here.

I watch as Hadley scratches Pixie behind her ear and almost falls on her ass as the dog crowds Hadley's personal space, desperate for more attention and an opportunity to lick her face, her hand, or anything she can come in contact with.

My heart beats faster, practically galloping in my chest, but still, I don't move. I can't. It's like a spell's been cast, and it's one I don't want to break. If I move, she'll disappear. I'll be alone again. And any spark of hope that hit when I saw her standing next to Hawthorne will dissipate into wisps of smoke. I can't let it happen.

Oblivious, the rest of the band joins me on the stage, and the lights flip on. Blinding me. Convincing me I'm hallucinating, and there's no way in hell the love of my life is here. Not after she left me.

I turn to the audience, shielding my eyes and blinking slowly before turning back to Hads. My Hads.

She's still here.

My new band watches me curiously, waiting for me to greet the crowd and play the first song in our set, but I'm too stunned to do anything but stare. I watch as Hawthorne leans down and murmurs something to Hadley. She shakes her head but takes his offered hand and stands up. He says something else, though I can't hear a word over the cheering audience.

With bright red cheeks and scuffed up black converse

shoes, Hadley's gaze connects with mine as she walks toward me. On the stage. In front of thousands.

And I can do nothing but watch. Her swaying hips. The short wisps of hair framing her face. The way her white teeth dig into her lower lip as she looks at the ground instead of her surroundings. Like she's anxious. Shy. I can't figure out if it's because she's on stage in front of a massive crowd or if it's because of me. Because of how we left things. How I screwed up. How she broke my heart.

When she reaches the center of the stage, she takes a slow, unsteady breath and looks up at me. "Hi."

"What are you doing here?" I rasp, my words echoing throughout the stadium, and I realize the microphone is only a few feet from us.

I sigh, remembering where the hell I am, and take a few steps away from it.

With her arms folded, Hadley follows me, looking small and vulnerable. "Hawthorne wanted me to tell you, you're kind of supposed to be performing right now, and we can sort our stuff after."

"And he sent you out here to tell me that yourself?"

Her tongue darts out between her lips. "Yes."

"So you're not going anywhere?" I ask.

She shakes her head, the first ghost of a smile causing her lips to slant as she peeks up at me again from behind her black frames. "Sorry, Fen, but after a short conversation with your brother and a long-ass flight all alone, I'm afraid you're stuck with me."

"Is that right?"

She nods and steps closer to me, closing the last bit of distance between us. Her fingers are delicate and unsure as she cups the side of my face and rubs her thumb along my cheek. "Yeah. I'm sure we can get into this when we don't have an audience watching our every move, but I love you, and I'm so sorry for abandoning you and for not being willing to listen. I was scared. And I know it's no excuse, but I'm here now. And I'm not−−"

I slam my mouth onto hers, and the crowd goes wild. Cheering. Clapping. Whistling. But it all fades away until I'm left alone with nothing but Hadley and the feel of her curves pressed against me, the soft sweetness of her lips, and the knowledge she isn't going anywhere. Not anymore. Not after everything we've been through.

She loves me.

Me.

My lungs force me to stop kissing the shit out of her, and I pull away, resting my forehead against hers as we both catch our breath.

"You're not going anywhere?" I repeat.

She shakes her head.

"No matter what?"

"It's like I said. You're stuck with me."

"Even when I'm broken?" I challenge, waiting for her to deny it. To tell me her love is conditional, and I'm not good enough. Will never be good enough. Because I won't. Not for a girl like her. A girl who deserves the world but is stuck with my sorry ass. Because I'm not letting her go. Not anymore. Not now that she's here. With me. For me.

I wrap my arms around her waist and squeeze her tighter, still convinced I'm hallucinating. But I know how she feels when she's pressed against me. I've memorized her curves. Her fruity scent. The way her eyes crinkle behind her glasses when she smiles at me. And right now? I'm witnessing it first hand.

She's here.

She's really here.

And she loves me.

With the same smile that's haunted me for weeks, she

cups my cheek again. "We're all a little broken sometimes, Fen. But I think, if you can forgive me and we stick together, we just might be able to fix each other too."

I close my eyes and rest my forehead against hers. Again. Like I can't get close enough. "I love you, Hadley Rutherford."

"Love you, too, Fender Hayes." On her tiptoes, she reaches for my mouth and kisses me softly. "Now, go get 'em, Tiger."

So I do.

And it's one hell of a show. A high I've never felt before. But when they scream for an encore, I shake my head and rush offstage.

I have a girl to get to. And when I'm with her, it's a high unlike anything.

It's even better.

EPILOGUE

HADLEY

"I want to thank everyone for being here tonight, especially my amazing girlfriend, Hadley." He motions to the side of the stage where I'm currently sitting with Pixie at my feet. "Without her, I wouldn't be here. She's saved me so many times. I'm not sure she even understands what I mean when I say I'd be lost without her. I love you, Hadley Rutherford."

He plays the intro to a new song he's been working on, and my grin widens as I listen to the lyrics, humming along since I've found my own writing mojo likes listening to him play while I work.

Fender and I flew home for a short trip, officially moved in together, and caught another flight to catch up with the rest of his band so we wouldn't miss any scheduled concerts during the tour.

Things have been perfect. So much so, I was finally able to write "the end" on my latest novel, and my editor loves it. In fact, she said her favorite addition to the story was a certain love interest who thought he was broken but wound up having an excellent character arc. Her words. Not mine.

I've decided to open a new pen name, spending my time writing more love stories almost rivaling the one Fender and I found.

Almost.

And Pixie? She's still Fender's sidekick, watching over us every minute of every day while refusing to leave either of our sides. Unless his favorite running buddy stops by.

Speaking of Mia, she got accepted into LAU's nursing program. Even though she still has a lot to work through, including abandonment issues and shitty taste in guys, she's trying to put herself back together again.

The final note rings throughout the massive stadium, and Fender lifts his arms into the air, his lime-green electric guitar hanging from the strap across his shoulder, and says his goodbyes while the crowd cheers for another encore.

"You think you'll ever get sick of his sappy declarations of love during every show?" Gibson asks beside me as he and the rest of the band wait for their turn to set up. Broken Vows was invited to meet up with Fender a few weeks ago. Hell, even the infamous Donny Hayes decided to tag along and be a guest singer during a show or two. It's been nice getting to know Fender's family. They've adopted me as one of their own. And the fact they're all writing songs for River and Reese's new movie? I'm pretty sure it's the cherry on top of a fantastic future.

"You ever going to get sick of pausing halfway through a song to kiss the crap out of your co-singer?" I counter, tearing my gaze from my sexy boyfriend to his brooding brother beside me.

Gibson laughs. "No."

"Then, no," I reply with a grin. "I won't ever get sick of Fender's sappy declarations."

"Good. Because I have a feeling they're not going anywhere."

My grin widens, and I look back at the sexy musician on stage I get to go home with every night. Seriously. Could I be any luckier?

The crowd continues screaming, cheering, and clapping, causing a deafening roar as the stage darkens. Fender jogs toward me with Pixie padding right beside him.

"You were amazing," I tell him as I wrap my arms around his damp neck.

The crowd was begging him to take off his shirt as soon as he walked on stage, but he kept it on, gifting them with his signature smirk and sexy voice instead. And once he started playing, they didn't complain. Because they saw the *real* Fen, and I'll give him this much…the guy definitely still knows how to put on a show.

There were good things about Fen before he went to rehab. Lots of good things. Like his love of music. And his protective nature. And his loyalty to family and those he cares about.

It's been interesting to sort through, but I'm glad we've been taking the time to find the pieces of the old Fen that are *so* worth keeping.

But what I'm even more grateful for? One of those pieces which made me fall in love with him in the first place is his lust for life. For chasing his dreams. And for weaving them with mine.

"I love you, Fender Hayes," I tell him as I rise onto my tiptoes and kiss his cheek.

"Love you too, Hads." He snatches my mouth with his own. "So damn much."

Don't Let Me Fall
Prologue
Ashlyn

My head bobs up and down to the radio as I wait for the red light to turn green and fiddle with the heater in my car. Even though it's late in the afternoon, the temperature is dropping, and I know that as soon as the sun slips beneath the horizon, it'll get cold. I just finished my last class for the week and am ready for a nice hot bubble bath with a side of ice cream. After the week I had, I need it. Big time.

Tapping my fingers against the steering wheel, I make a mental checklist of my upcoming assignments in my classes, when a massive pickup truck pulls up beside me on the road.

From the corner of my eye, I peek over at it, catching a glimpse of a chiseled chin and a corded forearm resting against the steering wheel. I crane my neck a little further.

Hot damn.

Clearing my throat, I look back at the stop light. Because, ya know, it's rude to stare.

The light's still red.

My tongue clicks against the roof of my mouth for a few more seconds before I glance at the guy beside me again, unable to help myself. As I take in his silhouette, my mouth practically waters.

Who is this guy? He doesn't look familiar.

Not that I'm surprised. LAU's campus isn't exactly small, but when your boyfriend's on the hockey team and is LAU's golden boy, you get to know people. A lot of people, actually.

But this guy?

Yeah, I definitely don't know him.

He has dark sunglasses propped on his nose, and full lips that are mumbling the lyrics to whatever song he's listening to. And boy, are those lips attractive. All pouty and kissable. His dark hair is somewhat wavy, and is pushed away from his face, showcasing his tan skin and stubbled jaw as he stares at the stoplight in front of us, oblivious that I'm most definitely checking him out when I most definitely shouldn't be.

I gulp.

The guy's good looking. I'll give him that much.

His mouth quirks into a smile as if he can read my mind before he looks down at his lap. I glance back at the stoplight––which is still red––before peeking at the stranger again.

Is he texting someone?

My phone dings with a notification, and I flinch at the obtrusive sound, my heart kicking up a notch as if I just got caught doing something I shouldn't, which, I guess, isn't exactly off-base. Digging the phone out of my purse, I scan the notification before my lips part, and my cheeks burn red.

Holy crap on a cracker. It's an airdrop notification. From someone I most definitely don't know.

Colt Thorne would like to share a note.

Colt Thorne?

Is *he* Colt Thorne?

My teeth dig into my bottom lip as I glance up at the truck again, but the space is empty, and the stoplight is green.

A loud honk reverberates from behind me before I press the gas and drive through the intersection, indecision gnawing on my lower gut. Because if my intuition is right, and Colt Thorne is the tall, dark, and handsome stranger in the truck––*and* he decided to airdrop me something–– should I be stupid enough to accept it? What if it's a dick pic? Or a list of names from his latest killing spree, since ya know, I don't exactly know the guy, and Ted Bundy was attractive too, or––I shake my head.

Calm the hell down, Ash, I remind myself.

My thumb hovers over the "accept" button for a solid ten seconds before my curiosity gets the best of me, and I tap the button.

The notes app opens, and the message sent from the sexy stranger pops up.

This message is for the cute girl in the beater who was staring at me at the light. Hope this is you.
You should text me.
547-555-4119

My jaw drops, and I swerve on the road when another car's horn honks at me, followed by my phone dinging with an incoming text message from my boyfriend.

I toss my phone onto the passenger seat like it burned me, then drive the rest of the way home, and park into the driveway while attempting to erase the last ten minutes from my life like it's a dirty bathroom in need of bleach.

Unfortunately, it's a waste of time.

Because even though I'm in a relationship, it's nice. Being wanted. Appreciated.

I haven't gotten a guy's number in years. Probably because most of them know I'm in a relationship with Logan, so it would be a waste of their time, but still.

A guy just gave me his number.

A good looking guy.

A *really* good looking guy.

My lips pull into a nervous smile at the memory before I shake my head, and shove the feeling aside.

Get a grip, Ash.

It doesn't matter how good looking the guy is, or how flattered I am that he reached out. I'm in a relationship. And I'm not going to jeopardize it for a stranger, no matter how attractive he is.

Once I'm perfectly safe in front of my house, I reach for my phone again, and pull up the message my boyfriend had sent, anxious to move on with my day and get the stranger as far away from my thoughts as possible.

Logan: Hey! You coming tonight?

With a frown, I close my eyes. I don't need to ask where Logan's referring. I already know.

Me: Next time, okay? I had a long day, and want to just chill at home tonight.

Logan: Come on, babe. Live a little. It'll be fun.

Me: Theo's parties aren't exactly my thing, Logan. You know that.

Logan: But what about us? I want to see you.

Me: You're welcome to come over, and watch Netflix or something, but I kind of just want to take it easy tonight. This week was rough.

Logan: I already told the guys I'd hang out, and I don't want to bail on them. Come on. You should come over.

I roll my eyes and rest my head against the headrest, nearly choking on the groan in my throat.

Theo's parties are...a lot. A lot of booze. A lot of dry humping. A lot of loud music. And a lot of headaches the day after.

They're just...a lot. But I've also been avoiding them for

KELSIE RAE

way too long, and it isn't exactly fair that Logan keeps inviting me, and I always keep seeing no.

After all, relationships are all about give and take, right?

Puffing out my cheeks, I unlock my phone again, and type a quick response.

Me: Next time, okay? Promise. Have fun with the guys. We'll do something tomorrow. Love you.

Logan: Love you, Babe.

With a sigh, I pull up the note from the mysterious Colt Thorne, and delete it, no matter how flattering the sentiment is.

Besides. I'm in a relationship.

And that's that.

Want to read about Mia and her experience in college? You can catch up in
Don't Let Me Fall

ALSO BY KELSIE RAE

Kelsie Rae tries to keep her books formatted with an updated list of her releases, but every once in a while she falls behind.

If you'd like to check out a complete list of her up-to-date published books, visit her website at www.authorkelsierae.com/books

Or you can join her newsletter to hear about her latest releases, get exclusive content, and participate in fun giveaways.

Interested in reading more by Kelsie Rae?

Wrecked Roommates Series

(Steamy Contemporary Romance Standalone Series)

Model Behavior

Forbidden Lyrics

Messy Strokes

Risky Business

Broken Instrument

Rebel Roommates Series

(Steamy Contemporary Romance Standalone Series)

Don't Let Me Fall

Signature Sweethearts Series

(Sweet Contemporary Romance Standalone Series)

Taking the Chance

Taking the Backseat - Download now for FREE

Taking the Job

Taking the Leap

Get Baked Sweethearts Series

(Sweet Contemporary Romance Standalone Series)

Off Limits

Stand Off

Hands Off

Hired Hottie (A *Steamy* Get Baked Sweethearts Spin-Off)

Swenson Sweethearts Series

(Sweet Contemporary Romance Standalone Series)

Finding You

Fooling You

Hating You

Cruising with You (A *Steamy* Swenson Sweethearts Novella)

Crush (A *Steamy* Swenson Sweethearts Spin-Off)

Advantage Play Series

(Steamy Romantic Suspense/Mafia Series)

Wild Card

Little Bird

Bitter Queen

Black Jack

Royal Flush - Download now for FREE

Stand Alones

Fifty-Fifty

Sign up for Kelsie's newsletter to receive exclusive content, including the first two chapters of every new book two weeks before its release date!

Dear Reader,

I want to thank you guys from the bottom of my heart for taking a chance on Broken Instrument, and for giving me the opportunity to share this story with you. I couldn't do this without you!

I would also be very grateful if you could take the time to leave a review. It's amazing how such a little thing like a review can be such a huge help to an author!

Thank you so much!!!

-Kelsie

ABOUT THE AUTHOR

Kelsie is a sucker for a love story with all the feels. When she's not chasing words for her next book, you will probably find her reading or, more likely, hanging out with her husband and playing with her three kiddos who love to drive her crazy.

She adores photography, baking, her two pups, and her cat who thinks she's a dog. Now that she's actively pursuing her writing dreams, she's set her sights on someday finding the self-discipline to not binge-watch an entire series on Netflix in one sitting.

If you'd like to connect with Kelsie, follow her on Facebook, sign up for her newsletter, or join Kelsie Rae's Reader Group to stay up to date on new releases, exclusive content, give-aways, and her crazy publishing journey.

Made in United States
North Haven, CT
09 May 2023

36406175R00147